Dear Readers,

I set out for France to research this book directed by a very unusual guide: a long-dead soldier. Tucked under my arm was Brigadier H. R. Sandilands's red-and-gold-embossed account of the story of the Great War as fought by his regiment, the Northumberland Fusiliers. Using his hand-drawn maps, I followed the young captain's staggering footsteps as, shot through the shoulder fighting in the rear-guard at Mons, he gritted his teeth and pressed on, retreating in a forced march south before the overwhelming might of the German army.

Exhausted, soaked to the skin, without supplies or a chance to sleep, they marched on, covering sixty miles in the first two days. The only brightness in this nightmare came from the local people: the owners of the château where he was billeted in Resson supplied him with "an excellent dinner, champagne and cigars," he records, and, in Crisolles, he spent the night in the cottage of a labourer and his wife who gave their young guests cider and two fowls. "One could wish," says Sandilands with a sensitivity unusual for the professional soldiery of the time, "that these poor folk could have known that their simple acts of kindness were to be recorded for all time in the pages of a regimental paper."

Four days later, they reached Chatres, where they collapsed, too weary even to sleep. Then they re-grouped, turned their faces to the north and fought their way back again to the coast. The "Miracle of the Marne" had begun.

The beauty of the countryside and the warmth of the local people made a lasting impression on the Allied army and, although at a low ebb, fearful and dispirited, Sandilands finds time to wonder at the loveliness of the forests, hills and rivers. Here, clearly, was a country worth fighting for. Thousands of men died or disappeared in the hills of Champagne, and I found many graves of Sandilands's fellow soldiers, of

Canadians, of Americans and Indians. The columns of white crosses line the hillsides, as lovingly tended as the rows of champagne vines. This seductive landscape smiles back at the visitor, confident in its well-ordered fertility, and it is hard to imagine that it has survived two devastating invasions in the last century.

The resilience of this part of France is personified for me and for anyone who visits Reims, its capital, by the carved stone figure known as the Smiling Angel who stands to the left above the portal of the cathedral. He was blown apart when the building was targeted by cannon in the Great War, but the people of Reims had him re-carved and set back in place. And here he stands, genial and civilised, offering the stranger a welcome to Champagne. As long as the crowds of all nationalities who gather at his feet value his smile and instinctively return it, there's hope for humanity.

I raise a glass of the last of the champagne I brought back with me from the Marne and have saved for the publication of this book and toast you, Reader. I hope you enjoy the book which is at heart a love story and a story of hope. And, with a second sip, I salute those women and children of Champagne who worked against huge odds ninety years ago to preserve the wine-making expertise acquired over centuries. Santé! And thank you!

Warmly,
Barbara Cleverly

"An excellent addition to this unique historical series."
—*MLB News*

"Spot-on characterizations and descriptions . . . Cleverly effortlessly calls up post–Great War France and the war's victims. . . . Clever plotting and an ability to evoke the past."
—*Richmond Times-Dispatch*

"Cleverly depicts well the 'tug of war' of her story. . . . The reappearance of Dorcas Joliffe from *The Bee's Kiss* contributes quite a bit of pleasure, spice and commentary to the story. She is a worthy honorary niece to Joe and an equally worthy partner in sleuthing. Next book, please, Ms. Cleverly." —*Mystery News*

The Bee's Kiss

Nominated for a Macavity Mystery Award for
Best Historical Mystery

"Stellar . . . As always, [Cleverly] scrupulously plays fair, and the careful reader who puts the pieces together will be gratified with a logical and chilling explanation."
—*Publishers Weekly* (starred review)

"*The Bee's Kiss* . . . certainly satisfies." —*Entertainment Weekly*

The Palace Tiger

"Cleverly's research brings even the most exotic places and people to full credibility, and she balances her ingredients—including a steamy dose of romance—with the skill and imagination of a master chef." —*Chicago Tribune*

The Damascened Blade

Winner 2004 CWA Historical Dagger Award—Best Historical Crime Novel

"Spectacular and dashing." —*New York Times Book Review*

"[*The Damascened Blade*] is set to bring the author into the big league…the writing and accuracy of scene are astonishing." —*Bookseller*

"This marvelous historical delivers." —*Publishers Weekly*

"This excellent historical mystery gains immediacy in light of the recent events in the region." —*Booklist*

Ragtime in Simla

"Captivating and enchanting. Attractive, magnetic, duplicitous women grab all the best roles in *Ragtime in Simla*. Between the natural beauty of the setting and the seductiveness of the women, it's a wonder that Joe Sandilands gets out of Simla with heart and mind intact." —*New York Times Book Review*

"*Ragtime in Simla* contains enough scenes of smashing action in and around the marvelously invoked Simla to delight even Rudyard Kipling." —*Chicago Tribune*

"Ms. Cleverly deftly transports readers to an exotic locale filled with intrigue, suspense, and characters skilled in the art of deception. This is a perfect travel book for historical mystery fans." —*Booklist*

"Cleverly gets credit for a fresh and fascinating setting. She gives her tale a final flip that will leave readers guessing and surely keep Joe Sandilands busy for many books to come."
—*Rocky Mountain News*

The Last Kashmiri Rose

"A spellbinding debut mystery. While classic in design, the whodunit formula is embellished by the vivid colonial setting ... and enriched by characters too complicated to read at a glance." —*New York Times Book Review*

"An impressive debut ... Cleverly weaves an engrossing tale of serial murder and the impending decline of the British Empire." —*Publishers Weekly*

"An accomplished debut novel is a historical mystery that has just about everything: a fresh, beautifully realized exotic setting; a strong, confident protagonist; a poignant love story; and an exquisitely complex plot." —*Denver Post*

Also by Barbara Cleverly

ℰ

The Last Kashmiri Rose

Ragtime in Simla

The Damascened Blade

The Palace Tiger

The Bee's Kiss

The Tomb of Zeus

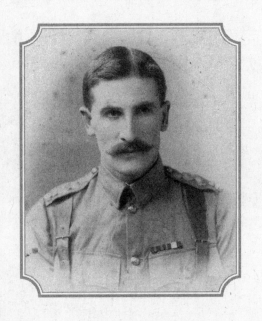

—DETECTIVE JOE SANDILANDS,
NORTHERN FRANCE, 1915

Tug
of War

Barbara Cleverly

DELTA TRADE PAPERBACKS

TUG OF WAR
A Delta Book

PUBLISHING HISTORY
Constable & Robinson hardcover edition, UK / September 2006
Carroll & Graf hardcover edition / June 2007
Delta trade paperback edition / May 2008

Published by Bantam Dell
A Division of Random House, Inc.
New York, New York

Book design by Virginia Norey

Library of Congress Catalog Card Number: 2007050551

Delta is a registered trademark of Random House, Inc.,
and the colophon is a trademark of Random House, Inc.

ISBN 978-0-385-34183-7

Printed in the United States of America
Published simultaneously in Canada

www.bantamdell.com

BVG   10 9 8 7 6 5 4 3 2 1

Tug
of War

Chapter 1

Champagne, northern France, September 1915

Aline Houdart got off her bicycle and stood still, holding tightly to the handlebars. At this moment she needed to have her feet firmly on the ground and she fought down a ridiculous urge to take off her shoes, the better to connect herself to the earth. Surely she was mistaken? The sound she'd heard was a tree crashing to the ground in the forest around her. Or thunder. A snap of her starched headdress in the breeze as she rounded the bend perhaps. The explanations she snatched at were elbowed away by a single word: cannon. But at such close quarters?

Aline thought at once of her parents. They would have been able to identify the make, calibre and direction of fire. Her parents knew all about cannon. In their distant youth they'd been trapped in Paris during the Prussian siege of 1870 and, round a good fire in the wintertime, they still vied with each other to convey the horrors of bombardment by von Moltke's fifty-ton siege gun. Aline tried to recall their

lurid accounts of the hellish din with its earth-trembling accompaniment.

The sound came again. She got her bearings and, as she
stood with her face to the north, the late afternoon sun over
her left shoulder threw a shadow to the east and north in
the direction of the blast. She stretched out an arm, extending the line, trying to remember what lay over there.
The plain of Champagne, stretching for wide miles around
Suippes and over to the bristling fortifications clustering
around Verdun. She could deceive herself no longer. This
was heavy artillery, but were the guns French or German?
Perhaps General Joffre had begun the longed-for offensive
to clear von Bülow out of Champagne, but at all events the
war was coming closer. No longer static, bogged down in
trenches, not even creeping up quietly but advancing openly,
snarling, in leaps and bounds. Soon they'd hear its roar in
the mountains to the south, one day perhaps in the hills of
Provence. And by then her world would have been con-
sumed, this perfect place reduced to rubble.

She'd been lucky in her choice of day last month when
she'd ventured north to look at the battlefield. It had been
a quiet day at the front. She'd persuaded old Felix to get out
the carriage and the one decrepit nag they had left in the
stables and drive her up to the very edge of the high country
overlooking the plain with Reims at its centre. They'd
found up there an ancient chapel which, unscathed so far,
appeared to have enjoyed the protective sanctity of an even
more ancient Celtic grove and, from its shelter, they'd
stared out in silence, too shocked by what they saw to try to
share their thoughts. The skylarks and wood doves had
been making more of a clamour, she remembered, than the
guns that day.

Framed by a canopy of beech leaves, under a hot August

sky, the land of Champagne should have stretched out its smooth curves languorously, seductively, as it did in the coloured picture postcards. For nearly two thousand years it had been a bountiful vineyard. Vines planted by Roman soldiers had thrived, the land had prospered.

It had taken less than one year to bring the ordered countryside to this obscene state of devastation.

Arrogant pigs, like all armies, the Romans at least had understood the lands they had conquered; they had trodden lightly and worked hard, leaving behind fertile and civilized provinces. Unlike the present invaders. The chalky lines of their trenches tore hideous scars across the terrain, each countered by an allied trench but all advancing towards the centre where stood, blackened and fire-bombed, roofless, its towers still raising defiant fingers at the enemy, the mighty Gothic cathedral of Reims.

The trenches. Clovis was there. Not riding, lance at the port, across open country towards the enemy but, in this modern war, bogged down, hedged in, crouching in the sketchy protection of one of those scars. She'd blinked and stared at the distant battlefield swimming before her eyes. It was distorted, not by tears, but by a heat haze shimmering over the plain. She made an effort to concentrate her thoughts on her husband, to feel his discomfort. After all these months of battle, his uniform would be quite worn out. Blue captain's jacket and red trousers—it was designed for cavalry officers peacocking about on chargers, a musical-comedy costume unsuitable for men wriggling on belly and elbows through mud and dust. And the steel helmet with horsehair plume dangling down his back—what protection was that Napoleonic flourish against bursting shells and German snipers? In this heat the cuffs of his jacket would be chafing his wrists, his high collar would be too tight, his feet blistered.

His physical state was easily imagined but with his thoughts and emotions it was more difficult to attempt a connection. Did he raise his head and glance behind him to the hills looking towards the home he was fighting for? Were his eyes seeking the familiar outline of the grove on the hill, all unknowing, at that very moment, as she gazed down? What would he be thinking? Aline smiled. A smile soured by a dash of irony. She knew what Clovis would be thinking. He'd be calculating the number of hods per hectare this wonderful summer would produce. If there were only hands available to fetch in the harvest. If there were still grapes to be harvested. He wouldn't know.

The vineyards surrounding Reims had been destroyed in the desperate German push to the south the previous summer. For two agonizing months, von Bülow's troops had swarmed down over the Marne in an impetuous and unscheduled dash, ravaging, destroying, stealing whatever resources they could lay hands on. Aline had fled with her son before the guns sounded, obedient to Clovis's instructions. But their cellar-master and his men had stayed on guard. No command, no plea, no reasoning from Aline had been able to shake these men, elderly but stout-hearted, from their resolve to stay and guard their life's work. A deserted château is the first to be pillaged, they'd maintained. The best vintages had been carefully concealed behind hastily erected and plastered walls in the miles of tunnels in the chalk under the vineyard and the bottles immediately on view to a pillaging army were the less-good wines, deceptively relabelled.

And their determination had paid off. Being well beyond the protecting bulwark of the Montagne de Reims and some miles distant from the river crossings, their remote valley and the *vignoble* had escaped with the lightest of

German attention. General Joffre, calculating that the enemy forces were impossibly overstretched, had reversed the retreat of the French from the north and unleashed his Fifth and Ninth Armies against the invaders. With the support of the British Expeditionary Force and the gallant dash of the French cavalry tearing into the gap between the two halves of the German army, the Boche had regretted their incursion and made off back across the Marne to the north again. They had been unequal to the task of hauling spoil from such an awkward piece of country, across a formidable river whose bridges had been blown up by the British, and the compulsion to lay greedy hands on heavy loot was more easily resisted when there were much richer pickings to be had on the accessible plain around Reims.

And now the *vendange* had come again. The second of the war. The grapes were safely in and how ironic if this year of misery and destruction were to yield a good vintage. Smaller but of a better quality perhaps than the legendary one of 1900? A daydream! Everyone said a war always began with a poor crop and ended with a good one. Nature's way of showing her disapproval of Man's activities, Aline thought, though the villagers said—God's way. Clovis would be concerned that his estate should be running as well as could be without him. He didn't trust her to manage it. At the last moment before leaving for the war, as he'd turned to mount his horse and ride off at the head of his small squadron of cuirassiers, he'd swung on his heel, breastplate glittering, hand negligently on sword-hilt, and called her over to him. The soldier's farewell. She knew what was required of her. Suppressing the tears and tumbling endearments which would have come more naturally to her, she went to him calmly and presented her cheek for a last kiss. He had taken her by the shoulders and murmured: "Copper

sulphate, my dear. Absolutely vital that you keep up supplies. Should you encounter difficulties you will have to
apply to our cousin Charles."

If Clovis knew that she'd taken four days off and wasted
Felix's time driving up on a fruitless expedition to gape at
the battlefield where perhaps he might be fighting, he
would have called her into his study and wearily delivered a
ticking off. Her Parisian ways had lost much of their charm
after six years of marriage, she knew that, but she could
change. She was determined to change. This war would
leave no one as they had been before. And, perhaps, when finally he was allowed to come home on his much overdue
leave, he would notice what she'd achieved. He'd notice, approve and love her for it. Perhaps.

On leave. She'd seen him only once since this war broke
out and he'd told her firmly not to expect him again until
she heard that it was all over. Leave was hardly ever accorded
to officers in his position. The thought of seeing him again
was as alarming as it was attractive. She feared that the war
would have demolished the barriers they had so carefully
built between them over the years, leaving them without
cover to see each other as they truly were—or had become.
Would the lubricants of convention and good manners ease
them through the demands of a four-day pass? She was un-
sure but at their next encounter she was determined she
would hold up her head and speak with pride of what she
had done.

Every available person, male or female, young or old,
living within ten miles of the château had been lured by
her—Parisian charm had its advantages on occasion—into
coming to work on the estate. The oldest recruit, Jean-Paul,
rheumatic and toothless at seventy-five, had come out of re-
tirement and found the energy to shuffle every morning

along the rows in the vineyard, pruning, training and singing to the vines. The youngest recruit was her own son, five-year-old Georges, who scampered about screaming defiance and throwing stones at the invading birds.

She'd raised a squad of thirty willing but sporadically available workers. The vineyard had even had the good luck to avoid attack by the phylloxera pestilence which had ravaged production on the great estates to the north. Aline paid her workers with the little cash she could lay hands on, with eggs and milk from the home farm and with promises of a share of the wine production. Well—why not? It was better shared out. If they had to leave it in the cellar before fleeing away again there was every chance it would be drunk by a regiment of swaggering Boches bombing and gassing their way south. And she had devised a scheme to outflank the enemy. If they could just be held at bay until the first cold snap of the winter came, stilling the fermentation, she could arrange to have some of the barrels shipped south to a cousin's estate to await maturity in a Provençal haven. A mad notion. She could imagine his wry comment: "Not, perhaps, one of your more considered ideas, Aline." But it was the product of her resolve to preserve a vestige at least of Clovis's world. And evidence of her own achievement. She would have felt defeated if the one gap in the run of vintages for hundreds of years had occurred during her stewardship.

More practical was her plan to find out from Jean-Paul, while he still had the memory, how to take shoots, samples, cuttings—whatever they were—of the strongest and best of their undiseased crop and to make off with them to safety. Aline hadn't discussed these plans with Clovis. She hadn't mentioned them in her letters, fearing she might irritate and distract him from the business of war; anxious also to appear confident and capable. It would be all too easy to make a foolish remark, betraying her ignorance. He had never expected the war to go on for so long or to loom so close. Would he be pleased at her foresight or would he shake his head, pitying her innocence and wild optimism?

A third booming crash had her once again on her bicycle and pedalling fast for the château.

It lay sunning itself in sleepy elegance, ancient and lovely, its two wings extending, she always thought, with their perfect symmetry, to enfold anyone approaching in a welcoming embrace. But it seemed she wasn't the first person to be welcomed down the carriage-drive this morning. A battered old transporter lorry with army markings was sitting, cocking a rusty snook at the white marble sweep of the staircase up to the double front doors which, unusually, were standing slightly open.

And something else was wrong. She looked for Clovis's dog. When she left the château and cycled off to do her weekly stint in the military hospital the greyhound always went on watch, positioning itself with bored resignation to cascade elegantly down the top three steps. But today the familiar form was absent from its post.

Aline's heart began to race as the implications became clear. Of course, he'd been driven home on leave. She slapped away a quick tug of doubt as a more sinister reason for a military presence raised itself: he'd been killed and someone had been sent to report his death. No. That couldn't be. They always sent a telegram or a letter or even the mayor. To announce the death of someone of Clovis's standing the Prefect himself might be paraded. She propped her cycle against the wheel of the lorry and ran up the steps. She called out for the housekeeper before remembering that it was Madame Legrand's afternoon off. The hall was dim and deserted but in a distant back room a door banged and she caught a blast of hearty male laughter. A maid, pink and giggling, hurried shyly towards her, fluttering with the responsibility of taking on the housekeeper's duty.

"Madame! Oh, there you are! We've been looking out for you for ages! They've arrived! A message came to say they were on their way an hour after you'd left. The Captain said not to send after you...better to let you go ahead and do your duties. He could wait..."

Aline almost collapsed with relief. She was hardly listening as the maid chattered on. "We didn't know quite what to do...the state they were in! But it's all right... we've managed! They're all bedded in and we've got their mucky uniforms off their backs and into the tub."

Aline spoke calmly to counter the girl's gushing excitement. "Quite right, Pauline. And—lye? Have you used plenty of lye? You'll find supplies on the bottom shelf of the pantry. Pay special attention to the seams. I understand that is where the lice gather." This was the *maîtresse de maison* speaking. At last she allowed herself to ask: "Now, tell me—where is the Captain?"

"He's out the back. Gone to take a stroll round the estate with Master Georges. He said as I was to tell you where he'd be the minute you got home. I put the men in the summer salon. Six of 'em. They're in there playing cards. Seem glad enough to be under a roof. I hope that was all right, madame?"

"Yes, of course. Offer them tea, Pauline. There's a caddy full on the top shelf of the housekeeper's dresser."

She dismissed the girl with a nod, turned and managed six stately steps before breaking into a run. As she tore along, she pulled off her bloodstained apron and her auxiliary nurse's cape and threw them to the floor. Her starched cap followed and she shook her hair loose as she went, weaving her way down cool corridors heading towards the stable yard. She knew where she'd find him. Clovis wouldn't have wasted time waiting for her to return. He'd be at work already.

At an open door she heard the clank of a pail, a cheerful whistling and a child's excited squeal. And then, there he was, the familiar tall shape at the end of the corridor, his fair hair freshly washed and gleaming in the sunshine, his dog at his heels. With his uniform discarded and in the tub, he'd put on his old working clothes and yard boots. And, naturally, he'd been out to inspect the cellars; he was returning, carrying a bottle of champagne in each hand.

All hesitations and doubts abandoned, shaking with excitement and caught out by an unexpected rush of affection, she called out his name. He was blinded by the sunlight and it was a moment before he saw her standing in the shadows. She ran to him, hugging him, breathing in the familiar smell of his brown linen shirt, moving her arms up around his neck and teetering on her toes to reach his lips.

The bottles crashed to the marble floor, frothing in scented eddies around their feet as he put both arms around her and lifted her up, swinging her round and laughing with delight.

Chapter 2

The War Office, London, August 1926

"I'm sorry, sir. Truly. Of course, I would have liked to oblige but…no…the answer has to be—no. I'm afraid it simply can't be done. I have to plead a prior engagement."

Joe Sandilands stirred uncomfortably in his seat. He was unused to refusing to fall in at once with a requirement, order, wish or whim from a superior officer. And Brigadier Sir Douglas Redmayne was a very superior officer. No one ever got into the habit of denying Sir Douglas anything. A second opportunity never presented itself. The Brigadier seemed equally surprised and discomfited by the feeble rejection. He bristled at Joe across the breadth of mahogany desk, bushy eyebrows gathering in attack with moustache coming up in support.

His hand reached out and he pressed a buzzer.

Joe rose to his feet and turned to face the door. He braced himself for the entry of a matched pair of the heavy brigade he'd caught sight of standing on duty in the corridors of the War Office on his way up to the fifth floor and prepared himself for the ceremony of ejection from the premises. It would be embarrassing, of course, but not entirely unwelcome. In fact he'd need an escort to find his way out of this imposing baroque building with its two and a half miles of corridor. Everything around him from the shining white Portland stone cladding on the pillared exterior to the heavy gold and ivory desk furniture was designed to overawe.

To Joe's surprise the two expected thugs made no appearance; the door was opened by one small female secretary.

"This would seem to be as good a moment as any, Miss Thwaite," said the Brigadier with a nod. "If you will oblige?"

Miss Thwaite favoured them both with an understanding smile and disappeared.

"Resume your seat and hear me out, Commander." Redmayne smiled and selected another card from his strong hand: "Perhaps I should have mentioned that I am seeing you with the knowledge and permission—encouragement even—of your Commissioner. From whom I continue to hear good things. Liaison between our departments, I'm sure you'll agree, has ..." Into the slight pause, Joe knew he was meant to slide the thought: "until this moment." "... been cordial and effective."

Joe sat down again, eyeing Redmayne with what he hoped was an expression at once undaunted but unchallenging. The officer was, he reckoned, ten years older than himself, probably in his early forties, lean, active and professional. His title was as impressive as his appearance: "Imperial General Staff, i/c Directorate of Military Operations and Intelligence." As baroque as the building, Joe reckoned. He'd always known it as "Mil Intel." A survivor of the war, Redmayne had worked his way to his present eminence, it was said, thanks to more than his fair share of luck. But Joe would have added: intelligence and a speedily acquired un-

derstanding whilst under fire of the changing nature of war-
fare. And, if the stories were to be believed, a strong streak of
ruthlessness had stiffened the blend.

"Now, be so kind as to hear me out, old chap!" said
Redmayne into the silence, trying for a tone of bonhomie.
"I'm perfectly aware of your travel arrangements." He poked
at and then straightened a folder in front of him, a folder
containing as the top sheet, Joe was sure, the outline of his
holiday plans. "Nevil was kind enough to send over your file
before he left for Exmoor."

Out of courtesy and custom Joe had sketched out his
itinerary beginning with departure early tomorrow morning
from his sister's house in Surrey where he would pick up a
package and make for the Channel port, and going on at a
speed dictated by the performance of his car and the state
of the roads all the way down to the south of France. He'd
even given estimated dates of arrival at hotels along his
route. But his plans further than Antibes he had not
confided for the simple reason that he had none. He was
looking forward to a blissful two weeks of wandering around
Provence before starting for home again.

"I see you've elected to take the Dover crossing to Calais
and then on down through the battlefields, fetching up at
Reims." The Brigadier looked at him with speculation.
"Many chaps would have gone Newhaven–Dieppe to Paris
and avoided all that."

"Avoiding 'all that' is not something I would ever want
to do," said Joe quietly. "I have respects to pay. Memories to
keep bright." In embarrassment he added, "And you have to
admire what the French and the Belgians are doing by way
of transforming all those hellish bone-yards into memorials
and cemeteries. There are some quite splendid monuments
designed by Lutyens I should like to take a look at…"

"Good. Good. Well, I see I'm not sending you out of your way then. Not at all. You'll be passing through Reims. Centre of the once glorious champagne trade. All I'm asking you to do is break your journey at this address instead of staying at a hotel. Here you are."

He passed over the desk two small white cards. Joe looked first at the visiting card and read in curlicued, florid French lettering: *Charles-Auguste Houdart, Château de Houdart, Reims, Champagne.* The second card was a merchant's copy of a wine label. A spare architectural sketch of a small château nestling between beech trees showed ordered lines of vines marching up a slope behind and disappearing into the distance. Across the top was printed the name of the champagne house, which appeared to be *Houdart Veuve, Fils et Cie.*

"Your wine merchant, sir?"

"Yes, that, but also my friend. Charles-Auguste. Splendid fellow. You'll like him."

"And is your friend Charles-Auguste the son of this house?" Joe asked, intrigued despite his unwillingness to show the least co-operation with this scheme to divert him from his plans.

"No, he isn't. I suppose you could say he's billed as *Cie—la Compagnie.* He runs it, after all. On behalf of the aforementioned Widow and Son. Ever heard of this brand, Sandilands? No. Can't say I'm surprised. It's a very small house . . . not one of the *grandes marques* like, oh, Moët et Chandon, Ayala, Bollinger, Veuve Clicquot. But to a connoisseur the name Houdart speaks volumes. Interesting history. Especially recent history. You'll remember the two battles of the Marne damn nearly scoured this country out of existence? Some of the larger estates are only just beginning to get back to pre-war production levels, but this little château managed to survive practically unscathed. And all in spite of losing the owner and moving force of the enterprise to the war. Clovis. His name was Clovis. He rode off to war, disappeared and was posted 'missing, presumed dead' in 1917. He left a widow and a seven-year-old son behind. But quite a widow as it turned out! Gallant, in the tradition of Champagne widows. Nothing loath, she rolled up her sleeves, kicked off her sandals and trod the grapes, so to speak, alongside whomever she could get hold of to work the estate. And it paid off, it would seem. Nothing prospered, of course, in that dreadful four years but it survived. And now it's prospering like anything!"

"I've identified the Veuve, and the Fils—her son—must be about sixteen now? But where does your friend, who I see bears the family name, come into this?" Joe's interest was polite and professional but no more than that.

"Charles-Auguste. He's a cousin of the chap who disappeared on the battlefield. When it was clear that Clovis had been lost he came up from Provence, where he had a small winery himself, and took the reins from the doubtless weary hands of the widow. With huge success. But you shall judge for yourself! Thank you, Miss Thwaite!" he shouted cheerily to his secretary, who entered bearing a tray set with champagne glasses and a bottle in a silver ice bucket.

Joe's mouth tightened. All this careful stage-setting boded ill for him. He scowled critically at the wine he was offered and listened to Redmayne's hearty toast: "To the Widow!"

"To all widows," Joe murmured in response. "God bless them."

He sipped the wine and sipped again with pleasure. It was as good a champagne as he had ever tasted and he said as much. Redmayne appeared pleased. "This is the 1921 vintage," he said. "Only just been released. Reports are that last year's will be even better. While you're down there, Sandilands, I want you to be sure to register an order for a certain quantity to be shipped to me when the moment comes. Charles-Auguste will advise you. Very much to my taste. The bouquet is excellent—don't you think so? People are so intrigued by the bubbles they often forget to appreciate it, you know. And the degree of dryness is spot-on. They get it right. What do you make of the colour?"

Well, if this was the game, Joe could hold his end up. Hiding a smile, he raised his glass to the light and squinted at it. "Rather deeper than one is accustomed to—a brilliant intense gold." He swirled the wine gently, put his nose to the glass and sniffed briefly. "And a bouquet to match. Spices, would you say? Vanilla certainly but...cardamom? Yes, a whisper of cardamom...and fruit...Something here from my childhood...got it—quinces! Quinces cooking with apples under a buttery pastry crust."

Redmayne stared and blinked and Joe wondered if he'd overdone it but the only response was a dry: "Indeed? Mmm...And *I* detect a touch of Proust, I think."

They drank companionably together, Redmayne talking knowledgeably of blending, first and second pressings, *remuage, dégorgement,* while Joe waited for the blow to fall.

"More wine, Sandilands?"

"Thank you. Would *this* be a good moment, sir," he said genially, "to tell me why you've summoned me here? My detective skills lead me to suppose you wouldn't have called in a Scotland Yard Commander to hand him a shopping list for champagne. I'm wondering what service, exactly, Monsieur Houdart would be expecting me to perform— were I to accept this chalice, which I suspect will turn out to be heavily laced with some poison or other?"

Joe held out his glass.

Redmayne smiled as he poured. "As a matter of fact there *is* something you could do for him. Just a small favour.

Army involvement, of course. French, possibly British. This thing landed on my desk, diverted from the Department of the Adjutant General, the Directorate of Prisoners of War and Personal Services—if you can believe!—but mainly it's the French police you would be helping. The request for assistance came, in fact, from them. From the very top. Oh, yes. Police Judiciaire involved . . . and rather puzzled to be involved, I gather. At all events, they handed it swiftly to Interpol and you'll be only too aware, after that last lot, that we owe *them* a considerable favour. *Your mob* owe them a considerable favour. The least we could do, I thought, when they approached me, was to send someone along to liaise with them. Interesting case. You'll be intrigued."

Not quite at ease with his presentation, Redmayne got up and strode to the window, hands behind his back. He pushed up a pane, the better to catch the bugle call coming up from Horseguards below, and looked out with satisfaction over to the crowding green canopy of trees in St James's Park.

He cleared his throat. "Of course, it's the press involvement that stirred the whole thing up. And now the country's in a frenzy. Nothing like a mysterious death and a grieving widow to get the Froggies going! The whole population dashes out in its slippers every morning to buy a paper and read the latest instalment of the drama. Haven't seen anything like it since the death of Little Nell hit the news-stands."

Joe had, as a child, ridden without permission a horse which, he had very quickly realized, was out of his control and heading for the hills. The same sick feeling was growing as Redmayne talked.

"Sir! A moment!" He attempted a tug on the reins. "Police? Interpol? Mysterious death? This doesn't sound like a matter I can attend to between sips of champagne and polite conversation. Whilst flighting south for the summer.

There's an officer in my department, exguardsman—Ralph Cottingham. I know he would be delighted to get away for a week or two."

Joe had overstepped the mark.

"Thank you for the suggestion, Commander," came the curt reply. Redmayne turned and glowered. "Cottingham's name came up, of course. I always choose the best man for the job and in this case, with your wartime experience in Military Intelligence and your knowledge of the language, you are he."

His words had a finality which depressed Joe but then the Brigadier unbent and gave a tight smile. "And I don't forget that you were right there—on the spot as it were. Caught up in the battle of the Marne, weren't you? Your local knowledge may come in handy. And, better yet—since you're travelling under no one's auspices but your own, your section will avoid any belly-aching from accounts in the matter of extra departmental expense. We're all accountable these days to pen-pushing pipsqueaks of one sort or another. It irritates me to have to take these petty restrictions into consideration and I expect it's much the same with you but—this way neither Nevil nor I will be expected to foot the bill. Some might consider the offer of a weekend's hospitality at a château a more than adequate quid pro quo."

"And so it would be, sir, if I were free to accept it." Joe's voice had an edge of desperation. "But, you see, there's a... an... impediment. For the outward leg of my journey, at least, I am not a free agent."

The Brigadier returned to his desk and poked again at the file. "Something you haven't declared?"

"Not something, sir. Someone. I shall not be alone. For the journey down to Antibes I shall be travelling with a female companion."

Chapter 3

A questioning flick of Redmayne's eye towards the file betrayed, to Joe's satisfaction, that the official records evidently did not contain full coverage of his private life.

"A lady, you say?"

"I think I said *female,* sir. Not sure the word *lady* would be appropriate."

Redmayne was, for a moment, disconcerted. But only for a moment. His expression adjusted itself into one conveying comprehension and collusion. "Look here—is the presence of this, er, companion absolutely essential to the success of your vacation, I wonder, Sandilands? You refer to her as an impediment. Quite understand your position. Most chaps would be only too glad to use the opportunity of an emergency posting abroad to get off by themselves. I'll be pleased to put it in writing... tiddle it up and make it look official if that would smooth a few feathers... ease your path. I'm sure I don't need to remind you that female companionship—if that's what you're after—is available and of a superior style in France."

Redmayne sat back, pleased with his solution. He exchanged an old soldier's knowing smile with the handsome young man sitting opposite. He didn't think he'd assumed too much. As well as the details he'd picked out from Sandilands's file he had had a full report from Sir Nevil and, indeed, had even met the man in a social context on one or two occasions. You never quite knew where you were with a Scotsman but first impressions had been most favourable. Undeniably a gentleman, impeccable war record. He was, to date, unattached and that suited his department. With no wifely or domestic concerns, he had always shown himself ready to move at a second's notice from his bachelor apartment in Chelsea without demur, travel any distance and take on any task, Nevil had assured him. But this was a state which could not, realistically, be expected to last. The Brigadier sighed. This promising chap would soon, inevitably, announce his decision to settle down in some green suburb with wife, children and Labrador. Redmayne dismissed this gloomy picture. With a bit of luck he might just turn out to be that useful thing—the eternal bachelor. Still in his early thirties, fit, active and charming company. Thick head of black hair, neatly barbered. Quiet grey eyes. Pity about the face. The war wound. Still, there were those, mainly women—and Lady Redmayne one of them—who maintained that the crooked brow was most intriguing and gave a certain mystery to the otherwise clear-cut features.

Sandilands was speaking again in his low voice which still retained a slight Scottish huskiness. Another of the man's attractions apparently. But, on this occasion, he was intrigued to hear an unaccustomed note of hesitation.

"Quite agree, sir, and I only wish it were so easy but the scenario is quite a different one. You see, the female in question is a child. My niece. At least, my honorary niece. Little

Dorcas Joliffe, the daughter of Orlando, the painter whose sister—"

"The Wren at the Ritz! That Joliffe? Beatrice Joliffe? Done to death three months ago...Yes, of course I know about that disgraceful affair. Good Lord! Are you saying you're still in contact with that rackety family? Believe me, Sandilands, you owe them no consideration. Your professional attentions ought properly to have ceased at the closing of the case. Surely Nevil...?"

"Orlando is an entertaining and talented fellow and, yes, I'm proud to count him my friend. His children, who, as you know, are motherless and live like gypsies, have been taken under the wing of my sister Lydia, who lives quite near to them in Surrey. The oldest girl, the impediment referred to earlier, this Dorcas, is, oh...fourteen? (Not sure she knows herself.) She's become particularly attached to my sister's family and seems to be living with them in the capacity of third daughter. Waifs and strays have always gravitated towards my sister and she's made something of a project of young Dorcas. Clever little thing. Most unusual. It was *her* observation and insight that led to the uncovering of her aunt's murderer."

"What extraordinary company you keep, man!" said Redmayne. "And what's all this nonsense about 'waifs and strays'? Hardly a description of the Joliffe children, I'd have thought? Pots of family money in the background. Good home in leafy Surrey. Yes? Death and treachery swirling all around, as all admit, but a respectable grandmother to keep the lid on. I understand she has wisely done her best to minimize the impact of her daughter's scandalous behaviour and sudden death. And it suits us to support her in this. Beatrice Joliffe died in the course of a robbery...we must all hang on to that. The old lady, at least, seems to have got the picture. Should be enough to protect those children from the public opprobrium which might otherwise have come their way."

"Deprivation can take many forms, sir, and these children have been rejected by their grandmother—on whom they are materially dependent—on account of their illegitimacy. Rejected with inexcusable and unnecessary cruelty, some might say. Their father, fond though I have become of him, is feckless—not uncaring but inadequate . . . say rather, perpetually distracted. When his model and current mistress, herself heavily pregnant, set fire to his caravan (and Orlando inside it at the time, under the influence of something or other) the eldest child, Dorcas, suffered burns whilst helping to rescue her father. Sister Lydia leapt in, scooped up the whole brood and took them home with her to introduce them to the civilized life."

"Don't recall hearing any of this penny-dreadful, Perils-of-Pauline stuff from Nevil?"

"No, sir. These skirmishings post-dated the premature closing of the case." Joe did not attempt to hide his disapproval.

Redmayne chose not to pick up the implied criticism of the military pressure which he was quite aware had been applied. "And the child is now loosely under the protection of your sister? A public-spirited gesture. Admirable woman! But I can't see why her self-sacrifice should extend to and involve *you*, Sandilands."

"Oh, people do occasionally talk me into undertaking unwelcome projects," Joe said genially. "Orlando gathered his remaining four children together with his current mistress, put them aboard a train and went off to the south of France as he does every year. He carouses all summer at a sort of awful artists' jamboree—returning in the autumn. He hobnobs with the likes of Georges Braque, Matisse, Picasso...Augustus John, I shouldn't wonder...All egging each other on. At this time of year, my sister travels in the opposite direction, going north home to Scotland, and Dorcas, discovering this, kicked up a fuss. She thinks of herself as a Child of the South, which, indeed, she very much appears...girls with her dark looks are thick on the ground in Arles...and I was cajoled into escorting her down through France to whichever villa they've all descended on and there I hope she will rejoin her father."

"A sorry tale. I fear you allow yourself to be used too readily, Sandilands. Disappointing that you have let yourself become so embroiled in *that* family's affairs. They must all, inevitably, be tainted in *some* minds..." Redmayne swept a warning glance up to the ceiling. This was his way of referring to the shadier elements of the government departments concerned with aspects of national security who were rumoured to have offices complete with the latest in listening technology situated in remote parts of the building. "...tainted with the scurrilous behaviour and treachery of that woman," he finished with tight-lipped distaste.

Joe had noticed that the few people who needed to refer to Dame Beatrice did so in a hushed voice and called her "that woman." The words "espionage," "blackmail" and "traitor" were always in mind but never spoken.

"Hum...Look, take the girl with you."

This was an order, not a suggestion. "Might work in our favour. Give an impression of a cosy family visit, policeman on holiday with his niece, relaxed, convivial. You could well learn a lot more—and faster—that way. And let's not forget Houdart Fils! He's, as you calculated, sixteen." Redmayne smiled with satisfaction. "Does this Joliffe child speak any French?"

Joe recalled with dismay the fast and colloquial street French Dorcas had picked up trailing about after her father in the loucher parts of the Riviera. "Fluently," he said diplomatically.

"She does? Good. Yes, this might all work out to our advantage. Look here, don't hesitate to telephone us if there's anything we can supply. Full back-up guaranteed. Shan't be at my desk myself unfortunately. Like your sensible sister, I'm going north for a week or two." He glanced at the dramatic Victorian paintings of stags at bay and frothing Scottish salmon streams hanging on his panelled walls and sighed with satisfaction. "But there'll be someone here keeping communications open."

"Telephone?" said Joe morosely. "Do they have the telephone down there?"

"They certainly do. Halfway between Paris and Reims, you'd expect it. Things have changed, Sandilands, since you were dodging German shells over there eight years ago. No one like the French when it comes to reconstruction. Still, when you come to think of it—they've had a lot of practice, poor souls. Look at it this way—sorting out Charles-Auguste's little problem is the teeniest bit of last-minute reconstruction. Least we can do, wouldn't you say?"

At this point Joe, mystified and discouraged, sighed and surrendered the pass.

"Now. To business!" At last the file was opened and Redmayne pretended to riffle through it. He had clearly made himself familiar with the contents and barely needed to refer to it during his briefing.

"Know anything about shell-shock? Or the condition we must now call 'neurasthenia' or 'war psychosis'?"

"I've encountered cases, sir. I can't say I've made a study of it."

"Well, you're going to have to. We have, naturally. In fact I've managed to put together a few papers here outlining the very latest thinking on the condition. Make yourself familiar with them. It may help you in your enquiry."

"My enquiry? And does it have a subject, my enquiry?"

"Of course. But not what I gather to be your usual kind of subject. No rotting corpse on offer, no member of the aristocracy done to death in mysterious circumstances. No, the reverse, in fact. You'll be helping to solve the mystery of someone who's decidedly (and rather inconveniently) *alive*."

He produced from the file a cutting from a French newspaper. The article occupied the whole of the front page and carried a large portrait photograph. Joe took it and translated the headline. "*Do you know this man?*" He studied the photograph for a few moments and looked up. "Of course I know him. Doesn't everybody?"

"What! Are you serious?"

"But his face is everywhere in London at the moment. On billboards ten feet high. It's Ronald Colman."

Pleased to have puzzled his boss he added kindly, "The film actor, sir, but a Ronald Colman after a heavy night out on the tiles, you'd say. Looks rather beaten up. You haven't seen him in *Her Night of Romance*? . . . *Lady Windermere's Fan*? And most recently *Beau Geste*? Oh, an excellent film! I do recommend it. I'm sure Lady Redmayne could tell you all about him. The gentleman is English by birth, wounded in the war and now making a name for himself on the silver screen in America."

"Do be serious, Commander."

Joe smiled. "The resemblance is, actually, quite striking." He looked again at the finely drawn, handsome face with its neat moustache.

"Interesting. Ramble on, will you. First impressions are usually worth hearing. When they're not flippantly delivered."

"No, I agree, sir, this could not possibly be a screen actor. This man is unaware of or indifferent to the camera. He's not seeing the photographer, you'd say. He's not looking in that slightly embarrassed way we have to the side or past the lens or narcissistically into it. His expression is impossible to read. A mask. There are signs of a wound along his jaw and I'd say he was about two stones underweight." He began to read out snatches from the accompanying text. "The man of mystery was found wandering around a railway station...It's thought one of a batch of late-release prisoners from a German prisoner-of-war camp for the mentally ill...Poor chap. That would account for his vacant expression. The man cannot speak, has lost his memory and has been passed along from one asylum to another, fetching up at Reims, where he is thought to have originated. The director of the asylum...um...from a swift perusal of this report I'd say he would seem to be a splendid fellow...has interested himself in the stranger's case and taken this unusual step to try to establish his identity and locate his family."

Joe looked up more cheerfully. "Well, I can't see a problem there. A man with such striking looks must have been instantly identified, wouldn't you think?"

Redmayne sighed. "And *there's* our problem, Sandilands. Would you believe—over a thousand families from all over France have claimed him! They've mobbed the asylum demanding to take him home with them. And, as you might guess, most of the claimants are female! Mothers, wives and sisters by the dozen. All desperate to get their man—or perhaps *any* man—back from the front after all these years. Poor devils."

"Easy enough to rule out most of the candidates, I'd have thought. Just a matter of process. Now I'd have—"

"Yes, yes. Whatever *you* can think of, the French authorities have already done. Height five foot eleven, fair hair, blue eyes. Well, in a country of largely dark-haired, dark-eyed inhabitants, those facts ruled out ninety per cent of the bidders for a start. He didn't feature in their Bertillon files so—no criminal record. Unless he went uncaught during his career, of course. There's always that. The French police only record the sportsmen they've actually apprehended and put behind bars."

"Fingerprints, sir? Have they explored the possibilities? I know the system hasn't captured the French imagination—so much invested in the Bertillon recording method—but surely a comparison would be possible and most revealing? I understand their police laboratory in Lyon to be in advance of anything we can supply ourselves here in London."

Joe heard the touch of eagerness in his own voice and sighed.

Redmayne hurried on, playing his fish with confidence. "Other physical details like limbs broken before the war… presence or absence of… eliminated a few more candidates and the upshot is—the authorities were left with a solid core of four claimants who will not be discouraged. They are all perfectly certain that the man belongs to them. Here's a list."

Joe took the sheet of paper and read out one by one the names and addresses of the claimants. "Number one: Madame Guy Langlois. A grocer's wife—or widow, do you suppose? From a village near Reims. Claims to be his mother. Her son, Albert, disappeared during the first battle of the Marne."

"'Missing in action. Presumed to be dead,'" supplied Redmayne. "But no *body* was ever found and no identification medallion handed in."

"Number two: a Mademoiselle Mireille Desforges of Reims, claiming a 'certain relationship' with the mystery man from before the war, vows she can identify him to everyone's satisfaction by particular physical characteristics not yet revealed to the public. 'A certain relationship'? Rather coy phrasing from our confrères?"

"Yes. Family newspaper. Probably means he was her what d'ye call it?... her pimp? And the 'satisfaction' she promises would undoubtedly be her own. Chap probably made off with her money in the way of those gentlemen and the lady wants to retrieve some of it."

"Number three: a whole family, evidently. The Tellancourts. Small farmers from the Reims area. Brother and sister adamant that this is their older brother Thomas."

"Some urgency to their claim. Sad case. Lost almost everything in the war. Father and mother are still alive and equally certain of their identification. They present a strong claim. Whole village has come out in support. Papa Tellancourt is very ill and not expected to last much longer. They are vociferous in their cries for an early decision. They were actually caught in the act of smuggling the chap out of the institution," Redmayne smiled, "in their eagerness to acquire him."

"Number four. Ah... Now I see why I'm here and about to ruin my first holiday in three years!" Joe cocked an amused eyebrow at the Brigadier. "Madame Clovis Houdart. Of the champagne house near Epernay. The invalid could be her husband, Clovis, posted missing in 1917. Do you wish, at this point, to declare an interest, Sir Douglas?"

"Well, of course!" He rapped sharply on the desk. "But an interest in finding out the truth! You must hear, Sandilands, the facts of the matter ... be *aware* of the pressures and expectations then you won't fall foul of them. I was approached by my friend Charles-Auguste when he heard of the involvement of the British authorities. He appeals to me to do what I can to ensure that the widow's claim is rejected. Proved false. He is quite certain that the man in question is not his cousin. And he is deeply suspicious of the widow's motivation in all this. Aline. Her name's Aline. It's no secret that the two in-laws do not get on well but more than that I can't tell you. They're perfectly polite to each other in their French way but you never can tell what's bubbling under the surface, can you? Awkward, what!"

"Sir, it occurs to me that we have the same theme running through each of these claims. And I don't refer to the affection they may or may not have for a dear and supposed departed one."

"Go on."

"A very prosaic and unromantic but deeply compelling motive. And particularly so in these hard times in France. Money, sir. I fear each of these claims could be based on financial gain."

"What an unworthy thought! Had the same one myself. Mm ... yes ... been researching this. Save you some time. If he is ever identified to the authorities' satisfaction, the man will, of course, even though he's out of his head and unaware of anything, be qualified to receive a very generous allowance from the state. A sort of war pension, calculated from the time of his vanishing to the present day and beyond. Froggies are quite a bit more openhanded than we are when it comes to paying for damages. His family, whoever they are proved to be, can count on receiving—shall we say—eight years' back pay. A fortune to some of the names on that list."

"Park the poor fellow in a rocking chair in the corner and they can go on drawing his pension as long as they can keep him alive," said Joe. "I would expect he qualifies for a disability allowance? But your friend Houdart? Some other financial advantage there, surely, I would guess? If the widow's claim were to be upheld, 'Clovis' would be restored to the family estates and Charles-Auguste's presence would be in question, probably redundant. 'Thank you so much, dear cousin, but you may leave now. I will do all that is necessary from now on.' Not confident I could navigate the intricacies of the Gallic laws of inheritance but obviously spanners would be thrown into works with a resounding clang."

"In a nutshell. Yes. It may come down to inheritance."

"But you mentioned something, sir . . . just now . . . which intrigued me. You say your friend contacted you with his plea for assistance *after* the police and the British authorities were made aware? We may assume his approach to be subsequent to—and perhaps dependent on—the official representation? I'm wondering why they should be bothering you with this affair at all."

Redmayne was happy with Joe's perception and his increasingly obvious involvement with the puzzle. "*Rem acu tetigisti,* Commander. Spot on the problem!" He leaned back, confident that his investigation was launched. "This director of the asylum, you had correctly identified as a good egg. Scientist by training, medical man, student of Charcot and Freud, I understand, not a civilian placeholder. You're to liaise with him. He's the target of much sniping from various French government departments for reasons you can probably guess but he has an interesting tale to tell. He got his voice heard largely because the new information he had to offer rather suited them, I'm thinking. But then, I have a very suspicious mind."

Joe remained silent waiting for the final twist and jerk that would land him firmly in Redmayne's net.

"This medic has lavished care and attention on our mystery man, whose case seems to have caught his imagination. He has made copious notes on his condition and tried, by experiment, not electrical shocks—the doc is a humane man, it would seem—to find out the nature and cause of his illness. One night, a week or so ago, he was called by a nurse to the man's room. The patient was reported to be having a particularly alarming nightmare and crying out in his sleep. Fascinating, of course. Normally completely dumb, perhaps, under the influence of the nightmare, he might well reveal some information? A useful name or two... *'Odile, mon amour, tu me manques! Maman, ton fils, Robert, te cherche!'* Something of that nature."

"Yes? And did he make out any words?"

"He did. Most surprising. And how lucky for us that this director is an educated man. He recognized the language at once. The patient was screaming out a stream of words. And this is where *we* find ourselves involved, Sandilands. The words he was screaming were *English*."

As Joe paused in the doorway to readjust the bulky file under his arm, Redmayne called out: "By the way, Joe... a last word of advice. The name 'Houdart'... know what it means?"

"No idea, sir. I've never heard it before."

"No. Most unusual. Charles tells me it's a very ancient one from two Germanic roots." He frowned in an effort to remember. "*Hild*, meaning combat and *hard* meaning... well...hard. Hard in combat. Tough fighter. And although Aline wasn't herself born with that surname—I believe she started out as a de Sailly—she's certainly grown into it. Oh, and Aline Houdart, you'll find, is a damned attractive woman."

The glance he directed at Joe was avuncular, amused. "Have a care, my boy!"

Chapter 4

As Joe ran downstairs towards the open door of the breakfast room he glanced at his luggage, set in the hall the evening before, ready for an early start. His two suitcases had been joined by one Gladstone bag and a pile of books done up with string.

Cheerful voices and a clatter of dishes warned him that breakfast was well under way and he checked his watch, annoyed to note he had overslept by half an hour. He paused by the door to collect himself and prepare for the good-natured teasing that would greet his late appearance. As he listened he took a furtive step back, startled by what he was hearing.

"Well, my money's on this Houdart woman," Lydia was saying firmly. "Sounds to me like someone who knows what she wants and gets it. She'll do a deal with the authorities, pull strings…pull Joe's strings too, I shouldn't wonder! And she'll have this poor man for her nefarious purposes."

"Can't say *I'd* mind being had for nefarious purposes by a glamorous champagne widow," said Joe's brother-in-law. "She can have her wicked way with me any day. Oh, I don't know. Let's add a sporting dash of excitement! Why not? I'll go for the dark horse…Mademoiselle from Armentières… what was her name? Pass me that sheet, Dorcas." There was a rustle of paper. "Mireille, that's it. Yes, if you're making a book put a tenner for me on the Tart from Reims."

"Marcus!" Lydia protested automatically. "Language! Ladies present!"

"You're both wrong," said Dorcas. "Aunt Lydia—do I still get my weekly pocket money while I'm in France? Good! Then, will you put a shilling for me on the Tellancourt family?" Raising her voice, she said casually, "I'll pour some coffee for Joe and ring for more. I'm sure I heard him come downstairs just now."

Joe snapped the catch of one of his cases noisily then entered looking distracted. "My file? I say, has anyone seen…? Could have sworn I'd left my file with the luggage last night…Oh, I see I did…There it is between the Cooper's Oxford and the Patum Peperium…Good morning, everyone! Anything interesting in the papers this morning?"

Marcus and Lydia looked at each other and smiled guiltily.

"Not really," said Dorcas. "We had to read your rubbish for entertainment. I can see why you didn't bother to hide it. Hardly confidential. Not a single body on any page. I wonder when you were intending to tell me of the change in our itinerary, Joe? Sounds exciting—though I'm not sure I'm prepared for a weekend living *la vie de château*. What do you think, Aunt Lydia?"

"Oh, goodness! Of course! We must pack your best dress— the blue one you said was too fussy…so glad we bought it! And you may borrow my pearls…Stockings! You'll need silk stockings. Gloves! We didn't think of gloves!"

Joe groaned and took the coffee Dorcas was handing him. Fortified, he reached out and gathered in the scattered pages of his file, reprovingly scraped a blob of marmalade from the top sheet and replaced them between the covers.

In frantic but silent communication, Lydia and Dorcas rose to their feet, hastily putting down their napkins. "Porridge in the pot, Joe...eggs, bacon...the usual," muttered Lydia. "How long have we got?"

"Half an hour," he said. "Wheels turning by nine?"

"Dorcas, scoot along, will you, and find your dress and anything else that comes to mind in view of the change in plans? You'll need another suitcase—ask Sally to fetch down one of mine. I'll look out some suitable jewellery and other folderols."

When Dorcas had charged out of the room Lydia turned to Joe wearing her big-sister's expression. "A word, if you please, Joe."

He looked at her warily.

"You may be a senior police officer and a pillar of society, as all would agree, and never think that I'm ungrateful for your offer to escort the child down to the Riviera but—"

"My *offer*! Come on, Lydia! I listen for your next pronouncement in the hope of hearing the words 'sorry,' 'twisting' and 'arm' in that order. 'Coercion' would be acceptable."

"Don't be pompous! You ought to guess from my circumlocutions that, just for once, I am actually trying hard to choose my words so as not to give offence."

He looked at his watch, hiding a smile. "Twenty-five minutes."

"Very well, then." She hesitated and went on firmly: "In England no one will look with anything less than indulgence at an uncle chaperoning his niece down to her father. And that's all very well. But I'm not so sure of customs and manners in France."

"It's a bit late, isn't it? To be having such qualms? Pity it didn't occur to you when I was trying to wriggle out...But let me put your mind at rest, Lyd. There'll be no problems of a social nature. So long as the child remembers to wear her gloves and speak when she's spoken to, say 'yes, Uncle' and 'no, Uncle' at every verse end, I see no problem. People will approve. I'll be held up as an example from Calais to Cannes of self-sacrificing uncle-hood."

"All the same, I do feel myself responsible."

Joe grinned. "You always did, Lydia. It can be infuriating. Look, love, stop fretting. Dorcas always comes out well, you've discovered that. She'll be just fine."

"Of course she will! It's not *Dorcas* I'm fretting about, you chump! Oh, Marcus! You'll have to speak to him!"

Left alone, the two men rolled their eyes in affectionate complicity and sank thankfully into a companionable silence, giving their full attention to plates of kidneys and bacon with copies of *The Times* and the *Daily Herald* on the side.

"Stockings?" Joe looked up, struck by a sudden thought. "Hasn't the child got supplies of socks?"

Marcus seemed to be having difficulty with a piece of toast and coughed behind his napkin. "You haven't noticed, have you, old boy? She's growing up fast."

"Well, of course I'd noticed! She's put on about two inches in every direction since you had the keeping of her. Good food, regularly offered. Makes a difference."

"Exactly. A difference. Glad you're aware. Lydia couldn't be quite certain that you were. Well, there you are then. I'll tell her. 'Joe's aware,' I shall say!"

Joe pondered on this for a moment. "I say, do I consider myself spoken to?"

"Can't imagine you'd want me to elaborate. I will venture

to add a word of advice of my own though...a thought or two from a man of the world, family man, father of girls and all that: if our perusal of the file is correct, I assume you'll be taking young Dorcas with you to stay with this family? Yes? Well, you could hardly park her in some hotel in war-torn Reims while you go off by yourself. There'll be a warm reception and—Lydia noticed—the company of the young son of the house. Dorcas will want to make a good impression. Wouldn't expect her to come down to dinner in the shorts and sandals she'd packed for the south of France, would you? The whole thing may be a bore and a distraction for you, Joe, but I can tell you, for the girls it's a romantic interlude. Let them enjoy it and don't be so stuffy!"

"And that's your advice? You hand me the fruits of your years of fathering and it amounts to—'Don't be stuffy'? Wouldn't fill a book, would it?"

Marcus gave Joe a long look over the table and spoke in a voice of rough affection. "It's a long way down to Antibes. It will seem twice as long if you antagonize Dorcas." And, seeing Joe was about to explode with indignation, "Take it easy, old chap. You're wound up tight as a spring. Can't help noticing. I'm saying she's rather like a partly trained little wild creature—think of a ferret...Remember Carver Doone?" he added lugubriously. "Lyd's done her best—so have I—but there's some way to go yet before we can present her at Court. Or for tea in a Joe Lyons Corner House, come to that.

"Well, that's it. I've said my piece." Marcus sat back, relieved to hear no riposte from Joe. "Listen, old man—those buggers at the Yard work you too hard. Lydia and I are always concerned for you, considering the life you lead... always mixed up in murder and mayhem of one sort or another. It will be a relief to *us* to know that for the next three weeks at least you're not dicing with death."

Chapter 5

"Did you lay this on specially, Joe?"

Dorcas, sitting in the passenger seat of the Morris Oxford cabriolet, looked up from her guidebook and stared with disbelief at the scene in the street before them.

"Certainly didn't," said Joe impatiently. "The street'll be blocked for hours!" He glanced at his watch. "We'll be late. You'd have thought my opposite number...what's his name? Inspector Bonnefoye, that's it...would have warned me this was happening. He must have known."

"I expect he did know," said Dorcas easily. "You'll find it's a dastardly Gallic wheeze to put you in your place and, for the French, your place would always be one step behind and on the wrong foot. It's manipulation...Joe, what *are* those beasts we're looking at? What are they doing in the middle of the city and how fast do they go?"

"Rather splendid, aren't they? Oxen. White oxen. Eight of them pulling each dray at about a hundred yards per hour and there would appear to be drays as far as I can see until they disappear round the corner of the Avenue. Look, this one's dedicated to the wool trade and the next is the biscuit-makers' float. Champagne houses after that..."

"There's a banner! *Reims Magnifique,* that's what we're seeing." She squinted into the distance and read: "It's *la grande cavalcade* and it's celebrating the resurgence of the city after the exigencies of the Great War. Well, it's quite a nuisance but you have to say—well done them!" She looked around her at the cheering crowds, the marching band, the buildings under reconstruction or already rebuilt and still shining clean. "Eight years, Joe, that's all the time they've had to build the city up again from the rubble the German army reduced it to. Look, there's a picture in my book of the cathedral in flames. September 1914. The Germans were over there," she waved an arm vaguely to the north, "and they just took pot shots at it with fire bombs. Some scaffolding around the north tower caught alight and the whole building went up in smoke. Many of their own German wounded who'd been sheltering in the nave were burned to death along with the nuns who were nursing them."

She looked up from her book, face puckering with distress. "They'd been here in the city only days before. They'd seen the beauty of the cathedral right there in front of them. How could they retire a few miles off and deliberately destroy it? I can't understand."

Joe had no answer. He'd felt her increasing sadness as they'd driven south through remembered battlefields and, in the end, had set aside most of the places he'd intended to see as unsuitable for a sensitive young person. He had not anticipated the force of her reaction to the memorials and had watched, disturbed, as the child had stood in floods of tears in front of the very first one they had visited, patiently going through all the names, insisting on pronouncing each one in her own private ritual, unable to move on until each man had been faithfully acknowledged.

"Have you never been this way before, Dorcas?" he'd asked. She reminded him that her father was a pacifist and a conscientious objector who'd spent the war years in Switzerland. They had always travelled through Dieppe and Paris and the war was never referred to. Orlando saw no reason to remind his children of this sorry episode.

In the end Joe had reduced their visits to two places of re-membrance. Mons, where it had all started, and Buzancy, not very distant, where for him it had all finished in that bloody July four months before the end. He'd chosen Buzancy be-cause it represented the combination, at times uneasy, of the allied forces. French, British and American had all fought here. But, above all, he'd chosen it because the small stone monument, a cairn in his eyes, had been hastily built up from material to hand after the battle; it was simple and affecting and bore no heartbreaking lists of the dead. Erected by the 17th French Division in honour of the 15th Scottish, it marked the place on the highest point of the plateau where had fallen the Scottish soldier who had ad-vanced the farthest. A simple two-line inscription said it all, Joe thought:

> *Here the glorious Thistle of Scotland will flourish forever*
> *amid the Roses of France.*

Now they'd arrived in Reims, he was determined to put nostalgic thoughts aside. Put out though he was by the hold-up, he was cheered by the sight of so much determined gaiety around them echoing his mood.

"But look at the town now, Dorcas! It's almost back to-gether again. A triumph of civilization over barbarism you might say. That's worth celebrating. Sit back and enjoy the show! And tomorrow I'll take you to see something really special. Something symbolizing for me and for many others, I know, the spirit of this part of France."

They paused to clap and cheer as another cart creaked past, overflowing with flowers, fruit and vegetables, the produce of the market gardeners of Cormontreuil.

"I'll show you an angel. Not just any old angel. You know…holy-looking…eyes raised piously to heaven… suffering a frightful stomach-ache. This one is smiling. You'll find him by the great door to the cathedral. He's smiling at someone at his elbow, caught, you'd say, in the middle of a conversation, or even telling a joke. And I always look for the glass of champagne in his hand. No—it isn't there, but you can imagine.

"And the Germans didn't have it all their own way! In their hurried retreat from the town—they'd been here for four days—some of the troops got left behind. They were carousing and failed to hear the bugle sound. Sixty of them were taken prisoner single-handedly by the innkeeper. There are tales of French derring-do on every street."

"How about a spot of English dash on this street?" Dorcas suggested. "Look—there's a gap between the floats— they're having problems with that tractor and the policeman who stopped us seems to be rather distracted by the lightly clad young ladies from the Printemps display. Why don't you…?"

Joe had already put his foot down and was surging forward through the gap.

"Left here and second right," shouted Dorcas and, for a moment, Joe was almost glad she was aboard.

* * *

Satisfyingly, they arrived at the Inspector's office a neat five minutes before they were expected and Dorcas had sufficient time to run a comb through her tangled black hair and fasten it back with a red hair ribbon. In short white socks and a red candy-striped dress tied up at the back, English guidebook in hand, she was perfectly acceptable, Joe thought. He introduced her as his niece on her way south to join her father and the young Inspector gave her no more than one brief look, offered her a chair in a corner of his office and politely asked if the young lady spoke French. On impulse, Joe said, "Unfortunately not." The Inspector was clearly not surprised to hear this admission and remarked with only the slightest touch of condescension how unusual it was to hear French spoken so well by an Anglo-Saxon. Where had the Commander learned his French?

He appeared intrigued to hear of Joe's involvement in the later stages of the war with Military Intelligence and his months of working as liaison officer with some distinguished French generals. His eye was drawn for a moment to the discreet ribbon of the Légion d'Honneur which Joe had fixed to his jacket as they mounted the stairs. Joe thought Bonnefoye looked too young to have participated in the war but, from his bearing, he judged he might have at some stage undertaken a military formation. He decided to treat him with the clear-cut good manners of a fellow soldier.

They were politely offered refreshment. Tea? Coffee? Joe deferred to Dorcas who, to his annoyance, went through a pantomime of wide-eyed "What was that, Uncle Joe?" and then produced a triumphant: "*Café*. I'd like *café*, please."

A tray was sent for and the two men settled to business. Files were produced. Dorcas opened her book.

With a few pointed questions the Inspector satisfied himself that Joe had made himself familiar with the facts of the case and was taking it seriously. Joe, in turn, filled in some gaps in his information and noted down the time of the interview the Frenchman had arranged for that afternoon with the doctor in charge of the case. He obtained further details of the four claimants and the Inspector's written permission to interview them at the addresses given if he wished. This was handed over with only the slightest of hesitations. A hesitation which was, however, picked up at once by Joe. With a slanting glance of complicity he took the sheet Bonnefoye was handing him, folded it negligently, sighed and tucked it away in his file. He made a phantom tick against an imaginary checklist on the front page of his file and directed his full attention back over the desk again. After a further few minutes of polite sparring, Joe nodded and closed his file, putting his pen away in his pocket.

"Good. Good," he said, smiling. "Well, I'm sure I shall be able to supply the help I think you're seeking." He stirred in his seat and raised an eyebrow, catching Dorcas's attention. "Ready, my dear?" He turned back to Bonnefoye, halfway out of his seat, hand extended. "Oh, before we go, perhaps you could just give me a clue as to what the position of the French authorities—the Pensions Ministry, shall we say?—might be in this affair should our poor unfortunate prove to be an Englishman?"

To his surprise, the Inspector put back his head and laughed. "I think you know that very well but I will confirm: they will say thank you very much, and post the parcel on to you. Thus saving the department thousands of francs in a country where resources are short! But a positive identification would be most welcome on other grounds. You will be aware of the overheated interest of the press?"

Joe nodded.

"Naturally, everyone from the Senator downwards is under pressure to resolve the problem. And the claimant families are increasingly a force to be reckoned with as they thread their way through the intricacies of bureaucracy, learning a trick or two as they go. They are showing a determination, a tenacity and a talent for trouble-making which no one could have anticipated. I can tell you—they're time-consuming, demanding to the point of aggression and they're becoming a damned nuisance! They've found out about each other's claims and competition's hotting up. Third battle of the Marne about to explode about our ears?" The Inspector shuddered delicately.

"I hear they're even taking bets on the outcome back in England," said Joe sympathetically.

The Inspector's neat black eyebrows signalled mock horror. "Not over here to nobble the favourite...fix the odds...I hope, Sandilands? Seriously, sir, I must emphasize the folly of becoming too closely involved with any of these individuals." He held up a hand to deflect Joe's instant rebuttal. "I do not exaggerate the difficulties. To have survived with their case intact to this point, they must of necessity be determined characters. You must appreciate that. I speak from personal experience when I tell you that they are *involving* and, each in his or her different way, convincing. And they are spreading their net, gaining public support for their own faction. They seem to have tapped into a seam or a mood of national angst—if I may use a German word—and every Frenchman and -woman is passionate to know the outcome. There's more riding on this than the Prix de l'Arc de Triomphe."

"And, of course, the whole world loves a mystery," said Joe.

"True. But the moment it's discovered that the chap is really François Untel, a deserter from Nulleville, then the brouhaha will die off quickly. Even faster if he proves to be Joe (I beg your pardon!) Bloggs from London. As you say— it's the mystery that enthrals. The solution rarely proves to be of equal fascination."

"Yes. Take your meaning," drawled Joe. "And what a let-down it would be, were we ever to reveal the identity of Jack the Ripper."

Bonnefoye smiled. "I am heartened to hear that Scotland Yard is finally in possession of it. We were hoping you would show yourselves a little more effective in the pursuit of our own puzzle," he said. "We will all heave a sigh of relief. We await with interest the outcome of your inspection this afternoon, Commander. Who knows? Perhaps by tomorrow you will be booking an extra passage back over the Channel? And I shall be putting this file away and planning to counter some real crime!"

Joe stood up. "Well, let's remember what Uncle Helmut von Moltke said, shall we? 'No plan survives contact with the enemy for more than twenty-four hours.' Oh, I say... do you have a place where a chap might...?"

"Of course. Let me show you."

Bonnefoye led him to the door and pointed down the corridor. Sighing, Dorcas looked at her watch, opened her book again and waited.

"Well—what did you make of the Inspector?" Joe asked affably when they settled once again in the car.

"I liked him," she said. "Good-looking and he has lovely teeth. I wasn't happy to see you making such a fool of him. Are you always as devious as this?"

"What on earth can you mean?"

"Stop it, Joe! Come off it! I've a jolly good mind to tell Aunt Lydia that you've set me up as some sort of apprentice Mata Hari. She won't be pleased! 'The child doesn't speak French' indeed! How could you know he was going to make a phone call the minute you had your back turned?"

"Did he? Well, I never! I wonder who he rang with such urgency?"

"Two calls actually. You were gone a very long time. The first was to a superior, judging by his respectful tone." Her face lit with mischief. "He was passing on his first impressions of the English policeman. I understood most of it… *dur à cuire*… would that be flattering? He warned whoever it was at the end of the wire that he should not consider attempting bribery. He judged you unsusceptible to that sort of thing. I was longing to tell him you're really about as straight as a corkscrew! But, dumbly, I just had to listen to this ill-informed judgement. The second was to the doctor at the mental hospital confirming the appointment and asking him to spruce up the patient and make him look as attractive a proposition as he could."

"Spruce him up? Huh! They seem to think I'm going to sign a form or two, pop this man into the back seat and drive him straight back home to Blighty."

"Yes, I think so. And if that's what's going to happen, you might as well put in for the bribe, don't you think? I couldn't hear the doctor's response but he didn't seem to like the suggestion. The Inspector was getting exasperated with him."

"Always useful to know these things. Look, I think before we check into the hotel, I'll buy you a hot chocolate. Or a lemonade? Both? There's a *chocolatier* over there. And we can pore over the maps and work out my best route to the hospital. I imagine you'd rather stay behind and have a rest? I'll tell the receptionist to watch out for you and send you up some dinner. I'm sure that'll be all right."

"Joe?"

"Absolutely not! A mental institution is no place for a young girl. Don't even think of it!"

"Not in the least, Commander! Don't concern yourself. It is nothing but a delight to welcome such a fresh young presence inside these drab walls. Better than a bunch of flowers!" The director twinkled gallantly at Dorcas and hurried to draw up a chair for her. "And may I assure the young lady that she will witness no scenes of a distressing nature during your visit?"

From the reports, Joe had pictured a dour, earnest and competent clinician in a long white coat. He was surprised and intrigued by the figure who had come himself to the main door of the hospital to greet them. Impeccably dressed in a grey suit and formal stiff collar, Patrice Varimont was short and bustling, radiating energy and good humour. His dark hair was parted precisely in the centre and controlled by a touch of pomade, his cravat was pinned down by a discreet regimental tie-pin. Joe noticed that all the workers they passed on their way up to his office, medical and civilian, quickened their pace on catching sight of him and murmured a respectful salute before hurrying on.

Varimont settled behind the desk in his well-ordered room, rearranged a neat pile of folders and smoothed down one side of his trim moustache and then the other. He glanced at a wall clock. "Five o'clock! Perfect timing! We'll have English tea." And, without a signal given, the door opened to admit an orderly carrying a tray. "One more cup please, Eugène."

Eugène nodded and went off at the double to fetch it.

When the doctor was happy with the parade of crockery and the timing of the brew, he invited Dorcas to officiate and, while she busied herself happily with this familiar task, he launched at once into the case.

"Before I take you to see the patient, a briefing, I think? Tell me, to save our time, what you already know of our poor unfortunate."

Joe outlined his knowledge, rather underplaying the extent of it and claiming no acquaintance with the medical aspects of shell-shock. "I am here, sir," he summarized, "to explore the implications of your recent revelations regarding the man's country of origin. To try to answer the question, 'Is he English?' No more than that. If he proves to be such, arrangements will be made to convey him to a suitable establishment over the Channel and the onus will then be on the English authorities to assign and identity. Tell me—apart from the language used during the nightmare, are there any other indications that he may be something other than French? Many races took part in the war."

"None that I can discover." The doctor stirred uneasily. "Look—he's not a new arrival, you understand. This is not the first hospital he has fetched up at since repatriation. We are just the first ones to interest ourselves in identifying and solving his problems. He has been passed along, shedding, doubtless, any information…clues…clothing…at each move. I've attempted to back-track but it's hopeless. I've got as far as an asylum in the Ardennes in 1922. Records start there. It's thought he was a late repatriation from Germany. They merely record him as a French soldier sent back without papers or identity. He was wearing the usual

German-issue undergarments with a threadbare French army greatcoat on top. No insignia on it and, of course, it may not even have been his. The only clue—and it may be misleading—was a piece of card with German lettering on it spelling out the name 'Reims.' That one word was the instigation for the original local search. Though you are aware that the net has been spread wider thanks to the publicity afforded by the national newspapers. The man is aphasic. Mute. Until the nightmare no one had ever heard his voice. A typical symptom of war neurosis.

"It's a sorry case, Commander, but, as I would guess you know from experience—" he glanced briefly at Joe's head wound "—not at all unusual." After the slightest pause he said confidentially, "Can't help noticing that your surgery was not done by the hands of an expert. Hope you don't mind my mentioning it. If you would like to have someone unpick that, um, attempt and try again I can put you in touch with a friend in Paris who would rise to the challenge."

Joe smiled his thanks.

The doctor pressed on. "Three hundred and fifty thousand Frenchmen, Commander, were declared missing in combat during the four years of war. Blown to bits, vaporized, buried under tons of earth, some just wandered off quietly perhaps. Leaving behind in limbo countless grieving relatives. And these late releases from prisoner-of-war camps have cruelly led their waiting families to nurse a false hope that one day their loved one will be restored to them. People whose dear ones disappear find it genuinely impossible to believe that they will not come marching through the door at any minute. So much grief, so much yearning, and never an end to it."

"You touched a nerve, I think, with your appeal to the public?"

Varimont sighed and raised eyebrows to the ceiling. "Opened up a hornets' nest might be more apt," he said. "Can I say I regret taking such action, I wonder?"

"Not if you find this poor man a loving home, monsieur," said Dorcas. "If you can do that, it surely will have been worth the effort. I think it's a noble and worthwhile thing that you are doing."

Varimont was startled by the interruption but charmed by the sentiment. Joe was surprised too, by the ease with which Dorcas had spoken in perfectly acceptable French.

"Mademoiselle has a slight accent of the Midi, I detect?" said Varimont.

"My mother is from the south, monsieur. My father is English but we always spend our summers in Provence," Dorcas explained.

"The nightmare," Joe picked up hurriedly. "Has it been repeated?"

"Yes. Once more. After the first explosion I did wonder whether to administer a barbiturate. Calm him down. But my second thought was to let it flow on and camp outside his door to catch any recurrence from the start."

"And did our man have anything further to add?"

"Look here—we could go on calling him 'our man…this poor chap,' we could even refer to him as G27, which is the number on his door, or we could call him—as I do—Thibaud."

"Thibaud?"

"One of the first Counts of Champagne. Very popular name hereabouts. Also the name of my great-uncle whom he much resembles."

"Perfect," said Joe. "Tell me what Thibaud had to say for himself."

"The same short scenario played and replayed. I was able to write down the words—excuse the spelling!" He inclined his head to Dorcas, drawing her into the discussion. "We do not all have a facility for languages." He handed over a sheet from his folder and continued to talk as Joe read it.

"His dream was accompanied by actions as well as words. He sat up on his bed with a shout of alarm then leapt up and strode about the room, gesticulating madly, quarrelling you'd say, with someone he could see very clearly but who was invisible to me, watching from the door. Then he sank to his knees and screamed out in English: 'For God's sake, man! Don't do this! Forgive me! Forgive me!' The effect was very disturbing—very... theatrical. Does what I've written make sense?"

"Certainly does," said Joe. "This is an Englishman begging for his life."

"With some success," said Dorcas thoughtfully, "as he's still with us."

Varimont was silent for a moment then said hesitantly, "Yes, you'd say so. Begging for his life. But, Commander, the odd thing is that his subsequent actions belied the words. He pleaded for mercy with those words, in perfect English as far as I am any judge, but then he acted out a quite extraordinary scene."

The doctor got to his feet and moved to the centre of the room. The short, fastidious, suited figure should have produced the comical effect of a Charlie Chaplin movie as he launched into his mime but Joe and Dorcas watched in growing horror as the meaning of his gestures became clear.

Eyes rolling in a pantomime of rage, Varimont lifted his right foot and kicked out viciously at something (or someone) unseen three feet above the ground. With a snarl, he reached across his body and drew a sword from its scabbard with his right hand, then, holding it up in front of his face with a two-handed grip on the hilt in a hideous semblance of a priestly gesture, he plunged it downwards again and again.

Chapter 6

As they made their way along darkening corridors, following the fast-moving figure of the doctor, Joe was aware of Dorcas scurrying along at his heels, staying much closer than she would normally have done. The architecture would have detained him in other circumstances, its massive Gothic arches and stone-flagged corridors demanding attention. An ancient monastic building of some sort, he would have guessed, which, by being incorporated at a later date into the structure of the town's defences, seemed to have survived the bombardment. Though not entirely unscathed. Distantly, he heard the hammering and shouting of a building team at work on repairs and found he was reassured by the sounds of ordinary life going on in this disconcerting place.

Varimont turned a corner and walked down a narrower corridor, pausing finally in sepulchral gloom in front of a stout oak door. Before he could insert his key in the lock Joe commented: "Formidable defences. You must reassure me, Varimont, that your Thibaud presents no danger to visitors."

"Oh, none at all. These precautions are for his protection. Be reassured, Commander...mademoiselle. When he is not suffering a nightmare, he is calm itself. He sits, sometimes stands, looking into an internal distance. He has a slight re-action to some of his visitors. Some he obviously likes and he expresses this by reaching out to touch their arm, very briefly. Do not be alarmed should he do this, mademoiselle. It is a sign perhaps of his returning humanity."

"What does he do if he takes a dislike to someone?" Dorcas thought it prudent to ask.

"Rather embarrassing, I'm afraid! He climbs into his bed, pulls the blanket over his head and goes to sleep. Come and meet him."

The tall slender man was sitting on his bed, under the single window, hunched and quiet. Not presented in hos-pital pyjamas but duly "spruced up," Joe thought, in a white shirt and pressed trousers. The late afternoon sun caught his head, lighting hair that must once have been blond but was now streaked with grey. He was facing away from them and made no response to their entry or Varimont's cheerful bellow: "Hello there, Thibaud, old chap! And how are you doing today? Look here—I've brought you some visitors."

There were chairs in the sparsely furnished room but they didn't sit. There were brightly coloured posters on the grey walls but the visitors paid no more attention to the scenes of the Châteaux of the Loire than did the occupant of the room. They trooped in and stood awkwardly in front of the patient in a line watching him. Joe had once had to escort a terrified young lady from the cinema, passing in front of a row of people absorbed by the last reel of *The Phantom of the Opera*. Their faces had shown much the same expression as the one he was now studying with attention. The man's focus was elsewhere and someone passing through his field of vision was a momentary annoyance, no more. The doctor chattered on, behaving as though his patient perfectly understood him. In the middle of a sentence and out of joint with the doctor's speech, the man suddenly reached out and stroked his arm twice. At once, Varimont responded with the same gesture. Treating this as the establishment of some kind of communication, he drew Joe forward and introduced him.

Thibaud stared through him, his startling blue eyes expressionless, and made no movement. He must at one time have been an exceptionally handsome man, Joe thought. Even the distortion of the jaw, the pallor and the thinness of the flesh could not quite quench an impression of nobility. Joe spoke a few hearty and meaningless sentences and then floundered, running into the quicksand of indifference. Picking up Joe's hesitation, Varimont then introduced Dorcas.

To both men's surprise, she stepped forward without hesitating to stand directly in front of him. She made no attempt to speak. She put out a hand and gently stroked his cheek in greeting. Then she reached into her pocket and produced a rose-pink biscuit, one of the biscuits they bake in Reims to nibble with their champagne, Joe noticed. She must have brought it with her from the cake shop, he thought, as there had been no such confection on offer in the director's office.

They watched as she snapped it in two, releasing a seductive scent of vanilla and a cloud of icing-sugar, and, murmuring, offered half to Thibaud. Joe felt Varimont, standing close by him, tense as his patient turned his head slightly. He allowed her to open his hand and then close it again over the biscuit. Dorcas carefully moved his hand towards his mouth and he began to eat. Having swallowed the first half, he opened his hand and stretched it out. Dorcas gave him the second half and he crunched his way through that too, to her evident satisfaction. When he'd finished, she tenderly whisked a crumb from his chin, crooning to him in a language Joe had not heard before.

And then Joe heard the doctor gasp in surprise. Thibaud turned to her and looked at her as though he saw her at last and he smiled. A smile of utter sweetness and childlike pleasure. And, swallowing his emotion, Joe acknowledged that of the many smiles that would be directed at Dorcas in the coming years, this was the one above all she would remember. A hand came out again, hesitantly, and reached for her shiny black head. He stroked her hair gently twice.

Standing once again outside Thibaud's room, Joe detained the director before he could lock the door. "A moment, sir. That was all very interesting and involving but in no way does our encounter begin to address the problem of your patient's nationality. I wonder, would you permit me…?"

He outlined his plan and the director nodded in agreement. "Can't do any harm and may tell us something. Carry on, Commander."

Joe opened the door again and checked that the man had, as expected, settled back into his slumped posture, sideways on the bed, face turned away from the door.

In a loud and convincing rendering of an English sergeant major's voice, he barked out an order.

"Atte-e-e-nSHUN! On your feet, laddie! Stand by your bed!" More parade ground commands followed and each was received blankly, with not the slightest twitch of a muscle. Joe went to stand directly in front of him and snapped off a smart salute. "Reporting for duty, SIR!" This time the voice was that of an officer. Impossible for a trained soldier of any rank not to offer the reciprocal salute.

Not one joint of one finger moved in response. Joe looked keenly at the man's features, awake to the slightest shifting expression.

And, finally, Joe's efforts were rewarded. At last the face began to twitch. His nostrils flared. His upper lip trembled. His mouth opened. Thibaud gave a wide yawn, collapsed on to his bed and pulled the blanket over his head.

Chapter 7

Joe waited until he was navigating his course with certainty back across the city before he spoke to Dorcas.

"So—the doctor's efforts 'will have been worth it,' eh? And where, pray, did you learn to juggle the future perfect tense with such confidence, miss?"

He was aware that his question sounded ponderous but he was keen to hear her answer.

She left a silence just long enough to reprove him for his condescension. "Well, it *could* have been—if I'm allowed to use a conditional perfect without incurring disapproval—in the stables of the Vicomte de Montcalme last year. Indeed, I do remember now that it was."

"Oooh! Hoity-toity! If you're going to talk to me like an offended duchess—or worse, her lady's maid—I'm going to throw you out on to the cobbles right now. Are you going to elaborate on that throwaway remark?"

"I don't know where you get your information about me but you must have noticed that my father is a gentleman. He may well be a painter and an English eccentric but I can tell you that these qualities make him very acceptable to aristocratic or rich people who live in the south. He can paint in whatever daubist style is fashionable but what you may not know is that he's a jolly good portrait painter in a traditional way. His productions are 'lively and perceptive,' people say—and I'd add, more importantly, flattering. Last summer he was painting the Vicomte de Montcalme and I used to go along with him and play... *ride,*" she corrected herself hastily, "with the Vicomte's children. Two sons and a daughter. The oldest boy, Félicien, was my special friend. He'll be seventeen now. I'm quite good at copying accents, which is a help. Orlando's been summoned back again to do an equestrian portrait of the Vicomtesse. I can't wait to see them all again!"

Was all this nonsense true? He had no idea. Ought he to have been annoyed by her sharp tone, lacking the deference due from one of her age to a well-meaning adult and amounting, in fact, to a set-down? Joe smiled. Probably. But pulling rank and demanding respect were not his style. There were other ways.

"I see. But I still can't imagine the circumstances," he said innocently, "that would precipitate the use of complex tenses in a *stable*. I find horses respond best to a simple imperative."

Dorcas smiled slightly. "'In a year's time you will have forgotten me.'" She sighed a lingering sigh, remembering.

"Talking horses? Whatever next!"

After a startled moment she burst out laughing and he felt it wise to change the subject. "Tell me, child—whatever prompted you to treat our friend Thibaud in the way you did?"

"He reminded me of a boy in our village who's blind. I know the doctor said all his senses are unimpaired but there was something about his unseeing expression...I did what I normally do when I greet Robin."

"And do you take Robin biscuits?"

"When I have them to offer, yes. I take them from Granny's Chinese jar. Reid always tells me when he's just re-filled it. I was thinking that if this man is really from this area he might respond to a prompting from one of his other senses. Worth a try. A smell associated with his childhood might awaken some memories and, I'd guess, every child born in Champagne was familiar with those pink biscuits. It seemed to work."

"It certainly did. I think you achieved more in two min-utes than the medical profession in as many years."

"I was longing to ask, but I couldn't get a word in edge-wise—do you know if they've tried hypnotism?"

"What do you know about hypnotism, Dorcas?"

"There's a chapter in my book..." She held it towards him and a swift glance revealed it to be *The Wounded Mind* by Lt. Col. M. W. Easterby MD. "Aunt Lydia whipped it from a shelf just before we left. She's done a lot of voluntary work on the wards at St Martin's, did you know that? She thought it might help you out. It's only just been published. The *most* intriguing thing—I've marked the page for you—is the story of a shell-shocked soldier who had lost the power of speech. He began eventually to speak again and he talked in the London accent of the nurses and orderlies who tended him, but under hypnosis he suddenly astonished everyone by reliving his wartime experiences in a *northern* accent. Another patient recognized it as Wearside—you know, from around the River Wear. They tracked him down. He was a Northumberland Fusilier who'd gone missing on the Aisne. But the minute he came out of hypnosis he lost

his Geordie accent and became a Londoner again. I wonder
why the doctor's not hypnotized Thibaud?"

"It's not a popular technique in France, I believe. But it's
a suggestion worth putting if we see him again."

"Were you able to form an impression of Thibaud's nationality? Is he English, do you think?"

"Not proven, I'd say."

"But he spoke in English. We've seen the doctor's record."

"Yes. But I haven't heard him speak myself. I don't know
the doctor. I liked him and I think I'd grow to admire him
as I got to know him but I take no stranger's evidence
without checking, especially witnesses who are closely involved and may be pursuing an agenda of which I'm unaware. I've decided, if you don't mind, Dorcas, to take this
problem further. A day more of research in Reims, perhaps
two, before we go off to the château."

"Are you always as pernickety as this, Joe?"

"Yes. It drives the men mad. I check and recheck and I
make them do the same thing."

Dorcas pulled down the corners of her mouth. "I
thought I was coming on holiday with Mr Holmes—all flash
and flare, inspiration and dramatic deduction—and what
I find I've got is Inspector Lestrade."

Joe grinned. "The world can get along without Holmes,
I suspect, but it can't do without its Lestrades."

"But Thibaud *looks* English," Dorcas persisted.

"Looks are not a reliable indicator. Quite a few French
from the north have Scandinavian blood like the English
and fair or red hair is not uncommon. Like us, they were invaded by waves of Norsemen. Followed by English from the
west, Ottoman Turks from the south and Prussians from
the east."

Dorcas was looking about her as they threaded their way back to the centre. "The poor French! They've been invaded so many times. It's a wonder they stay French. But they do. Look at those clapboard houses, Joe." She pointed to a row of wooden buildings hastily erected amongst the rubble of an ancient market place. "You could imagine a shanty town in the Californian gold rush but then you see the beautiful lettering on the shop-fronts, the net curtains, the shining paintwork and the neat piles of produce and you know you couldn't be anywhere but in France."

"They came up from their cellars, rolled up their sleeves and just got on with it," said Joe. "And all the way through that misery they kept saying the same thing: '*On les aura!*'— 'We'll get 'em!' And in the end, they did," he said sentimentally. "But at what a cost!"

"And so many people paid the bill," said Dorcas quietly.

Joe stared in dismay at the blackened stumps on either side of the great doors on the west façade of the cathedral and felt foolish.

"It's gone! Of course . . . smashed to pieces by long-range artillery like the rest of the statues. I had thought that here on the western side they might have escaped. These portals were crowded with them . . . saints and angels. The loveliest of medieval sculptures and all very natural, quite unlike the stylized, elongated ones at Chartres. They used to be there." He waved a hand. "Standing about. You'd have said a cocktail party was going on. And there," he pointed above his head, "is where you'd have found your host—the smiling angel."

"There's work going on—listen!" said Dorcas. "It's bound to take time. It makes a lot of sense to rebuild the houses and shops before the churches. I'll have to come back in a few years from now if I want to see this famous angel."

Joe shook his head. "Impossible to re-create, I'd say. I think, sadly, I've looked my last on him."

"Oh, don't be so sure of that," said a jovial voice behind them and they turned to see a figure from the Middle Ages watching them. A miller was Joe's first impression. Surely not? He wore a miller's hat, white with dust, and an equally dusty smock of holland fabric down to his knees. Plaster-caked trousers were secured with string at the bottom and his feet were shod with clogs. Above a grey-streaked beard, sharp, kindly eyes twinkled at them through a pince-nez.

"Come with me and I'll show you a wonder! This way, young lady, over that plank and mind where you put your feet."

Intrigued, they followed their jaunty guide through a stonemason's yard and into the shell-damaged but service-able shelter of an outbuilding which might at one time have been a chapel but was now a workshop. Joe was enchanted by the medieval scene being played out all around them, a reassuring blend of bustle and order. Men looked up from their chipping to greet them and to smile warmly at Dorcas. Their work reclaimed their attention at once and claimed Joe's attention also. Figures from the façades and ledges of the cathedral were being recarved. The fine-grained lime-stone of the region was being used for repair or complete re-construction and by hands which were the equal in skill, it seemed, of their ancestors.

"Over here!" They followed their guide, whom Joe guessed to be a master builder, judging by the signs of recognition he was receiving from his crew as he passed. "There he is. The gentleman you were looking for, young lady."

He waved an introductory hand as Dorcas stood wondering, a tiny figure, in front of the seven-foot-high angel. A
perfect, gleaming new figure. Beneficent and urbane, he
beamed his remembered welcome.

"But how? Can it be . . . ?" Joe murmured.

"Not the original unfortunately. No. That was shattered
beyond repair. But—" he held up a finger for emphasis
"—the Monuments Museum had, years ago, had the fore-
thought to have a cast made and it was preserved in Paris. I
have replicated the angel using the cast as a guide for my
carving."

"What a beautiful result!" said Joe. "Worth every effort
and a witness for evermore of your talent, monsieur." His
admiration compelled an old-fashioned but spontaneous
bow.

The sculptor beamed in recognition of the compliment.

"And when may we see him back in his rightful place?"

"I fear this will be some time in the future. Money has
been short. What the town has it spends on rehousing its
inhabitants." He smiled. "You'd say every architect in France
is busy in Reims and all trying to express themselves in the
new style."

"Art deco, you mean?" said Joe.

"Is that what you'd call it?" said the sculptor with gentle
irony. "Not sure about 'deco' . . . or 'art,' for that matter. But
we'll see. I shall have to try to get used to it. Repairs to the
damaged fabric have been going on here at Notre Dame
though not as fast as some of us would like. But with the in-
jection of a very large sum of American dollars and some
English pounds, work—as you can hear—goes on apace.
Soon we may have a façade on which to mount him. Well,
there you are. I hope he does not disappoint the young
lady."

"I think he's the most wonderful man I've ever seen! Don't you think so, Joe?"

"Always have," said Joe.

They said farewell to their guide and made their way back out into the morning sunshine.

"Two special smiles in as many days," said Joe. "Any similarity?"

"Hardly any," said Dorcas. "Thibaud's smile was sweet but it was just a reaction. There was no thought behind it. It didn't really reach his eyes, did it? The angel was all bright intelligence and good humour. His brain was creating the smile. I really think Thibaud's brain is mostly dead or frozen up somehow. But I'll tell you this, Joe—if ever our forgotten soldier were to come back to the world again and if he were to smile... good heavens!... it would be a smile worth waiting for."

"Are we going back to the hospital?" Dorcas wanted to know as they regained the car.

"Ah, no," said Joe. "I thought I'd make a start on interviewing one or two of the claimants. With Bonnefoye's introduction and signed permission in my pocket I think they'll agree to see me. Though I rather thought I'd start by going off at a tangent. One of the names on that list is a bit of a dark horse and I'd like to take a surreptitious look at its teeth before I begin anything so formal as an interview. My first call is at a house a street or two away and there is no way in the world I will agree to your accompanying me there. I'm going to park the car a couple of doors down and lock you in with your book while I go in."

"Are you seeing one of the claimants?"

"No. I'm paying an unscheduled visit to someone who

may be able to shed light on one of them. A past employer, if you like, with...um...commercial premises in the rue de la Magdeleine. The lady may be able to furnish a reference and background information."

Dorcas's look of puzzlement cleared. "Oh, you're off to a brothel! On the trail of Mademoiselle Desforges." She nodded wisely. "That'll be the Rêves de l'Orient. Everyone's heard about that! It has quite a reputation in tourist circles. Well, don't get carried away by your research. I don't want to have to tell Aunt Lydia you parked me outside a Reims house of ill-repute for an hour while you visited. Oh—and I won't be locked in. Suppose the car caught fire? They *do*, you know! Look—park the car here," she said as they passed along an elegant shop-lined street. "There's things for me to look at. I can see the new Galeries Lafayette. You can walk from here. Leave me the keys and I promise I'll be here safe and sound when you get back."

She consulted her watch in a marked manner.

"If she tells me to 'run along now' I shall put her on the first train to Nice with a label round her neck," Joe vowed silently.

He strode along the pavement of the rue de la Magdeleine checking the blue enamelled numbers of the refurbished town houses, a run of elegant façades. Had he got the right street? And there it was at the end, set a little way back and looking very proper with its newly painted front door and fresh draperies at the windows. He avoided turning in through the wrought-iron gate and strolled on around the corner. A second entrance at the side of the house and giving on to a street leading towards the river showed signs of use. The iron handrail which led up to the door was worn to a ribbon slenderness, the steps slightly dipped towards the centre. He was quite certain that, in their discreet

French way of going on, there would be an even more reti-
cent back door if he were to pursue his exploration. As he
lifted the knocker and rapped he thought he could well be
visiting his doctor or his dentist. Only the brass plate was
lacking.

The door was opened at once by a maid in dark dress and
white cap. She took his hat and whisked ahead of him down
the tiled hall, calling to him to take care—the floor was just
washed and not yet dry. She showed him in to a parlour
overlooking the street. Joe looked around him. The furnish-
ings were sumptuous and very new and all were imported
from the East. A small jungle of large-leafed plants appeared to have broken out.

"Do sit down, monsieur. Madame will be with you directly," the girl said sweetly, and left him deciding what to
do with himself.

The air was stale with the scent of last night's Havana
cigars, last night's Soir d'Été perfume too, both beginning
to lose the battle with the not unpleasant smell of freshly
laid Wilton carpet and beeswax polish. A silk-covered divan,
which appeared to be the principal seating, was piled high
with cushions in raging shades of red and purple and was
disconcertingly low. He did not wish to be discovered
lolling. Nor did he wish to stand about in a menacing way.
His eye lit on two Louis XV chairs, one on either side of the
door, and he firmly carried them over to the window and
set them facing each other. He'd carry out this interview
knee to knee, eye to eye. A moment's study of the window-
locking arrangements, never simple in France, was produc-
tive; in six moves he had managed to raise the window a
foot and stood by it breathing in the fresh morning air.

"Monsieur makes himself at home?"

He hadn't heard her enter and turned to see a handsome

woman of middle age watching him. There was calculation in her eyes though the tone of her question had been light, almost teasing.

"I've never felt at home in a *kala jugga*, madame," he said, waving an explanatory hand at the greenery.

"Ah? Monsieur has lived in India?"

"For a short time."

"You are English?"

"Say rather—Scottish."

She appeared to be encouraged by this confidence and moved forward to take the chair opposite him. Lydia would have approved of the single row of good pearls and the dark linen pleated day dress which could have come from the hands of Mademoiselle Chanel. The head-hugging haircut with its emphatic fringe framed a face which needed no additional emphasis. The strong, over-large nose and black eyebrows would have been overpowering without the sweetly curving red cupid's bow of a mouth. She crossed her legs neatly at the ankles and leaned towards him. "Always delighted to welcome a Scottish gentleman," she murmured. A flash of interest in her expression made him think that perhaps her sentiment owed more to experience than flattery. She looked at him with increasing warmth.

A not unusual reaction. He'd learned to use this French affection for all things Scottish to his advantage. For them, the English would always, though fighting and falling shoulder to shoulder with them, represent *le perfide Albion* but the Scots were a different matter. He'd first become aware of this perception of his fellow countrymen at a very low moment. Shot through the shoulder fighting a rearguard action at Mariette Bridge near Mons, he'd insisted on getting back into the thick of things as soon as he could struggle out of the hospital cart and, separated from his unit, had been sent along with the front ranks of the fast-retreating British Expeditionary Force south to...who knew where? He'd been instructed to act in the capacity of Staff Officer with knowledge of the language—never enough of these to be found—in order to facilitate the liaison of the French and British commanders—when they could be herded together. As these gentlemen appeared only too happy to avoid each other, Joe felt he'd been handed an uncomfortable duty. On the one occasion he'd met the Anglophobic General Lanrezac he'd been bursting to give the supercilious commander in whose unreliable hands lay the fate of an exhausted British Expeditionary Force a piece of his mind. His fingers had itched to turn the map upside down and tell him to get on with it. Lanrezac could, with his eternal back-pedalling, have given Quintus Fabius Maximus Cunctator a lesson in time-wasting. But Joe's duty was to stand unremarked in the background, listening and quietly seething as he murmured into the ear of his own commanding officer translations of Lanrezac's dismissive remarks and disconnected policy.

For the rest of the time in those desperate days when the British had force-marched their way, fighting every inch down the undulating white road towards the Marne, he'd made himself useful in the confusion, organizing supply dumps at crossroads, clearing the roadways, directing lost soldiers to their companies. He'd even caught a runaway horse and joined a cavalry patrol riding out to ambush and exterminate a German cavalry force threatening their right flank.

After eleven days with little sleep and food the men had slogged their way all night through the deep Forest of Crécy. They had emerged into the centre of a fairy-tale village with its small château, all untouched by the war and, in this idyllic place, someone had finally called a halt. The men had collapsed where they stood. Some who'd fallen on the road were dragged out of the path of wheels and hooves by their mates. They made it in their hundreds into the shelter of the apple and pear trees of an orchard and lay down more dead than alive.

This was it. This far and no farther. Here they would re-group, turn their faces to the north again and fight their way back. The retreat from Mons was over.

Joe had been in the village square conferring with the local mayor, supervising the available food supplies and sleeping arrangements, when his attention was demanded by a Valkyrie voice. A female voice. The mayor, at the sound, stopped speaking in mid-sentence, muttered his apologies and took flight. An elderly Frenchwoman, of some standing apparently, had arrived on a bicycle with her old groom in attendance, similarly mounted.

"You there!"

Joe automatically saluted the imposing figure clad, im-probably, in riding coat and brimmed veiled hat.

"I wish to see your billeting officer."

He had accompanied her to the schoolroom being used as billeting HQ. The officer in charge Joe remembered with affection. His name was Bates. A man with an amazing memory for names and a facility for making possible the seemingly impossible. Bates had leapt to his feet and saluted, as had Joe. The lady announced herself to be the owner of the nearby château and she suspected (correctly) that her property was on their billeting list.

"You will send me Scotsmen," she announced. "I will accept nothing but Scotsmen. I'm quite certain you have some."

Sensing their surprise, she thought to add an explanation: "My family, including six small grandchildren, have fled their home in the Ardennes and taken refuge with me. I am told that the Scottish soldiers are excellent child-minders and may be trusted not to break one's possessions."

Waiting until she had left and avoiding Joe's eye, Bates thumbed through his list, licked his pencil and made a few adjustments. "If that's how her ladyship wants it, we can oblige. What about that mob of hairy kilted blokes who staggered in last night? A dozen assorted Highlanders! I'll wake 'em up and send 'em along to the château. Right now!"

"Those kilted blokes are the handful of Gordons who managed to get away after le Câteau. The rest of their unit was shot to bits holding up von Bülow's lot for a day. We wouldn't be here if they hadn't watched our backs," said Joe quietly. "Let them sleep. But, yes, send them along to Madame la Baronne when they wake up," he added. "Why not? They've earned a bit of luxury."

The past, deliberately repressed for years, was floating in bubbles to the surface of his mind again, released by familiar sights and now, apparently, by no more than a sound—the simple sound of a Frenchwoman's voice pronouncing the word "*Écossais.*"

"Monsieur is from Edinburgh?" she asked.

"Yes," he agreed easily, "from Edinburgh."

"At all events—this is your first visit to the Rêve. You are on your way to the south?"

"Indeed." Joe nodded. "I hope I do not arrive at an inconvenient hour?"

"For us, monsieur, no hour is inconvenient. We have our late-night owls but we have our early-morning cockerels too."

Joe was almost disappointed that the description was undeserved. The image pleased him.

"And you will be unaware of the particularities of the house? Let me show you..."

She rose to her feet and took a folder from a gilded table. Returning to her seat she selected what seemed to be a brochure from the folder and handed it to him. In some surprise he leafed through it.

"Ah—the Turkish Harem. Yes, there it is, illustrated. Carpets, divans and the rest of it...The Japanese Room... looks the teeniest bit uncomfortable...but perhaps that's the point? The Rajah's Palace complete with tiger skins. The Sheik's Tent. Lacking only the smouldering presence of Rudolph Valentino...The Queen of Sheba's Bathroom... Good Lord! Can that possibly be authentic?"

Increasingly uneasy with his tone, she reached out and snatched the book from him.

"You are to be complimented on your ingenuity, madame. Unfortunately, I am here not to inspect or sample what you have to offer but to beg your assistance."

"My assistance?" The lady was puzzled and becoming more wary by the second.

Joe produced the letter of authority from Inspector Bonnefoye. To his surprise she laughed as she handed it back to him.

"Ah. My first thought was that perhaps you were a policeman."

"The feet?" he asked in some amusement. "Do the feet give me away?"

"Not at all. It is the arrogance. Not even the Senator would have the bad manners to rearrange my furniture and dismiss my presentation as a...a...menu! But—very well. If Jean-Philippe vouches for you, then you have my attention, Commandant. Tell me how I may help you."

"I want you to tell me whatever you can concerning the background of one of your employees. The Inspector tells me she works for you and has worked for you since before the war. A Mademoiselle Desforges. Mireille Desforges."

Her puzzled frown was sincere and he questioned further. "She *is* employed by you, I take it? I have not been misinformed?"

"Mireille does indeed do work for me and if it's her taxation standing you are interested in, I can assure you that all our paperwork is in good order. Though the records preceding 1918 are unavailable. We did not entirely escape the damage, you understand. You are welcome to inspect what we have, though how it could possibly be the concern of a Scottish policeman I cannot conceive."

"No. No. I wish only to hear what you have to tell me of the war years. Indeed, my enquiries may bring only good news and perhaps even a healthy financial prospect for the lady."

"Of course. You are examining her claim on the missing soldier." Relieved to have worked out the motive for his visit she relaxed and tapped his arm. "Believe her. That's my advice. Mireille is as honest as the day is long. Hard-working and virtuous. Yes," she repeated, sensing his surprise, "yes, virtuous. She may have had an affair with a cavalry officer and he a married man but she has remained faithful to him and his memory through all these long years. And now, of course, it's far too late for her to take up with any other man—even if there were supplies available. She must be in her early thirties, poor dear, and no longer a marriage prospect."

Joe was beginning to think he had lost any grip on this interview. He cleared his throat. "Before we go any further, madame, would you mind telling me, in your own words, in precisely what capacity Mademoiselle Desforges is employed by you?"

The sharp dark eyes narrowed and then flared in comprehension. He did not like to hear the shout of mocking laughter that followed. He listened in embarrassed silence as she jumped up and rang for the maid.

"Louise, I want you to fetch Mademoiselle Lakshmi. And Mademoiselle Benzai. They are both dressed and ready, I take it? Good. Tell them I wish them to parade for a Scottish gentleman."

Chapter 8

Joe's protests were waved away and the girls were swiftly in attendance. Looking completely at ease in their setting, they swayed into the room, arms gracefully about each other's waist, and Joe rose to his feet to greet them. Under their exotic disguises both girls were French, he thought, but it was easy enough to tell one from the other.

"Mademoiselle Lakshmi." He gave a slight bow to the slender dark girl wearing a startling confection of purple and shocking pink. The Indian sari was as perfect a sample as he had seen in a maharaja's palace. Convincing also was the gauzy veil she held flirtatiously over her lower face and the ruby forehead jewel gleaming on her smooth skin. "And Mademoiselle Benzai." He acknowledged the stiff white silk draperies of the high-waisted dress which could have graced a performance of *The Mikado* at the Savoy.

"I must ask you to keep your excitement in check, ladies," said his hostess drily. "The gentleman is window-shopping only this morning. I think he has seen enough to satisfy his curiosity. You may leave us now."

Joe was piqued to be so flippantly set aside and he found he was stung by the looks of smiling complicity exchanged by the women. As the girls turned to withdraw, he moved swiftly to open the door for them and caught their attention: "Mesdemoiselles! I am utterly charmed." He smiled merrily at the two girls. This was one of those occasions when he regretted he had no luxuriant moustache to twirl in a suggestive way. "Goddesses of Love, indeed! And may I say how I look forward to the moment when Time favours me and once again the Thistle of Scotland may flourish among the Roses of France?" he finished gallantly.

She turned an amused face to him. "Well, there you are. You may judge for yourself the artistry of Mademoiselle Desforges. A more enterprising girl could have obtained a position with the Ballets Russes. She has the flair of a Bakst combined with the practical skills of a Jeanne Lanvin. All our costumes come from her sketch pad and her needle. All our rooms, the design, the draperies, are of her creation. My dress—" she stood and twirled in front of him with the aplomb of a mannequin—"would have cost a hundred times more in Paris."

Enjoying his stricken silence she pressed on, helpful, informative. "She took over her father's tailoring business in the rue Baudricourt when he became ill just before the war. The war disrupted everything, of course, and she fled to Paris for a year or two but, on her return, she took up the business again and transformed it into the enterprise you may see if you pay her a visit. There are those who say her talents are quite wasted here in the provinces. But I am pleased to know her and glad that I have been able to encourage her. Women are learning to help one another out, Commandant, to snatch at the jobs men have jealously guarded for themselves. Perhaps the only good thing that will have resulted from those frightful years. But tell me, are you going to uphold Mireille's identification of her lover? She is not a woman to make a mistake. She lived with the man off and on for the four years of the war. She would know him whatever has happened to him in the meantime. And why is your friend and colleague," she smiled slyly, "Bonnefoye—so aptly named, wouldn't you say?—not capable of sorting out this dispute himself? He is a most able young man. Why does he have to apply to Scotland Yard for help?"

"I am here, not in the capacity of Metropolitan London detective, madame, but working under the auspices of Interpol. You are aware of Interpol?"

She nodded, puzzled.

"The French authorities investigating the problem have cast doubt on the man's nationality. There is a suspicion that he may, in fact, be English and Interpol called on us to check this. Being an ex-soldier myself and having some experience of this part of the land and the French language, I was deputed to look into the matter."

"And you start your enquiry with me? I am flattered by your attention, monsieur, but suspicious as to your motives. Mireille is a valued colleague and I do not feel easy discussing her private life with you. As soon as you leave I shall telephone her and warn her that you are sniffing along on her trail."

She would have delivered a further broadside but was distracted by the side-door bell which rang out, signalling more serious business. At once her anger evaporated and her professional mask of calm understanding descended.

Joe didn't wait to be dismissed. "The back door?" he said cheerfully. "I'll show myself out." He reached for her hand and held it. "I have heard all that you have said, madame, and am truly grateful for the time you have spent talking to me." On impulse, he clicked his heels, raised her hand and kissed it and made at once for the door.

Preoccupied with his encounter, he checked his watch anxiously on finding he'd taken a wrong turning and only managed to steer his way back to the car by remembering Dorcas's request to be parked in front of the Galeries Lafayette. He was a little later than he had hoped to be and was not surprised to see the car door being flung open impatiently for him as he neared it.

It was a moment before he noticed. "What's that strange smell?"

Dorcas waggled her head about and stared at him until he realized.

"Good Lord! What have you done with your hair?"

The wretched girl was wearing almost the same haircut as the madame he had just left.

"I thought I'd just slip into the coiffeur over there and have it trimmed. It looks far more modern, don't you agree? Estelle who did it said it was about time. No French girl has had long hair like mine for years. She trained in Paris, you know. This is the look all the mannequins have. She waved it with setting lotion—that's what you can smell. I'm very pleased with it." She glared at him from under the fringe, disappointed by his silence. "And so will be Aunt Lydia. She told me I might have it done if I wished. She even gave me some money for it," she lied.

"Yes, she's bound to like it, Dorcas. And so do I. I think. In fact, I'm almost sure. I suppose, as our friend the sculptor said, 'I shall just have to get used to it.' Bit old-fashioned, I'm afraid. But young Georges at the château will love it. Bound to!

"Now, if you're prepared, I think you could well accompany me to the rue Baudricourt to meet Mademoiselle Desforges, who turns out to be the entirely respectable owner of a tailoring and design establishment. Another example of post-war female enterprise."

Dorcas grinned. "Men had better watch out. Soon all that'll be left for you to do is fight each other."

Gold lettering on the dark blue fascia of a renovated shop announced her business: *Desforges, Tailleur. Confection de Dames. Paris Reims.* As an illustration, one window showed a single gown discreetly lit. A carved mannequin turned its back with insouciance on the window-shopper, showing off a black cocktail dress in mousseline de soie. The low-cut neckline dipped almost to the waist, silk ribbons floated from the shoulders and a long rope of pearls swung teasingly down the back. Dorcas stared in fascination.

The elderly servant who answered the bell was resentful of their presence on the doorstep. She greeted them, grudgingly acknowledging that Mademoiselle was expecting them. "She is very busy and can only afford you a short interview," she added.

"Thank you, Marie. I'll take our guests through to my office. You must be the Scottish policeman but I had no idea you had an assistant. Ah? Your niece. I'm delighted to meet you, mademoiselle." The voice was low and musical, the figure they followed along a corridor was youthful and slim, charming in its navy linen dress and white collar. She paused before a door and turned to them, a finger raised in warning. "Here I must ask you to step with care—we're about to pass through the machine room. The girls are busy with a rush order for a Paris nightclub. They are always rush orders! And it all moves so quickly these days. Every week a new cabaret opens and we'll have barely filled their first order before they've changed their star and the new prima donna demands an entirely different set of costumes."

To Joe's amusement the ten girls pedalling on treadle sewing machines were churning out a series of extremely short skirts in yellow and green. Mademoiselle Desforges laughed and picked up one of the outfits.

"This week it's bananas—with the odd discreetly placed green leaf, of course. Suddenly everyone wants tropical fruit. Next week...who knows?"

"Surely that's...?" Joe began.

"The divine Miss Baker. Yes. Costumes for her new show. Josephine designed the original—bananas threaded on to a string—but you can imagine the dangers! Energetic dancer that she is, that delicious derrière is in danger of exposure at any moment. And perhaps that's the point, but we are engaged to kit out a whole chorus line with something a little more substantial and durable." She tugged at the waistband to demonstrate the strength. "You see? We wouldn't want an unforeseen event on the front row stealing the limelight from the leading lady!"

A further room was crossed, this one crowded with racks and rails of colourful garments, an Aladdin's cave for Dorcas who managed, by loitering, to finger some of the satins and furs as they passed by. Catching her interest, Mireille loitered alongside identifying some of the costumes. "...and this one, all diamanté and red feathers, is a commission from Max for the Folies Bergères and these will be worn by Mistinguett...she opens in *Ça c'est Paris* at the Moulin Rouge later this year. Ah! Those are for the Dolly Sisters at the Casino de Paris..."

Joe's impatient throat-clearing and foot-tapping went unregarded and it seemed an eternity before they broke free of the frou-frous and entered her office.

The room was small and, in contrast with the previous display, spartan in appearance. Two of the walls were lined with shelves of ledgers. A third wall was covered with tacked-up music hall posters of a style and radiance that caught Joe's eye. Mistinguett, Barbette, Doriane flaunted extravagant confections of feathers and chiffon revealing tempting glimpses of long performers' limbs and bold eyes. "Your designs, mademoiselle?" he asked.

"I wish I could say so. No. I pin them there for inspiration. The artist is Charles Gesmar. Have you heard of him? He is depressingly young but a genius, I think."

The desk taking up most of the floor space was polished and clear but for a note pad and an elaborate black and gold telephone. An open French window gave on to a small courtyard bright with flowers. Joe settled to take his first steady look at Mademoiselle Desforges. Older than her silhouette suggested, she must have been about his own age. Her fine skin was beginning to line but the high cheekbones, the well-shaped mouth and the tilted hazel eyes would ensure that she remained a beautiful woman. Her gaze was intelligent, her gestures responsive. An actress. Yes, that expressive face, those controlled but slightly exaggerated movements were those of an actress. He was on his guard.

Most people he interviewed automatically put on a mask for the occasion even if they had nothing to hide. Nine times out of ten he would patiently prise away the mask only to find the same innocent features hiding underneath. On the tenth occasion something dark and hideous would be exposed.

But he thought he had never spoken to anyone less bent

on concealment than this woman. "You will, of course, want to know the truth of my relationship with Dominique. Yes, that is his name. He is Dominique de Villancourt. A cavalry officer with the Dragoons. A Parisian. Graduate of the Academy at St Cyr. He was my lover throughout the war years. He told me that he had a wife in Paris and that he did not love her. I can only assume he was telling me the truth of this because he spent every available leave with me. When the German army invaded Champagne in 1914 he managed to reach me and put me on the last evacuation train into Paris. He pushed an address into my hand and told me to go there. It was an apartment overlooking the Bois de Boulogne. I spent the more dangerous periods of the war years there and he came whenever he could. Sometimes we met here when things calmed down. We were lucky—this house escaped the shelling, you see.

"His wife, he said, knew nothing of the arrangement. The Paris apartment was in my name. He transferred the deeds from his name to mine. I kept all the documents and handed them to Inspector Bonnefoye for verification. He has, I understand, successfully authenticated Dominique's signature. After the war when he did not return I sold it and invested the money in reinvigorating my father's business here in Reims. I learned much in Paris. I was not a 'kept woman,' monsieur. Oh, no! I earned wages by working in the theatres. Starvation wages! But it was the knowledge and skills I was building to say nothing of the contacts I was making that have stood me in good stead." She waved a hand around her office. "I am doing rather well, you see.

"But I owe it all to Dominique. I still work—ludicrous, I know, but it's how I feel—for him. For a future together. I have never accepted his death…" She gave them both a challenging look. "It's pathetic, I understand that, and I see the embarrassed pity in your eyes before you look politely away, but the conviction that he is alive and will one day come back to me has always been so strong that it is quite useless to fight it."

"How did you meet this officer?" Dorcas asked, enchanted by the story. "Oh, I say, I'm sorry...excuse me... it's none of my business...Sorry, Uncle Joe."

Mireille turned and smiled at her. A smile to match Thibaud's, Joe thought.

"It was very romantic! I was working here—in the old shop, that is—helping my father with his tailoring when a dashing young officer came in. Literally dashing! He was in a hurry—his regiment was being sent north to harry the Germans and the sleeve of his tunic was hanging off. A respectable dragoon does not harry Germans looking like a scarecrow! He needed attention on the spot. The standard of tailoring in those days was appalling but so much to do in so little time...My father was away so I did the work myself. He stood in his shirtsleeves and watched me while I sewed. We talked. We flirted. We fell in love. He said he would return. I knew he would and he did. And I know he will again." She looked at them with speculation and came to a decision. "Come with me. I want to show you something."

She led them out through the French window, across the courtyard and into a recently built extension to her empire.

"This is where I live. I hope you like the modern style?"

"I visited the exhibition of Arts Décoratifs in Paris last year," said Joe warily, "and was most impressed."

He made further polite comments as she showed off her cool white interiors with their accents of black, grey and cobalt blue; he enjoyed the gleam of chrome, the sculpted lines of the black leather chairs, the feeling of generous space after the bustle and clutter of the commercial premises. "Your own design?" he asked.

"No. The work of a charming though expensive young architect from Paris. I bring you here to impress you, not with my success and my taste but to give you an idea of my grasp on reality. I want to demonstrate that here lives a woman who is firmly rooted in the modern world...a woman of common sense and energy who can look to the past and not ignore it and to the future and not fear it but who can—and does—live fully in the present. Oh, dear!" She smiled in apology. "I don't like to hear myself blowing my own trumpet but time is short. You are a stranger whom, for some reason of instinct, I wish to impress. Forgive me for showing off but you will understand that it is a necessary preparation for the next room I shall show you. This one is back over there in the old building and is indeed a re-creation of the living quarters of the old house. My father's old parlour. It is very special."

Joe guessed what she was attempting before he stepped through the parlour door. And stepped into a different age. It took a moment to adjust to the scene. He found himself in a room from before the war. Dim, cosy, overstuffed and decorated in the manner of the *belle époque,* was his first impression. A thick wreath of wood-smoke spiked with the orange peel and rose petal scent of pot-pourri was almost overpowering. Red plush curtains and potted palms, gold chandelier far too imposing for the room—after the clean geometric lines of Mireille's house, it was all an assault on the senses and very surprising.

There was a pair of well-worn armchairs, one on either side of the fireplace where a log fire smouldered, and it was towards these chairs that Dorcas strayed. Joe watched her take in the collection of items cluttering the top of a table by the side of one of the chairs: a pipe, still half full of burned tobacco, a tobacco pouch, a dusty brandy glass with the faintest trace of brown liquid in the bottom. From under a footstool a pair of black patent slippers decorated with bumblebees peeked out. A copy of *War and Peace* had been abandoned over one arm of the chair. The other chair was occupied. A fat white cat gave Dorcas silent warning of his displeasure at being disturbed and she crept away.

Joe breathed in the atmosphere of the room, torn between two reactions. Should he be seduced by the homely allure, the suggestion of every kind of masculine comfort on offer? He didn't doubt that upstairs there existed a similar shrine ready to provide solace for a weary returning soldier. His mind ranged briefly over feather beds, fresh linen, afternoon sun filtering through shutters, and flushed at the thought. Catching Mireille's slight smile he wondered if she had caught him out. Of course she had. And the woman's intelligence and awareness rendered invalid his alternative reaction. This was no Dickensian scene of mad longings never to be fulfilled. Mireille Desforges was no Miss Havisham. She understood herself, laughed at and forgave herself for this indulgence.

"This is the room he will return to?" whispered Dorcas, respectful as a pilgrim at a shrine.

"It's the room he has never truly left," said Mireille quietly, her eyes shining with suppressed tears. "He was happy here. If only I can bring him back, he will settle into his chair and pick up his book where he left off. He will feel secure with his cat on his knee. His cat will know him and welcome him."

She picked up the cat and hugged him but he struggled and made it quite clear that this demonstration was inappropriate. With a shrug, she replaced him on his cushion.

"Louis was a kitten when Dominique brought him to me as a gift. The trouble with cats—do you have a cat, mademoiselle?—then I'll tell you—you cannot compel or even expect their affection. And Louis has always understood himself to be Dominique's cat. Indeed, I do believe he understands Dominique to be *his* human. You'd swear that he holds me responsible in some way for his disappearance! He's getting old now but he'll remember. He'll leap on to his master's knee, purr in triumph and favour me with his narrow-eyed proprietorial sneer. And—believe me—I shall be delighted to see it!"

"You are both waiting," said Dorcas.

"Exactly. Louis despises me and I don't like cats. It's clear that we ought to have parted company years ago but . . . he's a link with Dominique. Can you understand this foolishness?"

"And this is your dragoon?" said Dorcas, pointing to photographs on a sideboard.

Mireille picked one up and held it lovingly in her hands for a moment before passing it to Dorcas.

Joe was intrigued to see the interaction between the two and perfectly content to stand quietly by and watch the scene play out.

Dorcas stared and gulped. "Golly! What a hero! And—yes—I can see the likeness. Do you see it, Uncle Joe?" She passed it to Joe.

"Yes, I do. It's very clear," said Joe.

The stern face was handsome, the pose a rigid and conventional professional portrait of a cavalry officer in full regalia.

"Taken sometime after 1916, I think? He's wearing the new-issue uniform in *blue d'horizon*. May I?"

She nodded her consent and he slipped the photograph

from its frame. The name of a Paris studio was printed on the back and a date: 1916. He looked again carefully at the soldier. "Your officer had been wounded by this stage of the war, mademoiselle?"

"You have sharp eyes, Commander," she said. "Yes indeed. And I gave a full report on what I remember of his wounds to the Inspector. Dominique had a sabre cut to his right upper arm. A flesh wound, the bone was not affected. It was for that he was given the wound chevron you have spotted sewn on to his left sleeve. But he has a later wound also. His jaw was broken, he told me by a rifle butt, towards the end of the campaign around Soissons. That was the last time I saw him. He could barely speak but he was determined to go off and rejoin his regiment. He was very distressed. I think he had had a bad time and knew he was about to have a worse. I believe he knew he would not return. He was returning to the Chemin des Dames, as we later called that disastrous encounter."

"And what was his rank, mademoiselle, the last time you saw him?"

"He had risen to be a Lieutenant Colonel. He was an officer of considerable standing by the end. The uniform in which he last fought—and perhaps died—would have borne that insignia, along with three, possibly four, service chevrons on his right sleeve and two war-wound chevrons on the left. I stitched the second one on myself," she said quietly, looking down at her hands.

She hesitated for a moment and then decided to confide in him. "I don't know how many of the facts of the case they have told you, Commander…I want you to know that I have no motive in claiming Dominique other than concern for his welfare. You have seen his circumstances. It is intolerable that such a man should have to bear that for one more day. I have seen him. I go every week to the hospital. He does not recognize me. Not yet. But I am assured that memory sometimes does return in these cases. I'm quite certain that I could bring him back to sanity again. I can care for him...I can afford to provide the best care for him. I have told the authorities that I make no claim on any pension or war recompense to which he may be due and I would insist that any such sums be placed in a bank account in his name and left there. It's important that you know that." She turned her face away from him and murmured, "I love him. I want him here with me. I know I can bring him back."

Joe nodded, understanding. "Tell me, mademoiselle, how well did Dominique speak English?"

She looked at him blankly for a moment. "I really have no idea. I never heard him speak English. There was never a reason why he should. Why do you ask?"

"Someone propounded a theory that, with his Anglo-Saxon looks, the patient in Reims could be an Englishman scooped up by the Germans, processed, misidentified—or not identified at all—and sent off to a camp in Germany for years. That is why I am here. Passing through Reims on my way south, I was asked to spend a moment or two looking into it. It's thought important to check all the possibilities no matter how remote."

"He's French. More particularly, he's a Parisian." The tone was firm, the response that of a businessman clinching a deal. She expected no argument.

Joe handed back the photograph and she put it back in its place, immediately taking another one from the line. "And this one is just a snapshot taken by a friend but it shows us together."

A youthful, round-faced Mireille, long glossy hair

bouncing on to her shoulders, stood, hat on head, gloves on hands, awkwardly accepting the embrace of recognizably the same man though he was not in uniform but wearing a smart suit and hat and shining boots. Posed as they were in front of the fountain in the centre of the town, they could have been any courting couple walking out on a Sunday afternoon before the war.

Before he could speak she held up a hand and smiled. "Yes, I know this is scarcely proof in the eyes of the unimpressionable Inspector Bonnefoye who gave me quite a speech on the frequency and positioning of war wounds on returned soldiers." The smile widened to a grin. "A speech illustrated by charts of the human body, would you believe? And a hideously dramatic demonstration of sabre-slashing! But I understand that there are other claimants who can produce equally convincing evidence that the unknown soldier belongs to them—and by ties of blood, which is something I could never claim. Though there is one indication which I had been hoping it would not be necessary to reveal...I would not wish to demean this poor person unnecessarily in any way. He suffers indignities enough in that dreadful place." She raised her head and finished defiantly, "But if I must fight for him, then I will use any weapon that comes to hand. I wonder, Commander, if you could ask your niece, Miss Dorcas, to go in search of the tray of refreshments I had ordered? Marie should be stumbling along the corridor as we speak. Perhaps you could go to her assistance, mademoiselle?"

Dorcas took her dismissal without demur though her eyes narrowed and she favoured Mireille with a long and meaningful stare.

Left alone, Mireille faced him, almost laughing. "Goodness! She could give lessons in suspicious staring to my cat!

I almost expected to feel her claws! She is very protective of you, I think? I'm sorry. I sent her off awkwardly but I am not aware of how much a woman of the world she is, your charming niece, Commander. I would not like to cause embarrassment in one so young by what I have to say, though…" She paused for a moment and added thoughtfully, "I suppose I was not a great deal older than she is when I made the discovery for myself."

Chapter 9

Didier Marmont, mayor of Choisy-sur-Meuse in the Ardennes forest, stood on the steps of the town hall heroically fighting back an urge to run a finger around his starched collar. His nervousness restricted itself to a swift twitch at the *tricolore* sash fastened around his comfortable stomach. Above or below? The bulge was making the positioning of his symbol of authority increasingly tricky. He glanced with a moment's envy at the still-lean shape of the uniformed American officer sharing the steps with him. The man hadn't put on an ounce since he'd stormed through the town as a lieutenant nearly ten years ago.

With the last note of the Marseillaise, following on the American national anthem rousingly played by the town band, their moment had come. Didier, the host, was the first to speak. He swept a commanding gaze over the upturned eager faces crowding the square and, as always, though he never counted on it, confidence began to flow. His voice boomed out, the grandiose phrases everyone waited to hear unfurled and he dashed a manly tear from his eye. Especially warm this year were his compliments to their US Army guests, the faithful band who returned year after year to the town that had welcomed them and billeted them. The last resting place of many of their comrades, the town was remembered with nostalgic affection but also with practical help. The doughboys had come mainly from the same small place in the States and, on repatriation, had set about collecting funds to send back to their adopted village in France.

The results of eight years' hard work were all around them as they stood in the hot August sunshine. The *mairie* itself, the school and the two bridges spanning the winding river Meuse owed their existence in large part to transatlantic generosity. And, in return, the French had built for the American dead the cemetery and monument they were on this day to hear the Colonel dedicate.

To the crowd's claps and cheers, the Colonel, a career soldier, stepped forward to respond to the mayor's introduction. Didier's son-in-law. It hardly seemed possible. Then he looked at his daughter standing in the front row of the audience, proudly holding up her baby son to witness his father and his grandfather sharing a platform. Though how much a six-month-old could make out he wasn't sure, and Didier rather thought little John ought to be tucked up at home in his cot, not sweating it out with the rest of them in this heat and noise. Didier had been overjoyed to see his first grandson though he had wondered about the wisdom of subjecting a small infant to a transatlantic crossing. America was so impossibly far away. He was always surprised that the people they loved continued to return.

His daughter was not the only local girl to be lured west by these handsome great fellows with their promise of excitement and an expanded life. The girls came back on their arm and you could pick them out in the crowd by their silk stockings, high-heeled shoes and pretty dresses. And, especially in his daughter's case, Didier acknowledged, by her happy face. He was thankful to see it. Yes, Paulette was happy.

The Colonel spoke briefly in English and then launched into French to a rising cheer from the crowd. He knew the strings to tug at and the emotive words rang out with pride and certainty: *l'entente cordiale, l'amitié éternelle, nos amis, nos épouses, nos confrères*...And he finished with a ringing reminder of the phrase which had been on all their lips ten years ago: *Ils ne passeront pas! Ils ne passeront jamais plus!*

The ceremony over, Didier made his excuses and slipped away. He hadn't the energy to confront his daughter and her forceful husband again just yet. He agreed there were many advantages to joining his only living relations over the Atlantic but he shuddered at the idea of the long sea crossing and he felt faint at the thought of the effort he would have to make to start, in approaching old age, on a life in a new land. He fled to the Promenade down by the river. A walk under the chestnut trees would cool him and help him to consider his future. What remained of it.

As he strolled deep in thought a sound above his head distracted him. He looked up to see an aeroplane looping the loop, stalling and beginning to drop from the sky. A paper aeroplane. To the accompaniment of excited giggles from the branches of the chestnut, he threw off his dignity and dashed about like a music-hall mime artist, chasing and finally catching the plane in his upturned top hat.

"Pierre! Alphonse!" He called the boys down. "What a useless pair! You'll never be aero-engineers on this showing. What's this you've designed? A Blériot special?"

"No, sir!" His suggestion was dismissed with scorn. "We're

designing something that will cross the Atlantic. Papa says there's a huge prize offered to the first man to cross without stopping. Papa thinks it should go to a Frenchman."

"Well, take the word of a trained engineer—this is never going to work. Look, why don't you put a paperclip on the tail to weigh it down a little? And while you're at it, think of refolding the fuselage. Like this. May I?"

Honoured to have the full attention of the mayor, the boys closed round, kneeling with him in the middle of the path, all eager interest. Didier began to unfold and smooth out the sheet of newspaper the frail craft had been fashioned from and stopped suddenly. His gaze fixed on the sheet, his voice stilled, his breath began to come in harsh rasps. He groaned and muttered something unintelligible to the boys.

"Are you all right? Sir? Monsieur Marmont?" Anxious, they looked at each other, startled by the abrupt change from bonhomie to distress.

"He's having one of his turns," said Alphonse. "Look, his lips are blue and he can't breathe. Ah, yes, he's clutching his chest," he said knowledgeably. "Seen my uncle do that... week before he snuffed it. You stay here. I'll run for my mum. She'll know what to do."

The rescue party, which included the local doctor, was soon at the spot. They found the mayor, breathing fitfully and in obvious pain, but still alive and, improbably, clutching the remains of a paper aeroplane to his breast.

"He'll be all right," pronounced the doctor to the worried crowd beginning to collect. "It's his heart problem, of course. But he's had this before and bounced back, haven't you, old chap? And this time—you see—he's smiling! Yes, he'll be all right."

Chapter 10

"A wart on the backside, was it, then?" Dorcas enquired without emphasis. "Aren't you going to tell me what makes Dominique so distinctive?"

She'd waited until her lemonade and Joe's black coffee had been served in the cool interior of the tea shop they'd used the previous day before she referred to their interview. A pair of elegant old ladies nursing matching apricot poodles were taking a very long time choosing the brand of tea they would have served in china cups. They spent even longer deciding which cakes their sculptured pets would prefer but at last, their order given, changed and given again, they settled to look around and smile indulgently at the kind uncle entertaining his niece at the next table. A civilized scene until Dorcas struck up. Joe wondered if they spoke English.

He breathed deeply. Would he ever become accustomed to this wild girl's free way of speaking, her irreverence bordering on rudeness? He blamed Orlando. His loose life and the dubious characters he chose to associate with had had a devastating and probably irreparable effect on a child who lurked behind sofas, listening, understanding and copying speech and manners that ought never to have been exhibited in her vicinity.

"No? Well, then—a birthmark in an intimate place? A dislocated penis perhaps?" she said, her voice rising. "There's a boy in our village whose father has trouble with his tyres and his tubes..."

He had learned the wisdom of cutting her off the moment she called in evidence "a boy from the village." More of them than he privately thought possible had uncles who'd passed through Port Said and sisters who'd worked in armaments factories. All had returned only too willing to share their worldly knowledge. And, at the end of the chain of information apparently, was Dorcas.

"One more attention-grabbing word and my lips are sealed for ever in the matter of Dominique's distinction," he growled. He waited for and accepted her silence with a nod, then went on: "Let us say... front elevation, left of centre, port-wine stain, so slight and so centrally placed as to escape the examination accorded by the medical establishment."

"Interesting! We shall have to return to the doctor and ask him to look again. I say, Joe, this seems to me like proof positive that he's who she says he is."

"Well, thinking ahead—as I've been taught!—I rang the good doctor when I slipped back to the hotel just now. While you were buying postcards." To his chagrin, Joe couldn't hide his pleasure at scoring a point over Dorcas. "I asked him to supply further and better particulars regarding Thibaud's nether regions. We're in luck. It's the day for the patient's weekly bath and delousing and Varimont agreed to bring forward Thibaud's time and instruct the orderlies who officiate at these ablutions. He's intending to supervise the operation himself and record anything interesting. I'm to ring him for a report this afternoon."

"So, we should know very soon that Thibaud is French and we can carry on with our journey?"

"I rather think we're committed to spending a day or so with the Houdart family," said Joe. "It's all fixed. I telephoned to say we'd arrive the day after tomorrow for the weekend. And besides—it would be a shame to pass up the chance of wearing your blue dress."

"You've made your mind up to see *each* of these claimants, haven't you? You're ignoring what the Inspector had to say. And what you said yourself—'I'm only here to establish whether he's English or not'—that was just so much blather. You can't resist a puzzle, that's what. And you can't bear to leave the solving of it to anyone else."

"I honestly don't believe that there is any way of establishing that he's English," said Joe patiently. "But, on the other hand, there may be a way of proving decisively that he is a Frenchman, which fills our aims just as neatly. And that's what I'm going to attempt to do. Yes, I'm going to take a look at the other claimants, hear their stories…I thought Thibaud was probably a fine man and I would like to see his problems resolved. And *I* don't fall victim to the first romantic tale I'm told. Now, when you've finished that…I'm off to see the widow Langlois. She claims that Thibaud is really her son, Albert. She lives in a small village a few miles away from here. Martigny. Do you want to come?"

The countryside rolled by, patchwork squares of green and gold seamed with narrow white threads of chalk roads as they drove eastwards. The caterpillar stripes of the vineyards gave way increasingly to fields of ripe corn where the harvest was well under way. Teams of heavy horses pulled fantastical pieces of machinery, toiling alongside workers a good number of whom were women in pinafores, headscarves and clogs. They stopped work at the sound of the engine and shaded their eyes to stare with suspicion at the oncoming motor car before responding to Dorcas's cheery wave.

"The natives don't seem particularly friendly," she said.

"If you'd had your village destroyed and the land laid waste by several warring armies swarming all over it you'd learn to take a long careful look at foreigners motoring through. And here we are. Martigny," he said, parking in the market square and looking around. "The new Martigny. Bit hit and miss. But it's an attempt. They've got their priorities right, you see—the café, the inn, the *boulangerie,* the school and the *mairie*...pretty bell tower...And the place we've come to visit is there on the corner opposite the *boulangerie*— the grocer's shop."

"*Le Familistère,*" Dorcas read out. "*Succursale no. 732. Guy Langlois, Patron.* Were you prepared for a *patron*? I thought we were coming to see a woman?"

"We are. Yes. The claim was made by a mother. Well, let's go and see if she's at home."

A bell clanged over the door as they entered and two customers turned from the counter to stare at them. Joe doffed his hat and gave the usual polite French greeting. There wasn't much to delight the eye in this dim and cluttered space. The staples of existence were on display in packets, tins and jars, their dull ranks enlivened by a smoked ham and a saucisson or two suspended from the ceiling. Joe guessed that the women of the village did their shopping for fresh food in the weekly market, the token line-up of wooden boxes of faded apples, wrinkled oranges and time-expired lettuce offering little temptation. When the ladies had finally snapped their purses shut, picked up their shopping bags and left, the elderly man behind the counter turned his attention to them, an ingratiating smile vying with curiosity to enliven his heavy features.

Joe introduced himself, watching the smile flicker and die as he proceeded. He handed over his letter of introduction and his Metropolitan Police warrant card and waited while both were inspected with the greatest care.

"So, you've come out all the way from Reims to see my wife? Why was this necessary? She gave her statement some weeks ago and she has nothing further to add. We await the Department's final decision on the affair. And it is a civil, not a police matter anyway."

"Your son's identity, sir—" Joe began, and recoiled before the interruption.

"*Not* my son, if you don't mind! My wife Henriette's son—and the man in question is most likely not even that," he said darkly. "It's nothing but a mare's nest. A waste of everyone's time. The lad's dead and gone...years ago...and I for one do not want the whole sorry business raked up again."

Joe let the man's explosion of bad humour roll away before replying mildly. He decided to borrow the ingratiating smile as window-dressing for his explanation: an international angle to the case had developed and, in confidential tones, he spoke of the involvement of the recently formed international police force with its headquarters in Lyon. Monsieur Langlois must be aware of Interpol? Even if he wasn't, Monsieur Langlois could not help but be impressed by the respect in Joe's voice as he mentioned it. And Scotland Yard's assistance had been sought by this august body in an attempt to resolve the question of the unknown soldier's possibly *English* nationality. This appeared to be not an unwelcome proposition to Langlois and he was just sufficiently impressed to fling up the hinged section of the counter which allowed access to the rear of the shop.

"Oh? Well, in that case, you'd better come through then."

He pulled back a curtain yelling, "Julie! Come and mind the shop!" and a young girl slipped by them to take up her place by the till.

They followed their guide through into a storage area full of tins, boxes and flour-sacks and at the far end of this a woman in a high-necked blouse and copious cambric pinafore was sitting at a table weighing out kilos of sugar. She turned to look at them, incurious and unsmiling.

Joe thought that the woman he now greeted as Madame Langlois was all that was conjured up by the word "drab." Her clothing was outdated and faded, her face was square, coarse and expressionless. Her dark hair, beginning to streak with grey, was divided precisely down the centre of her head by a parting through which the scalp gleamed like candle-wax.

"A policeman to see you, Henriette," her husband announced, and then, smirking: "It seems this loony of yours is actually an Englishman who took the wrong turning in the war. What a fuss about nothing! Well . . . things to do . . . busy man . . . I've wasted time enough on this silly business . . . I'm off to do my deliveries. I'll leave you, Commander, to spell it out to her. My advice: be firm and speak slowly. Be prepared to repeat everything. Don't fall for her nonsense."

He bustled off leaving them facing a woman no longer expressionless. The stony features, released from their rigidity by his departure, registered a hatred of such a startling intensity that Joe rocked back on his heels. She collected herself and, slowly assimilating the news so callously delivered, shook her head from side to side like a puzzled ox.

"Is this true, sir, what he says?"

Her bosom began to heave, she sniffled and rubbed a hand over her dusty face.

Alarmed by this show of emotion, Joe thrust his handkerchief at her and hurried to contradict the information fired at her by Langlois.

"So the truth of it is that nothing is yet decided? And you have seen my son? Yesterday? Tell me how he was. Are they treating him well? I should like to visit him but Guy will not spare me." She brightened and began to take off her pinafore and smooth her hair. "I should like to hear what you made of him. Albert. He's called Albert. Will you come through to the parlour and I'll ask my daughter to prepare us some coffee. Does the young lady drink coffee? Or would you prefer a glass of milk, mademoiselle, and some bread and chocolate?"

He had never had a more receptive audience, Joe thought as he sipped his coffee and accounted for his presence in her pin-neat parlour. He launched into a cheerful account of his meeting with the patient and told the story of Dorcas and the pink biscuit.

Once again the tears threatened to flow.

"Albert loved those biscuits!" she said. "He wasn't allowed to have them from the shop, of course, but I used sometimes when he was little to sneak a broken one for him when Guy was looking the other way."

"Madame," said Joe tentatively, "I can't help noticing that the patient whom you declare to be your son does not resemble you or your husband."

"He is not Guy's son," she said. "It's no secret. Albert is illegitimate."

She cast a wary glance at Dorcas and Joe reassured her: "My niece is au fait with the details of the case and is older than she looks. Quite the woman of the world, in fact."

She nodded and stumbled on. "You will have passed on the road in the neighbouring village an inn. The Croix d'Argent. A staging post between Reims and Paris. I was an orphan of the village and sent to work there on my fifteenth birthday. In 1889." She paused, choosing her words. "I knew nothing of the world…"

Joe sighed. He could guess the whole sorry tale.

"I was six months pregnant before anyone—before I my-self—realized what was happening. They threw me out into the street. I was taken up by Langlois. You will have noticed that he is an ugly man with the manners of a boar. He had had no success in finding a wife. He married me and I have been his slave ever since. He disliked Albert. He wanted sons of his own. Fate decided that I should produce daughter after daughter for him and after each girl his anger would increase. 'What kind of a woman are you? You can produce a son for a stranger and only girls for your husband?' He was never kind to Albert. And poor Albert! If only he'd looked like me! But the boy was born the spitting image of his father."

"You know his father's identity?"

"No. I only know that he was like no man that I had ever seen before. A beautiful man. Tall, fair, blue-eyed like Albert and—a German."

She grasped Joe's arm. "Sir, I have never disclosed as much to Langlois."

"I understand. Be reassured, madame—your information is for my ears alone. It must have taken some courage to defy opposition and start on your identification?"

"I could not have done it without the support of the

schoolmaster," she said. "It was he who came to us last spring, waving a newspaper. Monsieur Barbier had taught my Albert. He liked him and took a special interest in him because he was a clever boy and he pitied him in his situation with his stepfather. He showed us the photograph and assured us that it was Albert. He never forgets any of his pupils, Commander. And I recognized my son, of course. M. Barbier is not impressed by my husband and, in the way of bullies, Langlois defers to a stronger man. He allowed me, grudgingly, to go to Reims with Barbier to see my son. It was the schoolmaster who wrote out my official claim form for me. He always knows what to say."

"Can you tell me what evidence you submitted apart from the visual identification?"

"Photographs."

She went to a sewing table and automatically looked about her, although they were unobserved, before taking from the bottom three creased photographs and a bundle of letters.

"I showed these to the director."

The first photograph was a formal one taken on the steps of the pre-war school building on a clear, sunny day. The children, in their grey school smocks, were excited and over-awed by the camera. M. Barbier stood on the right, the proud shepherd of his flock. The flock was, with little variation, dark-haired and chubby. Albert, on the left, stood out from the crowd with his light build and fair hair. His ethereal features, framed by a neat white collar, tugged at Joe's heart over the gap of a quarter of a century. He wondered if Dorcas, stickily breathing chocolate fumes over his shoulder, had seen it: the same unfocused expression of dislocation and sadness, of other-worldliness that they had seen in Thibaud's face.

In the second photograph the Langlois children were lined up in height order in a studio, grinning at the camera over their right shoulders. Four dark girls with square faces and dark eyes. Adrift by a few inches at the back and gazing at the middle distance Albert hovered, an alien presence.

The third was also a posed photograph, taken in Reims. The grown Albert looked straight at the camera this time, alone, defiant, wearing with some dash the tight tunic, red jodhpurs, knee-high boots and saucily tilted casquette of an artilleryman.

"He loved horses, you see. He was very good with them. M. Barbier managed to steer him into the artillery."

Joe passed the photographs to Dorcas.

"What a fine man," she said quietly. "You must be very proud of him, madame."

"Always," was the whispered reply. "Always."

"Can you tell us when you last saw your son?"

"It was in April 1917. We'd returned after the 1914 invasion thinking it couldn't happen again. Papa Joffre had sent them all packing, hadn't he? But we were wrong. They came again and it was worse this time. Hardly a village survived the bombing and the burning. We were caught up in it all. And it was just days before that when Albert turned up suddenly on leave. He'd walked all the way from somewhere up by Laon . . ." She hesitated, trying to remember.

"The Chemin des Dames?" Joe supplied. "Was he involved in that battle?"

"That's the one. Chemin des Dames. He was in the Fifth Army under General Nivelle. Albert told us he was on leave," she added uncertainly. "Langlois said it was all a lie. They wouldn't have given leave to anyone at such a bad moment, he said. Albert must have deserted.

"Albert was wearing his own civilian clothes, helping us

to load our things on to the cart, when someone shouted, 'The Uhlans are coming!'" She shivered with remembered terror at the panic-raising call. "And the Boche flooded in. They shot the mayor who'd dared to confront them and rounded up fifty hostages. The usual behaviour. And when they retreated they set the houses on fire, marched the hostages out with them and fired cannon at the village until it was rubble. One of the hostages was my son. I never saw or heard from him again until I went to Reims last spring."

Joe, who had been discreetly jotting down dates, closed his notebook. "I wonder... is there anything at all, madame, that you could add to the information you have already given to Inspector Bonnefoye? Any detail of a personal and perhaps physical nature that might distinguish Albert? A scar or a birthmark of some description? A mark of which a *mother* might be aware?" He could think of no more discreet way of phrasing his question.

She looked embarrassed and awkward. She opened her mouth to speak and decided not to. Then, shrugging: "The usual childhood marks... scuffed knees... cuts and bruises from falling off horses and out of trees. That sort of thing. Would you like to see his letters?"

As Joe agreed to this sudden shift of focus Dorcas stood and asked politely if she might be excused. She'd like to go back into the shop to buy some of the delicious dark French chocolate to take home... better than anything they could get in England and made here in the village? They readily agreed to this tactful withdrawal from the next stage of the enquiry which promised to be rather tedious for a young girl.

Joe was intrigued by the small collection of letters written in a good copperplate hand on torn scraps of writing paper. One or two of the messages were almost obliterated by ominous brown stains. At the start jaunty and optimistic (and addressed solely to *"ma chère maman"*), the letters had become progressively sombre and hopeless. The most recent one was dated April 1917, just a week or two before his last appearance in the village. He spoke with despair of stalemate, with anger of the deaths of men in his company, the never-ending bombardment, the foul conditions in the trenches. He ended by saying he was just about to be called up the line to the front ranks again.

Joe looked for signs of censorship but found none. A second reading impressed him with the clever wording. No militarily sensitive information, no names, no positions were given. The censor's pencil would have hovered and found no precise target and yet the tone, truculent and mutinous throughout, was deserving of censorship. It occurred to him that perhaps even the censor by this stage in the war had been of the same mind.

Had Albert, in his despair, nipped out the back way after all, as his stepfather claimed? It was probable, Joe decided. Or had he served his spell in the front line and been rewarded with an eight-day pass? It was at about that time that the army's grievances, increasingly loud, had been heard, Joe calculated from the little he knew about the French end-game. Pétain had replaced the failing General Nivelle in the campaign of the Chemin des Dames and conditions for the men in the field had improved. Home leave had been granted again. It was possible.

He said as much to Madame Langlois who drank in every soothing word. So absorbed had he been by the letters and the eagerness of the mother to share them with him, he had lost track of time and wondered at last what on earth Dorcas could possibly be doing.

Laughter down the corridor reassured him. She came in, pink and smiling and obviously the best of friends with what Joe took to be the youngest Langlois daughter.

"This is Julie, Uncle Joe."

Julie giggled and bobbed. She gave Joe a long and appreciative stare before her bright eyes flashed a message sideways at Dorcas.

"I've cashed up and locked the shop, Maman," she said in a voice which had none of the grating hesitations of her mother's. "Dorcas has been telling me all about London. Did you know she came from London? And we're the same age! She's sixteen too! Are all English girls so small?"

"Oh, I'd say Dorcas was pretty much average size for her age," said Joe easily.

"Uncle Joe, I hope you don't mind but I've offered Julie a lift into Reims. It's early closing today and she's visiting her married sister. She was going to catch the bus but I said we were going straight back and could drop her off."

"Well, certainly. If her mother agrees. Delighted," said Joe.

Slightly dubiously, her mother gave her consent, commenting that such an offer would at least save the bus fare and she didn't see how Monsieur Langlois could have any objection, and they set off with the two girls installed on the back seat whispering and laughing together.

Joe made no attempt to tune in to their conversation, pleased to hear Dorcas chatting with someone more or less her own age and relieved to be free to marshal his thoughts.

On arriving in Reims, Julie asked to be dropped off in the centre in the Place Drouet d'Erlon and, with warm exchanges of addresses and promises, she finally skipped away.

"Nice chat, Dorcas?" he asked as she slid over into the front passenger seat.

"No. Rather terrible in fact, Joe. You weren't listening, were you? Look, drive over into the Promenade, will you, park under a plane tree and I'll tell you."

Disturbed by her serious tone, he did as she asked.

"I was just trying to help. I thought that woman wasn't telling you the full truth. I thought I'd find one of the girls—in fact there's only that Julie, the fifth and youngest, left at home—all the others got married and went off as soon as they could—and try to find out a bit more about life *chez les Langlois*. She didn't know much about Albert. She was an afterthought. Born in 1910. So she was only four when Albert marched off to war. And she only saw him once or twice when he came home on leave after that."

"So her opinions may be misleading, you're warning me?"

"Yes. I think she echoes her sisters' views and they may have been influenced by their charming father. She dismissed her half-brother as 'that weedy Albert who disappeared.' But she does seem close to her mother. Julie wants to leave home as well. She's not really here to see her sister—did you guess? She's come to meet a young man she's walking out with. It's all right, Joe—her mother knows all about it. Madame Langlois is making her own plans, you see. Julie knows her mother's up to something. She thinks that if she's granted custody of Albert her mother will come into a lot of money from the state as well as his pension and Julie's certain she's planning to do a bunk. She's going to use Albert to finance her escape from old Langlois. They're blackmailing each other—you keep quiet about my plans and I won't split on you...that sort of thing."

"So the worm is turning after all these years? She's going to scoop up her son, run away and live with him on the basis of his pension? Shows a bit of spirit! I thought I'd glimpsed a certain steely resolve … well, tinny resolve, perhaps, in her demeanour."

"You didn't quite understand, Joe."

"What can you mean?"

"When you asked about the distinctive marks on his body I thought she reacted in a strange way and changed the subject. I mean … you might have expected: 'Oh, gosh, yes—that day when the nappy pin slipped!' or something like that. I thought she was covering something up. And she was."

For a moment she sank into dejection and uncertainty.

"And Julie told you … what?" he prompted.

"That Albert was beaten quite badly as a child. It's likely that he will have traces on his buttocks, isn't it? Would he still have scars after all these years?"

"It's possible," said Joe. "Look, I'm speaking to Varimont this afternoon. That should tell us more. Perhaps in their search for dramatic wounds—sabre cuts and the like—little domestic marks have gone unregarded. But they would represent incontrovertible evidence all the same."

Dorcas was hardly listening. "'Little domestic marks'? Joe, how can you speak so lightly?"

"I think you mean 'dispassionately.' If I let myself be moved by pain and death I would make mistakes. But this is information we must have, Dorcas. I know it's really none of our business—it's a French affair and let's hang on to that." And, rattled by her petulant silence: "What on earth do you expect me to do? Tell tales to Inspector Bonnefoye? Encourage him to go out, confront Langlois, and belatedly wag a minatory finger at the wicked stepfather? 'It's come to my attention, Langlois, that you were unkind to your stepson thirty years ago.' He'd laugh at me."

Dorcas sighed wearily.

"Old Langlois may have failed to charm us, Joe, but you can't dismiss him as entirely evil on the sample of behaviour we witnessed. Albert was beaten as a child, I'm certain of that, but it wasn't his stepfather who beat him."

Chapter 11

"*Not* his stepfather? Can you be certain? And, if you are, then who? Who on earth could take a stick to such a little angel?"

"The one who abused him as a child and is now planning to abuse him as a witless and helpless adult. His mother."

Joe lapsed into a shocked silence. "You're going to have to explain this surprising accusation, Dorcas."

"You could have interviewed Julie yourself but I don't think you'd have got any more information out of her than you managed to extract from her mother. Madame Langlois may not have been *born* a wicked person but—goodness, she had a bad enough start in life! Enough to drive anyone to despair and make them unstable, I'd have thought. That's if she's telling us the truth, of course. But Julie, who had no reason to lie to me, told me the family stories. The ones she had from her sisters. They were not mistreated. Only Albert. But, apparently, the old man, though he used to rage and storm at the boy and made his hatred very apparent, never actually hit him. It was his mother who beat him merci-lessly."

She was speaking quietly and trying, Joe thought, for the dispassionate tone he had advocated. "Does Julie have any idea why she would have behaved in this way?"

"Oh, yes. She thinks she did it to divert Langlois's anger. To turn his rage away from her and the girls on to the boy who counted for so little in that household. A sort of whip-ping boy, you might say. First in line for punishment when punishment was necessary."

"A demonstration of her loyalty and her acceptance of the situation between them?" suggested Joe.

"That's what the girls think," said Dorcas. "But *I* don't think that would be enough. Not enough to make a mother do such a dreadful thing, do you?"

"You have a different theory?" he enquired gently. The question of mothers would always be a tricky one with Dorcas, deserted practically at birth by her own.

"Yes. See what you think. There's a girl in the village… No! Don't shudder in that showy way!" she said crossly. "All right—I know I exaggerate sometimes… occasionally I lie. But I always know that I'm not deceiving you or I wouldn't do it. This is a true story, so listen! Have you seen Cora with the red hair who works in the chemist's? No? Well, she was a very pretty girl but she's never married. When she was just old enough she went to Godalming to do her bit for the war effort. The gaffer in the factory she was sent to was a no-good. She came home pregnant and only when the baby was born did she tell her father what had happened. She'd been raped. It's a good family. The mother wanted to bring the child up as her own and the father went straight off to Godalming and beat the man nearly to death. They arrested

Cora's dad and he was up on a charge of GBH. They put him away for five years' hard labour."

"A sad story. And not uncommon," said Joe quietly.

"It got sadder. When the baby was born they kept trying to persuade her to feed it. She wouldn't. Wouldn't even look at it. It kept howling with hunger and then it suddenly went quiet. When her mother ran upstairs to see if all was well, Cora was lying in bed just staring and the baby was by her side. Not breathing. It was dead. She tried to explain to the doctor who came that she hated the baby and couldn't bear to touch it."

"Terrible tale. Were there repercussions for poor Cora? I'm afraid she could have been facing a murder charge."

"There would have been but it was all hushed up. So hushed that nobody speaks of it outside the village." She added thoughtfully, "But the doctor is very highly respected. You often hear them say, 'I'd give my right arm for that man! He's a champion feller.' But the point is, Joe, if Albert's mother treated him as she did, don't you think there may have been a sinister reason for this? Vulnerable young girl attacked by stranger passing through? She might well, like Cora, have secretly hated the child. But that's not something a woman could ever confess to. She disguised the nastiness for our benefit."

"She was spinning us a tale, you think?"

"Yes. She gave us a much more romantic and acceptable version. Well, it certainly captured *your* sympathy, didn't it? Can't say you weren't warned! Old Langlois told you— 'Don't fall for her nonsense.' A woman in her situation must get used to lying convincingly. A way of life, I'd have thought. But I'll tell you what, Joe...however dispassionate you might think yourself, you can't let Thibaud be handed over to her. Can you? He'd be at her mercy! Think of the awful life he would lead."

Joe spoke sharply in a sudden rush of anger. "I'm a foreign policeman passing through. I have no authority, no magic wand. If the French can prove to their satisfaction that this woman is the patient's mother, that's it. Nothing I can do. Now, I'm grateful for your insights, Dorcas, never think otherwise, but if you're going to get so involved with these claimants I think you'd better kept at a distance. I'll go by myself to see the Tellancourt family tomorrow morning and leave you behind." He glanced at his wristwatch. "Half past one. I think I could probably make that phone call to the doctor now. He should have something for us. But first we'll go and have a well-earned lunch, shall we? We're a bit late but I expect they'll be able to put something together."

Varimont answered the telephone himself. His staccato tones had the added energy of excitement: "Sandilands! Glad you rang. Look—why don't you come round to my office if you're free? Soon as you like. Much easier to *show* you what we've found, I think, rather than explain. Oh, yes, we *have* found something. Not much but it could make all the difference, I think you'll agree."

Chapter 12

"Didier, my old friend, what more can I say? I *beg* you...No! For God's sake, what am I saying? I'm your doctor! I *order* you to stay on the train for another hour. An hour, that's all—it can't take longer than that—and go straight through to Paris. Why Reims? The best heart specialists are to be found in Paris and I'm giving you an introduction to the *very* best. I say again—why Reims?"

"Calm down, Christophe! You risk an apoplexy and there isn't another doctor for miles," said Didier, comfortably. "I've heard your advice and I'm truly grateful for it. And I'm glad you've called round. I was just going to make myself a mushroom omelette...I picked some of those little chanterelles in the forest this morning. And Dorine's given me a pot of her wild boar pâté...it's about the place somewhere...Would you like to join me? Good. In that case, I'll open a bottle of Hermitage and we'll have a farewell feast, the two of us."

"Didier, I can't think of anything I'd rather do. Thank you. You assume—rightly—that I can be distracted by the promise of one of your omelettes, but not to the point of forgetting my question! You have not answered my question."

"Reims has a reputation for excellence in medicine. I'm sure I shall find someone who can give satisfaction. You know I hate the capital. Four eggs or three?" He rattled the stove and turned his attention to the frying pan to hide his expression. He did not lie convincingly and Christophe was not easily deceived.

"Absolute rubbish! No one hates Paris even if he's on his deathbed. Which you aren't by a long chalk!" the doctor added hastily. "You're up to something. Are you going to tell me about it? Look, if you're doing a fugue—organizing a flight from your daughter and her barn-storming husband—just say so. I can help you. I can put on a grave face, wring my hands and tell them that in no circumstances could I possibly, as your physician, allow you to contemplate a trip across the Atlantic."

"I can't deceive you, Christophe." Didier smiled. "And I don't want what could be your last memory of me to be that of a cussed old idiot who didn't listen to good advice when it was given with care and concern. I have other things to do in Reims." He was aware that friendship demanded a less dismissive explanation and added awkwardly: "Unexpected. It's all most unexpected. After all these years of hoping...I may find a cardiologist though that is not the main object of my journey—I was just putting up covering fire to distract Paulette. Well, yes, and you! There's someone I have to look up. An old army chum. I've tried for years to trace him but with no success. I'd given up all expectation of seeing him again—had to admit he very probably hadn't survived that bloody awful business up on the Chemin des Dames in '17. But I was wrong. I have reason to believe he's alive and living in Reims."

The doctor relaxed. "Why on earth didn't you say so? That could all work out very well. You can see your friend—now don't go and get roaring drunk...I absolutely forbid it. One celebratory glass of champagne perhaps?—and then go straight on to Paris. Here, I'll put this envelope on the mantelpiece. I'm giving you an address and an introduction to an excellent chap."

"If God spares me and I have no success in Reims, I'll go straight there, I promise."

"Good. Good. Now tell me where you'll be staying in Reims."

"At the Continental. I thought I'd treat myself to a bit of comfort. I've got a *tarte tatin* to follow if you're interested. Not for me, of course—but I'll gladly watch you eat it. A glass of mirabelle with it?"

Left alone after the affectionate farewells and the last-minute advice and repeated instructions, Didier washed the dishes and put them back in their place on the dresser. He glanced around, checking that he'd left everything in good order. Soldierly habits acquired in the trenches had stayed with him. Even at the lowest moment of that degrading episode the men had shaved, cleaned out their billy cans, deloused themselves and maintained their equipment.

Good Lord! Equipment! He was getting forgetful. Time to get this over while he still had his wits. Didier went to his bedroom and pulled a chair over to the wardrobe. He climbed up and felt about under a selection of hats on the top shelf until he found it.

The six shot Lebel army revolver sat easily in his grasp. He'd handled and cleaned it regularly since the end of the war. He wrapped it in a silk scarf and pushed it into the centre of his suitcase, standing ready packed on the chest at the bottom of his bed. He added a box of bullets and closed it with a snap. He was ready. Looking up, he caught his reflection in the dressing-table mirror and drew in his breath, startled by what he saw.

He'd seen the same expression countless times on faces of comrades, an unforgettable blend of terror and resignation.

He was about to go over the top.

Chapter 13

"Birthmark? Yes, it could be. Or a mark acquired at birth? Not the same thing. Signs of a forceps delivery perhaps? Yes, again, it could be. I'm no expert in this field, you understand. Marks of this sort in the majority of cases fade away with time but they are not unknown in adults, I understand."

Dr Varimont handed Joe a sheet of paper. "Anyway, you shall judge for yourself. I just give evidence. Look, I've plotted the position and measurements on this plan of the body. The frontal mark is dark purple, the size of a centime piece, no more, and just where you said it might be, to the left of centre. That's the left as you look at him. It wasn't easy. Thibaud doesn't much like being handled—squirms and wriggles like a two-year-old—even though he is familiar with the orderlies who carried out the inspection. I chose the two who've had closest contact with him and briefed them to get out their combs and bottles of Sanitol and pretend to be carrying out the usual procedures. Routine calms him."

"Exactly as Mademoiselle Desforges described it, this mark," said Joe. "That would seem to be conclusive, then." He struggled to suppress a smile of satisfaction. "I'll convey this to Inspector Bonnefoye as tactfully as I can. Don't want to tread on toes, I'm sure you'll understand."

"Of course. We ought all of us to have come across this sooner. I can send him a sketch if you like and tell him it's come up as a matter of routine inspection...true enough."

"Thank you, Varimont. I would like that. But—am I missing something? Tell me, did you say *frontal* mark just now? Was that to imply that there is something else?" asked Joe.

"Yes, as a matter of fact there was." The doctor handed over a second sheet. "Difficult to see even if you're looking for it. A corresponding *rear* mark. Which is what makes me think it may have been caused by forceps used at birth. It's faint but it's there all right. A mother would remember."

"But you found no sign of ancient scarring—no signs of physical abuse?"

The doctor shrugged. "It's no baby's bottom down there but I think you could say—nothing dramatic. Wear and tear consistent with years in the saddle, I'd say. Or years in the trenches—everything from flea bites to shrapnel. He's as knocked about as any soldier of any of the armies."

"Thank you very much, Doctor." Joe held up the sheets. "This could well be a clincher. I say, may I..."

"By all means have them. I've had copies made. I'll send some with a covering note by messenger to Bonnefoye straightaway. And good luck with the rest of your enquiries. Do I take it that the field is still open?"

"Wide open, I'd say. I'm off to see the Tellancourt family tomorrow morning."

The doctor raised his eyebrows in mock alarm. "Family?

More like a tribe—a clan," he commented. "One for all and all for one. Have a care, Sandilands. Tell Bonnefoye you're going. If you're not back by midnight he can send out a posse. Not thinking of taking the little girl along, I hope?"

"No. She's happy to stay behind at the hotel and catch up with her diary entries, she tells me," Joe said. The word "happy" was a polite exaggeration.

"Take my advice, Sandilands," said the doctor, riffling through his file, "and make a telephone call to let them know you're coming. Give 'em a chance to chain up the dog. Farming family…busy time of year…there's no guarantee that they'll be able to parade for you without due notice and you don't want to have to go hunting about in the fields."

He scribbled figures on a pad, tore off a sheet and handed it to Joe.

"They have a telephone?"

"Not at the farm, no. The first of those numbers will connect you with the town hall. The mayor's secretary is a Mademoiselle Tellancourt, the cousin of the missing soldier, and the second number is that of the village café. The owner—yes, you've guessed!—is also a Tellancourt. The soldier's uncle. They are all utterly convinced that our Thibaud is their Thomas. And so eager are they to return him to his home before his awful old father expires, they arrived here at the hospital en masse one Sunday when I was off duty and they had our man halfway out through the gate with his head in a bag before someone stepped in—bravely!—to stop them. Good luck. Let me know how you get on."

Joe braked and pulled off the road on a lift of country overlooking what he took to be the valley where lay the Tellancourt farm. On his journey west and south from

Reims he had left the vineyards behind and was now contemplating agricultural land. Mixed farming apparently was going on and with some success. Cereals had been harvested and various animals wandered the fields. A number of fine white Charolais cropped the meadow grass under the willows by the river looking for all the world like a scene painted by Corot. The village in the foreground appeared to be in good condition. A squat church with Romanesque nave and transept stoutly shouldering a grey-tiled tower marked the centre. Red roofs of varying ages and states of repair radiated from it and merged into orchards on the outskirts, marking a settlement much larger than he had envisaged.

The church clock of St Céré-sur-Marne was sounding ten as he drove into the village square and Joe made at once for the café. It was a hot day, he had half an hour to spare and a sudden craving for a glass of Alsace beer.

In the dim interior two old men at a table were playing dominoes. They stopped their game to stare at him, hostile and mistrustful. A group of young men, the owners, he presumed, of the motor bikes parked proudly outside, were sitting in front of tankards of *bière blonde*. No point in trying to make a discreet entrance, Joe thought. He marched in with his officer's swagger, took off his cap and stood surveying the interior with polite greetings all round before deciding to approach the bar. He placed one elbow firmly on the zinc counter and with a crisp "Monsieur!" caught the barkeeper's unwilling attention. The man who served him was silent and unfriendly. When he had enjoyed his first two swallows of Fischer, Joe determined to break through his reticence. "That was welcome! Fine church you have," he said cheerfully, in a voice that included the rest of the clientele. "I must take a closer look at it. The village was lucky to have escaped much of the unpleasantness, I take it?"

No attempt was made to respond to his overture. The barman leaned over the counter and shouted over Joe's shoulder: "Jules! He's here. Get on over to the farm and tell your pa that the English *flic* is on his way."

One of the youths drained his glass and hurried out.

Joe found himself the object of a knowing, mutinous glower. "War's over, mister. Long ago. You're not wanted around here. You're not needed. Bugger off home!"

Joe put his beer down carefully and placed a coin beside it. His voice was polite, even pleasant: "Only too delighted to bugger off home, my dear chap. Sadly not possible until the English have pulled a few more French chestnuts out of the fire. Once again, it seems you need our help." His tone became more confidential: "Passed a cemetery on the way here. Chanzy. You know it? Four hundred and six soldiers of my old regiment are buried there. I paused to say a prayer or two. The memorial was interesting. Put up by the French and it says: 'In remembrance of the soldiers of the British Army who gave their lives for our freedom.' A very proper sentiment, in the circumstances, don't you think? I have always been impressed by French good manners."

The young men stared truculently into their beer but the old domino players began to cackle. One raised his glass of marc and in a defiant voice said, "*Vivent les Anglais!* Arrogant sods but they knew how to fire a rifle!"

The other one raised his glass and added, "To the *rosbifs*! It's true, Stéphane—you wouldn't be here pulling pints if they hadn't stood firm up there near Reims. Pay no heed to him, monsieur, he's suffered more than most. Can leave you a bit curdled, experiences like he's had."

Joe, disarmed by the bluff attempt at good humour, smiled and nodded. Swiftly judging the mood of the company, the barman poured and handed out glasses of marc for everyone and, taking one himself, threw a challenging glance at the visitor. Joe realized he was expected to say something. He raised his glass. "To a final end to this bloody war. May we forgive and forget and may the last soldier return safely to his true home."

"To a safe return," agreed the old men.

"He's ours, you know," said the barman. "My brother's lad. And we want him back before my brother snuffs it. He's not in good health. Doctor thinks he won't last another winter. Lungs. Poison gas did it. He should never have been up there fighting…over age…but he would go. Didn't last long. And it's cutting him up knowing that his son is stuck in a loony bin when he could be back here with his family. We can look after him."

"And he has a mother, your nephew?" Joe asked.

"My sister-in-law. Yes. Armande. She's not from these parts. She's from up north. Normandy. Came to work as lady's maid up at the château…oh, it must have been in 1888 or thereabouts. A right fancy piece! My brother fell for her airs and graces and her blonde hair. She wasn't the best choice for him but he was always in a rush and no one could tell him anything." He shrugged. "She's done well enough."

"Grudging sod!" commented one of the old men. "You've got to hand it to Armande—she's faithful. She's grieved for that boy from the day he…went missing…And since she's heard he's alive and likely to come home again she sits herself by the gate waiting and watching. Says she's always known her Thomas would come walking home down the lane one day."

"And both parents have identified the patient in Reims as their son Thomas?"

"Of course. We've all identified him. Signed statements. Hired a charabanc and we all went up, every last relation, and we all said the same thing: 'That's him. That's Thomas.'"

"He was always easy to pick out," chimed in the old man. "Go on, André, tell him!" And without allowing the more slow-speaking André to get a word in, continued: "Fair hair. He had this fair hair. And the blue eyes, just like his ma. The other children were more like their father, dark and not so tall. Of course Thomas stood out in the playground and life wasn't all that easy for him, he looked such a foreigner, but he was always a good-humoured lad—could make anyone laugh—and had a lively punch which was more of a help. We were all fond of the lad . . . the whole village . . . and we want him back where he belongs. It stands out a mile that this chap in Reims is Thomas. Changed of course, been through the mill, jaw bust, anyone can see that, but the main things like his height and his colouring, well, you can't argue. And," he added meaningfully, "a mother knows. A mother always knows."

Joe clung precariously, balanced side-saddle on the flapper seat of one of the motor bikes. A second round of marc had melted away any residue of bad feeling and loosened tongues to the point where one of the young men had awkwardly offered to take him to the Tellancourt farm. The car was better left in safety in front of the town hall, was the unanimous opinion of the company, instead of scraping down narrow lanes for several kilometres. As they bounced over the rutted ground, Joe was glad he'd spared his undercarriage by agreeing to this offer of outlandish transport. And he was glad to arrive finally at his destination.

Relieved and charmed. Some way distant from an already remote village in this chalky landscape, the farm buildings were grouped, he guessed, around a spring or water source of some description. It was at first glance impressive and extensive. They entered, throttling back, through a wide porte-cochère surmounted by a low-built wooden storey running the length of the transom, a useful construction which acted as a *pigeonnier* judging by the flocks of white doves perching there. The interior *basse-cour* was rectangular and spacious and lined on two sides by a barn and a stable block. Their arrival sent a guard dog into fits of rage and hens dashed to throw themselves under their wheels. Opposite stood the farmhouse, half timbered with walls of local limestone and dressed stone surrounds to the doors and windows. The roof was pitched at a low angle under a strong frame to bear the weight of heavy clay tiles. It was not lovely but it reflected the colours and fabric of the earth from which it sprang and it pleased Joe.

The motor cycle puttered to a brief halt at the door to allow him time to dismount. He did this with as much dignity as he could muster, aware of scrutiny from all sides and very much wondering how securely the still-raging dog was confined. He waved goodbye to his chauffeur and, approaching the door, made use of the heavy knocker. While he waited, he stepped back a pace to take a glance at his surroundings. The second look was less reassuring. Tiles had slipped and fallen from the barns and not been replaced. One or two doors and windows were broken, cracked or missing altogether. No paintwork had been renovated for years. In an establishment which boasted so many vigorous young men, he found this hard to account for.

The door creaked slowly open and he turned to smile a greeting but saw no one.

"Are you the policeman?"

The voice had come from low down and he watched in amusement as the child warily stuck a head around the door and surveyed him. He must have looked unthreatening as the boy came forward and opened the door wide. He was about six years old, Joe estimated, and was dressed neatly in baggy shirt with a white collar, knickerbockers and buckled shoes. Turned out to welcome and disarm the visiting policeman? Joe thought so.

"Oh, hello, young man. Yes, I am the policeman. I've come to see Monsieur and Madame Tellancourt. Here's my card."

He took the card and pretended to examine it. "Grandpa's expecting you. He said to take you through to the back parlour. Uncle Victor and Aunt Isabelle are there as well. Come this way."

He hurried off down the tiled corridor and Joe followed until he reached a door at the end and pushed it open. "In there," said his guide, and abandoned him.

Joe's first instinct was to tell the assembled company to, for God's sake, run for a doctor. He stepped forward anxiously at the sight of the grey-faced old man, alarmed by his rasping efforts to breathe. In spite of the warm weather he was swathed in rugs and shawls and the remains of a meal in jugs and bowls stood on a table at his elbow.

As the others, a man and two women, showed no immediate signs of panic, Joe calmed himself and addressed the old man. "Sir. Commander Sandilands of the London police and also with Interpol. How do you do?"

The younger man answered and took the card from Joe's outstretched hand. "I'm Victor, Monsieur Tellancourt's son. This is my sister Isabelle and this is Clothilde, the wife of my older brother Thomas, whom I understand you have seen in Reims. We'd be obliged if you could direct your questions through me. As you see, my father is in poor health and not able to sustain a conversation. Though he will understand all that you have to say, I'm sure." The tone was perfectly polite though there was no warmth.

Joe wondered if he'd heard correctly. A wife? Clothilde? This was the first mention of a wife, surely? He remembered that the official claimants of the unknown soldier were named as Victor and Isabelle Tellancourt. Recognizably brother and sister and both in their mid-thirties they stood together, dark of hair and complexion like their father. The wife of Thomas—or Thibaud—was a brown-haired woman dressed in widow's black, small and quenched. She did not attempt to return Joe's greeting.

For form's sake, Joe went through his rehearsed questions receiving exactly the answers he anticipated from Victor with occasional interjections from Isabelle. They knew their father's answers by heart but he confirmed each statement with a nod and followed the conversation with alert eyes. Their certainty that the patient was their brother was unshakable, their eagerness for a quick solution in their favour compelling. With slightly excessive nostalgia, they recounted stories of Thomas's young days, they produced letters he had written from the front and the inevitable portrait photograph. Joe took the much-handled sepia study and said into the expectant silence: "Ah, yes. A *fantassin*— would that be the word?" Joe could conjure up the colourful figure from his memory. The handsome young man was wearing the high-collared tunic of an infantryman under

the blue greatcoat, the *capote* with its two front hems but-
toned back like a butterfly's wings showing puttees and
shining laced shoes. He was wearing the soldier's round
blue helmet, an unflattering piece of headgear which hid his
hair, and the lower half of his face was almost swamped by a
flamboyant moustache. A *poilu*. Impossible on this evidence,
Joe thought, to rule the man in or out in the struggle for
Thibaud.

"An infantryman? Your son fought his war on foot, then,
not on horseback?"

His comment was received by puzzlement all round and
the reply came from Victor: "Of course he did. The cavalry?
Thomas? He was a farm boy like the rest of us. A peasant!
From St Céré not St Cyr!" Victor laughed at his joke.
"Couldn't stand horses. Had too much to do with them on
the farm. He could handle them all right—rode like a
Cossack but always said they were the stupidest animals
ever invented. No, he was nothing special. A trench rat.
Swept up for cannon fodder like the rest of us. Declared
missing, presumed dead, at Verdun. They never sent us his
name tag. But it seems they presumed wrong, doesn't it?
Taken prisoner and now returned to his home town."

Joe turned to the silent wife, standing apart from the rest
and looking through the window. "An emotional moment
for you, madame. To envisage the possibility of one's husband being restored after so long and in such a battered
condition..." he murmured.

"Well, of course it's emotional," snapped Victor. "But
she'll cope. She was always a good wife to Thomas. Devoted.
She'll go on caring for him. What's more natural?"

It was becoming clear to Joe that the tension he felt in
the room had its source in the woman whose voice he
had not yet heard and he sensed a mystery. He nodded his

agreement and turned his attention from the widow, taking the brother and sister down paths they were more keen to follow and noting down officiously points which they deemed important. Finally he snapped shut his notebook with a satisfied smile and began to thank the old man and his son and daughter warmly for their help and clarification.

Relief swept through the room. Victor hurried to the door, finding the small boy playing skittles in the corridor, and sent him to whistle up the Commander's transport back into the village.

"One last thing," said Joe without emphasis, "and perhaps Madame could enlighten me..." He bowed to the widow. "If you wouldn't mind strolling back to the gate with me there's a couple of questions better directed at a wife...I'm sure you understand, old chap," he finished, with a conspiratorial glance at Victor, who gaped and looked from one to the other with suspicion. Unexpectedly, the widow came at once to his aid, nodding and slipping out of the room ahead of him.

He followed her swift steps down the corridor away from the front door and in some surprise turned at her beckoning finger and climbed a set of back stairs. Two flights of increasingly narrow treads and threadbare carpet took them to the attic floor of the house. The sun streamed through a side window glinting off dust motes and, distantly, a dove cooed and was answered. It was uncomfortably hot up here under the eaves and Joe was feeling more uneasy by the minute. She stopped in front of a door: a door of solid oak and, unusually for this neglected house, freshly installed. There was a bolt on the outside. The widow wrapped a fold of her skirt over it to muffle the sound and pulled it back. With a gesture she invited him to step inside, listening intently the while. For noises of pursuit, perhaps? Her nervousness was catching.

His instinct for self-preservation made him insist that she enter the room first. He had no intention of being discovered, a mummified corpse locked in a French attic a hundred years from now. Standing in the open doorway, one hand on the latch, Joe looked inside and he understood.

Chapter 14

Bare, white-painted walls, a metal-framed bed with a thin mattress and one chair, it was more stark than the hospital room in Reims. Heavy bars fitted across the one small window.

She began to speak hurriedly. A rehearsed speech. Not a word was wasted. "That man's not Thomas! They're claiming him for the money—heaven knows they need it! The state would pay it to me, I think, but...well, you've seen them! They'd take it all in payment for my board and lodging over the years. But look at this!" She waved a hand around the room and her pretty face melted for a moment into pity. "They'll keep him prisoner here." The expression changed to one of petulance as she rushed on: "And guess who'll be expected to care for him? Me! I'll be running up and down those stairs with slop bowls until one of us drops dead. I'll be just as much a prisoner as he is. I'm no nurse, monsieur, and I don't want to spend the rest of my life cleaning up after some lunatic who's not even my husband." She seized Joe's hands, needing to make a physical link with him before she confided her next secret. The torrent continued: "I'm a widow. I have official confirmation. I can show you my papers. A widow. I may marry again."

"You have someone in mind?" he asked with equal brevity.

"There's a man in the village. Not a Tellancourt!" She almost smiled. "He's elderly but kind. He owns the pharmacy. We could make each other happy. You must understand that this man in Reims is not my husband!"

"You must try to give proof of that assertion, madame. It isn't enough merely to express an opinion and keep repeating it. Listen! Tell me—you were married for how long before he disappeared?"

"Three years."

"Did you have any children?"

"One."

"A girl or a boy?"

"A boy."

"How old?"

"He died before he was six months old."

The simple questions provoked swift answers and were followed seamlessly by Joe's next: "What distinguishing marks did your husband have on his body?"

She faltered. "What do you mean? That bayonet cut on his arm? Thomas never had a wound like that as far as I know."

Voices were heard shouting down below and somewhere distantly a motor cycle revved up. Joe eased his straining collar and took another lungful of warm air.

"Did he or didn't he have any special marks in, let's say, an intimate area? In a place where only a wife would be aware, perhaps? If you could furnish details of...a wart...a mark on the skin that Thomas had in a particular spot and the patient in Reims does not have such a mark then your case is made."

In the dusty dimness of the room he noticed she was blushing. She looked away in embarrassment and withdrew her hands.

"Inspector! My husband Thomas and I were modest people."

Joe pondered this for a moment and could think of no response. The shouting below increased. The dog joined in. Joe followed her back downstairs.

Encountering a dangerously angry Victor by the front door, Joe faced him with the lazy confidence and clipped tones of a commanding officer. "Well, Tellancourt, that just about wraps it up. Madame was kind enough to indulge my whim to check the accommodation. The accommodation," he repeated meaningfully, tapping him on the shoulder. "Sensible precautions taken, I see. And there's my transport in the lane ... Goodbye then, and I'll see you are the first to hear the outcome of this business."

He strode across the farm courtyard and the door banged shut behind him. As he passed under the dovecote he became aware on the far side of a dark figure seated on a bench. The old lady was staring down the lane, waiting and watching for her son to return, he remembered. He looked with curiosity at the black-clad widow sunk into her sorrow. Very likely ga-ga, he decided and prepared to pass by, quietly raising his cap. But as he approached she caught his attention. He wondered whether perhaps she had been expecting to see him. She glanced up at him, blue eyes unfaded, intelligent, even amused. A wisp of grey hair which might once have been blonde escaped from her bonnet. She had a book open in her lap and a bundle of knitting. So this was

Armande, the stranger, the smart lady's maid from Normandy. He stood to greet her and introduce himself.

After his introductory comments had established that she knew exactly who he was and what he was doing there, he made a polite compliment to the mother whose devotion would keep her watching for her missing son. Her eyes twinkled. "It's not such a penance, you know, Commander. It's a madhouse in there! You've seen them! And the children were shut away for the duration of your visit...If I couldn't look forward to my hour a day out here by myself in peace and quiet, I'd be as mad as they are. Now, what can I tell you about my son?"

Dr Varimont's words came back to him—"A mother would remember"—and he decided to venture once more to pose his sensitive question.

She listened to his convoluted phrasing with patience and replied at once. "Well, it's about time someone asked a sensible question. Of course! Do you know, I'd nearly forgotten! Perhaps I'm not such a saintly mother after all. Yes, my Thomas did have marks...birthmarks...no, I don't mean that exactly. Not the strawberry mark so many babies have...no. It was a difficult birth, Commander. My first child. The midwife knew her trade though and managed to save him—and me. But she had to use those—what do you call them?—forceps, that's it." She put out her hand in a pincer shape. "Like this. It left one mark on his front and one mark on his bottom. Purplish they were. Round and smaller than a cherry. On the left-hand side. As you look at him, I mean, so that would be his right." The hand demonstrated again. "Is this of any help?"

* * *

Joe was dropped off by the boy called Jules at the door of his motor car. After a silent acknowledgement of his passenger's thanks and farewells, Jules stayed on, engine ticking over, one foot on the ground, watching. Being seen off the premises? Joe was irritated. He banged shut the door, turned on the ignition and set about a three point turn to make his way out of the village square. With a nod in his direction the boy let in the clutch and roared off back the way he had come.

Joe took a long while over his turn, listened to the disappearing rumble of the motor bike and changed his mind. He parked again, facing outwards this time in case he needed to make a swift exit, and sat thinking. The boy's behaviour had been odd. Eager to be off and yet, he would have sworn, under orders to make certain the policeman had left. Joe glanced around the peaceful scene. What, hereabouts, or whom, did they want him not to see?

The central square with its plane trees, skittle alley, duck pond, town hall and inn could have served as the illustration to any school textbook encouraging pupils to learn the French language. *Combien de canards y a-t-il? Qui entre dans l'épicerie? Quelle heure est-il à l'horloge de l'église? Où se trouve le monument aux morts?* The stock phrases rushed to mind, delivered in the sharp tones of his dominie as he surveyed the peaceful scene.

The war memorial!

His glance flashed back to the effigy carved in granite, a bluish stone almost, in this bright sunlight, the shade of *bleu d'horizon* of the living soldier's uniform. A *poilu*, helmeted head bent, greatcoat pinned back, the bayonet of his rifle garlanded with wild flowers, he stood sorrowing for his fallen comrades. It was striking. Another memorial to add to Joe's list.

He turned off his engine and walked across to pay his respects. He took off his hat and bowed his head, always playing to the invisible crowd he assumed to be witnessing his actions. Under lowered lids he ran an eye down the list of the fallen. And there he was—the twentieth name down. Thomas Tellancourt. Put up very soon after the armistice, Joe guessed, so the family must at that time have accepted the death of their son readily enough to have agreed to his name featuring on the local memorial at any rate. Perhaps there was another long shot he could play?

Glad that he'd established an interest in the architecture of the church on arrival at the café, he looked ostentatiously at his watch, took an indecisive step forward, stopped and then went on towards the porch. He spent a few minutes admiring the carvings, stepping back the better to get them in focus and then walking on around the exterior. He wandered into the surrounding graveyard to scan the roof line and shielded his eyes against the noonday sun to view the tower. None of the gravestones on the north and east sides of the church bore the name of the family Tellancourt but when he got to the south side they started to appear. Many of them. They marched shoulder to shoulder in rows, dark granite decorated with ornate carvings and mementoes. Some had several occupants. Hardly possible to examine each one. He reckoned he'd get about as far as the third before someone took a bead on him from the café. Rifles had been hanging on the walls, he remembered, and perhaps they were more than harmless mementoes. Hunting accidents all too common in the French countryside, he understood. Many scores settled by that means. The agonized fear of snipers' bullets returned to strike him where he stood. His head went down, his spine bristled with a sudden chill and he had to clench his hands and breathe deeply to resist a forward plunge into the shelter of a gravestone. But here he was in full view of the village and, indeed, right by the town hall, that symbol of an ordered and lawful society. And then he remembered that *la mairie* was a forward listening post of the Clan Tellancourt, according to the doctor.

He was being ridiculous! Scotland Yard's ace manhunter creeping about a French cemetery in fear of the mayor's secretary's umbrella poking him in the ribs? And then he saw what his instinct had surely been telling him was there. At one of the graves close by, work seemed to be in progress. A canvas sheet of the kind that grave-diggers use was stretched over the plot and another was hanging casually over the granite stone. A wheelbarrow was propped against it to keep it in place. But there were no spades, not a crumb of displaced earth. Joe strolled over, eased back the wheelbarrow and tweaked aside the covering.

He read on the stone words he was clearly not intended to read. "Idiots!" he thought. "Should have left well alone!" By this ill-conceived attempt at a literal cover-up his attention had been drawn straight to the gilt letters: *Thomas Tellancourt soldat de la grande guerre. 1890–1916. Mort pour la Patrie.*

For one moment Joe wished that he had Dorcas by his side to enjoy the revelation.

"Well, well," he muttered, replacing the cover. "I wonder who exactly we have down there? How interesting it would be to find out."

Shaking his head, he hurried back to his car and moved off as smoothly as he could.

Chapter 15

Didier politely held the door of the lift to allow two people from his floor to dash in. An Englishman and a young girl. The usual strained attempts at conversation between strangers in the confined space of a lift ensued: "Ground floor all right for you?...Thank you, yes, we're bound for the dining room...Your first night here?... You'll enjoy the food...Ah, here we are."

Seated by himself at a table in the corner, Didier gave his full attention to the menu and then settled to look covertly at the other guests. Inquisitive by nature, he always enjoyed a little mischievous speculation about his fellow men. No surprises here: mostly men on business associated no doubt with the champagne trade and mostly, like him, solitary. There were one or two couples, the silent ones he presumed to be married to each other, the animated ones almost certainly to someone else. These were far more interesting. But his eye was continually taken by the Englishman and his companion. And here was a puzzle. The man was obviously too young to be her father and treated her with none of the paternal *froideur* you might expect of an Anglo-Saxon parent. Brother and sister? Hardly. The age gap was too great. And yet, superficially there was a family resemblance. They had dark hair and complexions, though on second glance the man had the misty grey eyes of a northern land while the girl had the unmistakable warm brown *marron* of the Mediterranean.

Didier recognized a fellow soldier. The Englishman, even without the give-away wound to the forehead, was easily identified as such by his confident stride and watchful eyes. He seemed, as far as Didier could gather from a distance of three tables, to be recounting his day. A day full of incident, judging by the reactions of his audience. The girl was fascinated, responding one moment with horror, the next with laughter. With not too distant memories of his own daughter and her friends at the same age as this girl Didier realized that what was missing was the element of adolescent playing to an audience, of flirtation. His Paulette would have been excitedly eyeing the waiters and the more youthful of the other diners and passing salty comments. This girl was completely absorbed by the conversation. At ease with her companion, she leaned over and brushed a crumb from his sleeve and refilled his water glass without a pause in her sentence. And Didier smiled. He had it. These two were partners. In what, he had no idea, but whatever their business, and it was clear to him that they had a business, they were conducting it on equal terms.

The Englishman had it right: the food was indeed very good. His doctor's advice set aside for the duration of his stay, Didier decided to treat himself to the rich northern dishes he really enjoyed and had for so many months forgone and he selected a bottle of Chablis and a bottle of burgundy to accompany them. So near the end of his road now, why not? Towards the end of the meal, familiar twinges made him begin to regret his indulgence. The trouble was he had regularly in the last year or so passed off what Christophe told him was angina as indigestion. And now— could he any longer tell the difference? Was one a trigger for the other? He wished he had listened more carefully to his doctor's explanations. He gripped the edge of the table as the crisis seized him, gasping for breath and trying to hold firm, battling with the band of steel which tightened across his chest. He must not black out here in public among strangers. He must not collapse so near to his goal.

"Are you all right, sir? Pardon my intrusion…my niece noticed you seem to be in some difficulty and sent me over. Look, you're obviously *not* all right. Shall I get the manager to call a doctor?" The Englishman leaned over him, shielding him from curious eyes, concerned but discreet.

Head to the wind, Didier crashed through a final wave of pain and managed to speak. "It's all right. Thank you. An old problem. Brought on by over-indulgence, I'm afraid. As you say—the food here is indeed very good. Too challenging for my decrepit old system. I have pills somewhere…" He scrabbled in his pocket for his pill box and shook out two. "I'll be all right again in two ticks."

The Englishman handed him his glass of water and stead-ied his hand as he swallowed. "Well, if you're sure…" But the man did not leave at once, duty done, as Didier expected. He slipped on to the chair next to him, one hand comfortingly on his arm, and sat through the crisis with him. Finally, "That's better," he said. "Less blue about the gills, I think! But, all the same, old chap, I'd see a medic in the morning if I were you." He held out his hand in an English gesture. "How do you do? Sandilands, Joe Sandilands from London. Policeman and busybody."

Didier managed a faint smile. "Marmont. Didier Marmont from the Ardennes. Mayor and gourmand. Thank you for your concern, monsieur, and I'll certainly take your advice. Oh, and thank your lovely niece, would you," he bowed his head in acknowledgement of Dorcas, whose eyes had not left them across the room, "for her awareness and her kind heart."

"Well, your Mayor Marmont actually seems to have taken your advice, Joe."

"I'm surprised you sound surprised! But what makes you say that?" said Joe, intrigued by the gleam of secret knowledge in Dorcas's eyes.

"As we were leaving the hotel just now, I saw him at the reception desk using the guests' telephone. Did you know you can overhear anything people are saying if you stand behind them—the partition's quite inadequate."

Joe groaned. "I left you alone for half a day yesterday and I'll bet you've produced a notebook full of potential blackmail material." He had been, since their first meeting, aware of Dorcas's eavesdropping habits. A necessary tool for survival in her difficult domestic circumstances, he allowed, but it could be an embarrassment if used in more civilized surroundings.

"I had more useful things to do yesterday," she said primly. "But listen—your new friend the apoplectic mayor was talking to a doctor as we were coming out." Joe remembered she'd slipped back into the hotel with a muttered excuse about checking their pigeon-hole for messages. "And I wondered if you or someone or other should help him? He seemed to be having no luck... 'But, Doctor, it's rather ur-

gent,' he said. 'Surely you can see me before next Monday?'
Think, Joe! Next Monday—that's ages! And then his shoulders slumped and he said: 'Oh, well then, if that's the ear-
liest appointment you can give me, I suppose I shall have to
accept it.' And he wrote it down in his diary. We shan't be
here tonight to keep an eye on him—we'll be at the château."

"Poor chap," said Joe. "But listen, Dorcas—he's a man of
the world. He's a mayor, for goodness' sake! Which, in this
country, means competent, efficient and fully able to nego-
tiate the channels of bureaucracy. They *are* the channels of
bureaucracy! If a mayor can't do it, it can't be done. Put him
out of your mind. You can't look out for every waif and
stray and heart-attack victim you encounter on life's road.
You've quite enough on your plate watching out for me at
the moment."

He spoke gently, unwilling to be critical of Dorcas's
quality of large-heartedness. At far too young an age she
had assumed responsibility not only for the well-being of
her three younger brothers and sister but also for her feckless father, whom she protected like a lioness. Not even Joe,
who was conscious of, though mystified by, his own special
standing with Dorcas, was allowed to criticize Orlando in
her hearing.

She grinned. "Did you remember to brush your teeth and
have you paid the bill? Goodness! Am I so annoying?"

"Yes! Worse than Lydia! From whom you have learned a
good deal of nonsense. And the answer is yes to both those
questions. I also took the trouble to enquire about rooms
for our return. When we leave the château, I thought we'd
spend a day back here in Reims tying up ends, making a
statement to Bonnefoye—that sort of thing. It'll be okay.
They have plenty of space next week. Now—Bonnefoye. Do

you feel up to encountering him again? Getting another look at those wonderful teeth? I have a date with him in half an hour. To discuss progress so far."

Dorcas blushed. "I'd simply love to," she said.

Joe looked her up and down with a critical eye. "Ah, yes, I do see that. New yellow dress, gloves . . . and aren't those silk stockings? Good Lord! Now what game are you playing?"

"If anyone's playing games, it's Bonnefoye," she said with spirit. "You know he's using you, Joe? He hasn't time or interest in this case, I think, and he just let you fish about in this murky pond vaguely hoping you might stir up something from the bottom that repays attention."

"Well, of course I realized. He was so keen to warn me off—to tell me how disturbed he would be by any interference—I interpreted this as a quite deliberate challenge, and he calculated that my response would instantly be to defy him and go my own way, risking the displeasure of the French police force."

"You're double-bluffing each other?"

"Exactly. A comfortable arrangement. And, should anything go wrong, anything embarrassing occur, each of us feels he can cover himself. Misunderstandings, misinterpretations—all easily explained by the foreignness of the other player in the game. I liked Bonnefoye. Very professional. I'd have done just the same. But I still think I'd like to quiz him on the information he's been holding back from us."

"Commander! How good to see you again." Bonnefoye did a gratifying double-take and added, "And Miss Dorcas?" He gave her the benefit of his slanting smile, dazzlingly accentuated by the sharp black line of his moustache. He took

Dorcas's hand and kissed it with unnecessary gallantry, Joe thought. "But a Miss Dorcas transformed!" he exclaimed, with an admiring glance at her hair. "I see you have bene-fited from the skill of our local coiffeurs? Charming! Charming!" Joe also noticed that he was addressing her in fast French. Communication on several levels had obviously occurred between the Inspector and the doctor. Just for once Dorcas was rendered speechless. She reddened and dimpled prettily. Joe sighed.

"Now, Commander, perhaps you could tell me what progress you have made? Have you proved to Dr Varimont's satisfaction that the patient is English? I have ready all the forms you will need if you feel we may now take the step of confirming officially his nationality and subsequently arrange for his repatriation." He poked at a file on his desk with the end of his pencil.

"Hold your horses, Bonnefoye," said Joe firmly. "I have little evidence and no proof that he is English. Further-more, I would say it's unlikely that this could ever, in the present medical circumstances, be established." He gave a brief account of his encounter with Thibaud, knowing that he must already have had a similar version from Varimont.

"But you believe the doctor when he tells you that the pa-tient spoke in English, surely?" Bonnefoye objected.

"I do. But I have not heard him speak for myself. I do not think a foreigner like the doctor could be one hundred per cent certain, from this hearing, that the language was used as by a native speaker. After all, *I* might replay a nightmare scene quoting bits of French but *my* accent would not de-ceive a Frenchman. Though a fellow Englishman might well be taken in."

"I see what you mean. It all comes down to speech, doesn't it?" said Bonnefoye, shrugging. "Just a few words,

that's all we'd need. If he were French, Varimont could identify his class and the part of France he comes from, I don't
doubt. We'd know straightaway whether he was an officer from Champagne or a sergeant from Brittany. Our
accents are as much a give-away as our faces. Communication! We've got to get the man to communicate." He pondered this for a moment. "I wonder if they've tried sign
language?"

"It's an interesting fact," said Dorcas, "that studies of
shell-shock have turned up victims—and I believe they *are*
victims," she added firmly, "who suffered from aphasia—
dumbness—*before* entering the war. After their neurasthenia
was diagnosed these poor men were found to be unable to
remember their sign language. Nothing wrong with their
hands as there is probably nothing wrong with Thibaud's
speech mechanisms—it's the *ability to communicate* that's cut
off. The root of the problem is what appears to be a paralysis in the brain."

"Indeed?" Bonnefoye looked at her in astonishment.
"Mademoiselle interests herself in psychotherapy?"

Dorcas looked uncomfortable for a moment then raised
her chin and favoured him with one of her best smiles.
"As a matter of fact, I do. I intend to study the subject at
London University and qualify as a medical psychologist,
perhaps a psychiatrist."

"A very worthy aim, mademoiselle. I wish you the best of
good fortune." Bonnefoye looked genuinely admiring, Joe
thought, realizing suddenly that he was not treating Dorcas
as a child but as a young woman. And Dorcas was lapping
it up. He decided to reclaim the initiative.

"So. Your best course, Bonnefoye, would be to prove by
some means or other that our man is definitely the relation

claimed by one of the four feuding families. This I believe to be the only clear solution open to us. Yes, I appreciate, of course, that this entails quite a bit of detective work. Work which cannot be undertaken by the usual government agencies which interest themselves in these matters. Awkward, really, and delicate stuff. Emotions running high, public opinion being manipulated by means of the press...I do understand. It's not police work. You have much more demanding affairs to deal with. So," he finished brightly, "I'm pleased to give you what I have. Make life a bit easier for you perhaps. And...if we were to pool our knowledge...how much more efficiently we would bring this affair to a satisfactory conclusion. Now..."

Joe slapped down on the desk the notes he'd taken in his three interviews. "That's what I've got. You're very welcome to it. And I'll fill in the gaps with your findings and we'll be getting somewhere. Case number one. Mireille Desforges, claimant. Says the man is one Dominique de Villancourt. Have you checked this man's details in the army records?"

"We have." Bonnefoye's tone was clipped and businesslike. "There was such an officer in a cavalry regiment. The 8th Dragoons. Born and educated in Paris, trained at the military academy at St Cyr. Well-to-do family." He paused. "Problem is...his only living relations, mother and father, are practically fossils. Not interested in staking a claim and positively deny that this could possibly be their son. Refuse point blank to co-operate with us. They live in the past. And for them life ended with the receipt of the letter telling them of Dominique's death. We have accounts from fellow officers written later to the parents and we can draw up quite a clear picture of his last days. He died in the charge on von Kluck's forces in the first battle of the

Chemin des Dames. Not the second affair in 1917, no, this was in 1914, early on, following on the first battle of the Marne before everything got bogged down in trenches.

"We know he crossed the Seine with the cavalry in the first days of September and rode north to the Marne to fight on the right flank of the British Expeditionary Force. The British and French fighting together," he said with a slight smile, "took advantage of an opening gap and cut their way through to divide the opposing forces. Just like us, you're thinking! The action led to the first allied victory of the war. But you were there, I understand?"

"Right in the middle," said Joe. "Effecting liaison be-tween the British GHQ and General Joffre." He swept a negligent hand over his eyebrow. "Souvenir of the Marne. If Dominique was 8th Dragoons he must have ended up in the French Cavalry Corps under General Louis Napoleon Conneau?"

Bonnefoye nodded. "We have a sighting of him on 3rd September, massing under Conneau behind the Petit Morin river ready to cover the left flank of the French Fifth Army. The next reference is an account from a fellow officer (I have a copy) describing Dominique's last movements. He'd sur-vived the Marne and fought his way north up to the plain at Sissonne, caught between the German First and Second Armies but hoping to storm the plateau between Soissons and Craonne."

"Huge casualties up there, British and French, in the second half of that September," Joe said quietly. He could never repress a shiver at the sound of the word "Craonne."

"His death was reported as taking place on 15th September, trying to break through the front between Cerny and Craonne. An eyewitness, again a fellow officer, wrote at length to the parents after the war, so we know there was no censorship. It was his moving account which led to the award of the Croix de Guerre for Dominique. He tells that they were out on patrol, a flying column of seven men and two officers, when they came upon a thirty-strong and very fresh German cavalry troop. The French horses were exhausted, their backs stinking with running sores, the men hadn't eaten for two days and they'd run out of ammunition. Only one thing to do!" His chin went up, jutting with pride. "They attacked."

Joe left a respectful silence.

"In the skirmish that followed, Dominique's horse was shot from under him and he was last seen grappling in combat with the German commander. Sabre to sabre. The French troop was wiped out with the exception of the letter writer, who was knocked unconscious and carted off for interrogation and three years of prisoner-of-war camp by the Germans."

"Terrible story. And you think our Mademoiselle Desforges is utterly confused? Her man whom she identifies convincingly and without prompting by his birthmarks was, according to her, present at the Chemin des Dames but I could have sworn she meant the second battle of that name in 1917. But, Bonnefoye, she even told me how many service stripes he would have had on his sleeve. Claims—and convincingly, I have to say—that she sewed his second wound stripe on his sleeve. The wound to the jaw. Result of a blow from a rifle butt, he claimed. It's all in the notes. She was firmly convinced she had continued to meet her Dominique until his disappearance in 1917."

"I'm afraid the evidence rules her out. A body—complete with identification, I have to say—was returned to the parents, was buried with no query raised in the family vault in Paris. In October 1914."

Joe was aware of Dorcas's disappointment.

"Can we be absolutely certain that it is his body?" Joe ventured to ask on her behalf. "In the chaos of war strange things happened..."

"We'll have to take it as established, I'm afraid. There is no way in the world we'll get permission to disinter a war hero. Posthumous Croix de Guerre and all that. The parents categorically refuse permission. And, the facts being what they are, I can't say I blame them. We'd be flying in the face of common sense and the evidence if we pursued this."

"Don't cross Mireille off your list yet!" said Dorcas. "Oh, sorry, Uncle Joe."

"I understand your sentiments, mademoiselle, and sympathize," smiled Bonnefoye.

"Talking of burials," said Joe. "If you look at my notes on the third lot, the Tellancourts, you'll see I discovered—you might have warned me!—that their Thomas is comfortably buried where every French soldier wants to be buried, in the shadow of his own village church steeple. Amongst a whole tribe of Tellancourts. So what is all this nonsense about their claim?"

"Ah, yes." Bonnefoye had the grace to look shifty. "Wondered if you'd trip across that. Are you aware, I wonder, of a rather disgusting type of business which has sprung up in these post-war entrepreneurial times? A business which is hard to suppress since there is such a continuing demand for it. There are companies which—you will find this hard to believe—have set themselves up as retrievers of corpses from the battlefields. It goes on. It still goes on. They dig about in mass graves occasionally finding bodies which still have the name tag of the soldier around his neck or wrist and they track him down and approach his relatives. Sometimes the families of the missing themselves, having exhausted all other channels—the Red Cross and so on—advertise for information in the newspapers, so desperate are they to bring their sons and fathers home to the village.

"It was in response to such a plea posted by the mother that one of these firms contacted her. They had found the boy, they declared, and had his tag to prove it. They could box up the remains in a coffin and return it to St Céré-sur-Marne. For a fee, of course. They charge a franc per kilometre, I understand. So, for a small fortune, a body was returned and buried in the family plot. And until that wretched photograph of Thibaud was printed, they were at peace, content to take their flowers along to his grave every Sunday. But now? Well, how certain can we be that the body in the grave is the Tellancourt boy? You tell me!"

"Not at all," said Joe quietly. "And I have to tell you, Bonnefoye, that the wife I was to discover he had when I arrived at the farm roundly declares that Thibaud is not Thomas. She didn't tell you that? No? Probably keeping quiet under duress from the rest of the family. I managed to get her by herself and found she was eager to communicate this."

"Silly woman! But that was well done, Sandilands. A denial by the wife! I'll fetch her in and take her statement. That'll amply satisfy the powers that be. Good, that's one more off our list," Bonnefoye said cheerfully.

"Wait! Not so simple, I'm afraid. I was to discover that the lady values her widow's status and means to remarry. The thought of remaining chained to a mental patient for the rest of her life doesn't appeal. And gives her a jolly strong motive for denying him."

Bonnefoye opened his mouth to exclaim, caught sight of Dorcas and limited himself to "Dear, dear! What a nuisance."

"But wait! You'll see I had a roller-coaster of a day—I also managed a private interview with the mother, though I can't be certain that she didn't do the managing… Anyway—when asked, she offered conclusive evidence as to the birthmarks. It's all in the notes. She was even able to describe the one on the rear which apparently escaped the attention of his *soi-disant* lover, Mireille Desforges."

"So, we rule out Desforges, leave in the Tellancourts and, tell me, what are your thoughts on the Langlois claim?"

"As with the Tellancourts, I suspect that the imperative here is a financial one. Dorcas has done some sound detective work of her own and discovers that Mother Langlois, having apparently mistreated her son through his young life, now wants him back in his damaged state to facilitate her flight from the family hearth. I can't blame her for formulating such a plan but I have to say it casts doubt on the foundation of her claim. Much, I'd say, rests on the statement of this schoolmaster who seems to be so sure of his ground and fighting her corner. Anything known?"

Bonnefoye nodded wisely. "You're nearly there, Sandilands. About as far forward as we are. But there are methods I can employ," he said mysteriously, "to get at the truth which are not available to a visiting English policeman. Leave it to me. I assure you I will tell you what we know as soon as we know it. I will just say that for the moment we must mark the Langlois claim with a question mark. That's one cross, one tick and one question mark."

He grunted with satisfaction. "Well, it begins to look very much as though the business is wrapped up," he said. "Unless you can unearth, I'm sorry, discover, something more sensational *chez les Houdart* this weekend. It *is* this weekend you're spending with them? Good. Well, let me know how you get on, won't you?" He gave a sudden and boyish grin. "You know how I shall spend the rest of my morning, curse you, Sandilands? Looking through your notes and ferreting about in this case. Waste of my time, I know it! My business is solving the problems of the freshly murdered (three corpses on my books at the moment. Three! Any chance…? No…?) not working out who the *living* may be! You have my number? Ring me at once if there's anything I can do or say, won't you? I want this solved and you out of my hair by next Wednesday. Clear?"

"Clear, old man," said Joe and, to Dorcas's barely concealed disgust, they shook hands in a matey way.

"Oh, one last thing," said Joe, hand on the doorknob. He pointed to his notes. "Last page and rather urgent. It's an outside chance but you never know. Just a suggestion. But I think you'd agree we should explore all avenues. And I'm sure the French technical services are up to it."

"Well, Miss Dorcas? Do you still admire the Inspector?" Joe asked as they made their way back to the car.

"Oh, yes," she said. "He'll do—for a police inspector. He'll do very well."

"And what was all that stuff about studying…psychology, was it? *Are* you intending to do such a thing? Because if so, we must take steps to get you educated first."

"Of course I'm intending no such thing! Live in London for three years? Urgh! But I had to say *something*!"

"Another naughty lie?"

"A distortion of the truth for politeness' sake."

"Ah. But I suppose I should be relieved that politeness is in the forefront of your mind with the weekend I see stretching in front of us. Lunch first to fortify ourselves and then we'll get started. I'm not sure what our reception will consist of, Dorcas. Be prepared for anything, will you? We could find ourselves entertained as honoured guests or we could be shown round to the tradesmen's entrance and fed on scraps in the back kitchen. I've encountered both extremes in my time."

"I've lived at both extremes in my time," said Dorcas seriously. "Don't worry, Joe. I'm a chameleon, you know."

Chapter 16

"Crikey! Were you expecting this?" Dorcas asked as they passed down an avenue of beech trees and drew up in front of the gates to the château.

"No. And what's more, I'm not even certain we've got the right place," said Joe, doubtfully. "Though we followed the direction from the village carefully enough. Don't forget I've only seen an artist's impression on a champagne bottle. And if this *is* the right place our artist has taken quite a bit of licence. The name for a start! I thought, in my simple unquestioning way, it was most probably named as on the bottle, the Château Houdart, but if you look at the old sign outside—a bit battered perhaps and those holes are bullet holes, I do believe—you'll see it's the Château de Septfontaines. Seven Fountains? I wonder if they're still to be found?"

He gazed from the stone arcade with its central arch guarding the forecourt of the château to the procession of tall chimney stacks in the distance.

"House rebuilt by Mansart in 1685, I understand," he

said. "Yes—it begins to emerge. I know what the artist has done—he's pared it down to its essentials, missed out all the interesting details and moved a vineyard several hundred yards to the north."

"Those creatures up there on the piers. What are they?"

"Gryphons? Would you say gryphons? Something couchant, gardant anyway. Might even be lions. Shall we take a chance?"

"Yes, let's go in. They can only set the dogs on us!"

Joe slipped the car into gear and they stole forward through the open wrought-iron gates, taking in the symmetrical wings decorated with classical urns and, in the centre, the main body of the house, its parapet carrying a cargo of gesticulating statuary. They crunched their way over the immaculately swept gravel and encircled a stone basin in which a stone Triton with a far from reluctant stone maiden in his arms tirelessly poured a jet of water from a stone shell.

"Do you think we could have one of those at home, Joe?" Dorcas whispered. "Lydia would love it."

Joe parked the car neatly in the shade and they set out to climb the shallow run of steps up to the wide front door. No knocker, no bell, but the door opened as they approached it. A manservant smiled a welcome and reached for the car keys Joe still held in his hand. "Good afternoon, Commander. Miss. If you'll permit, I'll have your things taken up to your rooms. Come this way. Madame Houdart is in the *petit salon* where she will be taking tea."

"Tea? In the *petit salon*?" Dorcas muttered. "Oh, I say! Awfully glad I put on my silk stockings!"

As they walked behind their guide they caught intriguing glimpses through open doors of a series of stately rooms. In one which appeared by its great size to be the main reception room, a mighty chandelier winked in the afternoon sun and the light was reflected from mirrors and gilded candle sconces along the walls. They ran the gauntlet of the cold marble gaze of a row of classical busts, one perched over each doorway and attending them in their progress along the corridor until they arrived at an image of Athena. At this door the manservant paused. He went inside and announced them. Dorcas scuttled back with a sudden show of nerves to stand behind Joe.

"Come in, come in! I'm delighted that you could come. Fabrice, we'll have tea straightaway. Will you drink tea, Commander? I can offer you lemonade if you prefer? You must have had a hot journey. Yes, Fabrice, bring a jug of Pauline's lemonade and have them put lots of ice in it. Oh, and summon Monsieur Houdart and my son in—shall we say—ten minutes' time?"

Aline Houdart fluttered towards them, a slight and attractive figure, hands outstretched in welcome. She was wearing a pale green silk tea gown and a simple silver necklace and looked cool and at ease, a decorative element of this white and gold, high-ceilinged room. Large grey eyes, a porcelain skin and a cloud of short chestnut hair were Joe's first impressions. Fanciful visions of Botticelli maidens sprang to mind and he realized he had fallen uncharacteristically silent. And he was staring and gulping like an adolescent youth. Redmayne's warning had not gone far enough, he thought. He ought to be bearing in mind that this woman who seemed to have all the unconscious allure of an exotic moth had worked to survive horrors that would have taxed the reserves of any man he knew.

Dorcas poked him in the back.

"Ah. May I present my niece, madame?" he said, clicking back on to the social track. "Miss Jagow-Joliffe. Dorcas."

Dorcas stepped forward, receiving a perfumed kiss on each cheek and a waterfall of welcoming words. Dorcas was the first to swim clear of the polite effusions swirling all around. "I wonder, madame, if you are going to introduce us to the stately gentleman reclining by the fire?" she said with a grin. "A boar hound, isn't he? Very handsome! I've never met one socially before."

"You are quite right—he is a boar hound. Do you like dogs, Mademoiselle Dorcas?" said Aline Houdart. "I can ask him to leave...Naughty Bruno! Bad boy! He knows he ought not to be here. I eject him ten times a day and he somehow manages to creep back. He is a trained guard dog and not very friendly with strangers but he will not attack you if you ignore him. Oh, do take care! Mademoiselle!"

Dorcas had advanced smoothly on the huge brindled dog stretched the full length of the hearth. She knelt, a small and vulnerable figure, at his side and spoke a few words into his ear. His heavy head went up in surprise but he made no objection when she proceeded to scratch him under the chin, murmuring the while. His tail thumped and he gave a strangled whimper of ecstasy. An embarrassing scene, Joe thought, and cleared his throat in warning but Aline appeared enchanted. When Dorcas went to sit on a sofa the dog heaved himself up and, with what Joe could have sworn was an apologetic glance all round, followed her, settling down uncomfortably on her feet.

"It's a talent she has," murmured Joe, recovering himself. "Runs in the family." He didn't want Dorcas to launch into one of her stories about the esoteric lore she had acquired from her father's gypsy friends, where he was fairly sure the party trick had come from.

At any rate the ice was broken. And perhaps that was one of the dog's functions he thought, cynically. The tea arrived and Dorcas, extricating herself, slipped easily into her role of stand-in hostess, dispensing it with quiet skill, leaving Aline Houdart and Joe the opportunity of starting their conversation. Aline did not beat about the bush. In less than the ten minutes before the men arrived she had outlined and delicately put a question mark by the friendly relationship between her brother-in-law Charles-Auguste and Sir Douglas and she had prepared Joe for the discord between the close members of the family, defining their allegiances and ambitions.

"So, you will find, Commander—I say, shall I call you Joe? I feel a ridiculous compulsion to salute when I use your rank!—you will find that I am alone in my claim that this man is my husband. Both Charles and my son Georges maintain that he is not. There is little enough peace in this household at the best of times and I would say that this is decidedly one of the worst." Her smile and her good humour suggested otherwise.

"May I just ask, madame, before it becomes inconvenient, what exactly is the position in law of the inheritance, should this gentleman prove to be Clovis, your husband?"

"Oh, very little change," she shrugged. "My son inherits the estate in its entirety whatever happens. Very soon, if Clovis is indeed dead. Rather later if his father returns, since he will have to await his death. But at all events he will inherit. Charles-Auguste is my son's guardian, no more than that. He has his own estate in the south but is kind enough to spend time with us helping to run the champagne business which is, you must understand, far more profitable than an estate producing a very ordinary *vin de pays*. In medieval times, Charles-Auguste would have been known as the *équyer* or *maître d'hôtel*. An honoured position in a noble household. Ah, here they come!"

She heard the sound of footsteps in the corridor seconds before Joe's keen ears picked them up. Her eyes flashed a warning, a finger hovered playfully over her lips for a moment involving them in her game.

It was deftly done. In minutes she had recruited them to her team. He'd known generals who would have benefited from this skill. And two who had it.

Charles-Auguste came in closely followed by a young boy who could at first sight have been taken for his son, though the boy was a good head taller. Joe experienced a moment of confusion, struck as he was by the resemblance between the handsome middle-aged man now holding out a hand to him and the lost soul they had seen in a hospital cell. Charles Houdart was shorter than Thibaud with the same greying fair hair and blue eyes, the same fair complexion. But there the similarity gave out. These eyes were focused, friendly and intelligent. The man crackled with energy. He brought into the refined room an eddy of fresh air with the slightest scent of the stables. Must be a little difficult to live with, Joe guessed and instantly dismissed the thought.

More introductions were made, kept efficiently to the minimum by Houdart. He looked about him, preparing to present the young people. Georges advanced and shook Joe's hand. A firm grip, an inquisitive eye. A shy smile.

"And you must meet the Commander's niece, Dorcas," said Aline. "A young lady as clever, I suspect, as she is pretty—which is to say, very!"

Georges followed her waving hand to the sofa where Dorcas was once again sitting in uncomfortable proximity to the hound Bruno. He stared and took in the scene at once. "No! Don't get up, mademoiselle!" he said, and went over to shake her hand. "We know better than to disturb old Bruno when he's settled." He sat down by her side with no further ceremony and began to talk. The boy smiled a lot, Joe thought, for a sixteen-year-old. He had thick chestnut hair like his mother but there the similarity ran out; his nose and chin might, flatteringly, have been called decisive. Not love's young dream, Joe was relieved to note, but better than that—his face was full of the promise of character. And a good character at that.

Dorcas smiled back and replied. The boy laughed and whispered something. Dorcas laughed. They both patted the dog. So far so good, then. Joe felt free to turn his attention back to Houdart and answered his keen enquiries about Sir Douglas and London, which he appeared to know well.

Conversation flowed and Joe was surprised to hear, distantly, a clock sounding five, the signal for the party to break up evidently. Aline rang for the footman to have them shown to their rooms, adding: "We will be dining at seven. Earlier than you are accustomed to perhaps? But this is the country not Paris or London and we have our country ways. Our country cooks too! I hope you like simple hearty food? *Foie gras?* Smoked haunch of wild boar? *Poulet au champagne?* Do join us for drinks in the salon when you come down."

As they climbed the stairs a step or two behind the footman, Joe leaned towards Dorcas and hissed at her: "That trick of whispering magic into dogs' ears, miss—does it work on boys?"

She gave him a knowing look. "Oh, yes, it does. Trouble is—you can only use it once on a human. I'm saving it up."

* * *

Joe woke to the insistent serenade of a song thrush perched on the parapet in front of his window and groped for his wristwatch. Seven. Eight o'clock breakfast had been declared so he had plenty of time for a shower. He scrambled out of bed and slumped on to the stool in front of the dressing table to check that he'd survived the night. Incredibly, he had no headache, not a sign of the hangover he had expected. And yet he'd drunk a large quantity of excellent champagne, he remembered. Jokingly, the family had chosen a different champagne from the estate to accompany each of the courses, promising the more usual parade of Pouilly and Clos Vougeot the next day.

He frowned at his dark unshaven features incongruously framed by the ornate gilded mirror and decided that the blue and white draperies of *toile de Jouy* did him no favours. He blinked and yawned and wandered off into the adjoining bathroom to start his day.

At ten to eight he tapped on Dorcas's door and tapped again, disconcerted to hear no reply. Odd. She didn't have many virtues but punctuality was one of them. She never kept him waiting. Had she overslept, worn out by the strain of appearing at a dinner party? They had sat down eight to dinner, the numbers swollen by neighbours chosen, Joe guessed, for their youth and animation. Dorcas, discreetly dressed in blue silk and Lydia's best pearls, had looked very pretty and she'd behaved, he remembered, impeccably, seated between Georges and Charles-Auguste; every time he'd glanced in her direction she had been listening or talking with enthusiasm, even laughing. A strain on a girl, anyway, and he wouldn't blame her if she was intending to have a lie-in.

The manservant of the previous evening hurried down the corridor. "Mademoiselle is not in her room, monsieur.

She went out riding at six this morning with Monsieur Georges."

"She did what? Riding? Good Lord! But what on earth would she have been wearing?" was Joe's disconnected thought.

With no sign that he found the question strange, the man replied: "Jodhpurs, sir, a shirt and a pair of riding boots which the young lady had in her luggage. She lacked only a hat but we were able to supply this item from stock." And, responding to Joe's discomfiture: "They expressed their intention of returning in good time for breakfast. At all events, sir, breakfast is a meal young Master Georges would always be prompt to attend. And it is a very informal occasion you will find. They suggest you join them. If you will come with me?"

The two young cavaliers were already settled at the long table in a beamed breakfast room towards the back of the house and halfway through their meal when Joe arrived. They were still wearing their riding gear and their only concession to civility was to have removed their boots and lined them up by the door. Georges rose politely to his feet and greeted him, stepping over in his socks to the buffet to bring him coffee in a large silver pot.

"We've got the place to ourselves," he said cheerfully. "Maman never comes down for breakfast—she has it in her room and appears at about ten. She's expecting to see you then, by the way, to show you the estate and tell you her side of the story. If she hasn't already."

"And your uncle Charles?"

"He's left to go and finish some work in the *vignoble*. It's coming up to the time of the *vendange* and the next few days are crucial. Conferences every morning with every hoary old expert in the vicinity! Milk with that? There's croissants if you'd like them? Boiled eggs? Ham? Baguettes? Butter from the farm? Cook's strawberry jam?"

"All of that in any order," said Joe, and, sniffing and looking around, "What's that disgusting smell? Smells like wet...oh, hello, Bruno, old man! I say, is he allowed under the table in his present state?"

"Don't try to move him! He got a bit wet rolling about in one of the seven springs. Joe, you must go and look at the stables," Dorcas said, and, turning to Georges, "Joe's a top-hole rider! Why don't you offer him a ride on Taranis?" she suggested slyly.

"I think I'd need to know what his name meant first," said Joe warily.

"Gaulish God of Thunder, sir," said Georges. "And your reservations are well founded. We never offer him to guests," he added reprovingly, with a forgiving grin for Dorcas. "But I would like to snatch a few words with you myself, if you wouldn't mind...Dorcas thinks I should speak to you, sir. I mean, don't let me put you off your breakfast or anything and I haven't much to say, I sup-pose..." He began to run out of steam and shuffled his large feet in embarrassment.

"Rubbish!" said Dorcas. "You've got important things to say and Joe's a good listener. That's what he's come all this way for—to listen. Go on, you're to tell him, Georges!"

Georges was pleased to be so encouraged but something was still holding him back.

"Not the easiest thing in the world—taking up a stance opposite to that of your mother," said Joe. His slight smile and sudden inward focus suggested a personal under-standing of Georges's dilemma. "But let me tell you I don't find it at all unusual or shocking or even disloyal. I've met three families in the course of this case and none of them have been in agreement over the identity of the patient in Reims. Everyone involved has his or her own genuinely held opinion or evidence to put forward and I'm working with the French police to collect and evaluate it. It's important that I hear your views. You are, after all, likely to be significantly affected by the outcome, aren't you? Pivotal, I'd say."

The boy nodded miserably. His good humour had faded and his young face, suddenly serious and drawn, gave a foretaste of the handsome man he would become. Still he debated with himself, unable to speak.

"Look, I'll come clean," said Joe encouragingly. "I have no authority in France. I'm just here to find out whether the gentleman in question may be English and to help Inspector Bonnefoye where I can in an advisory capacity. Sir Douglas…" The boy brightened and nodded at the mention of his name. The Brigadier was obviously a welcome and respected guest. "Sir Douglas sent me to offer a hand. We just want to arrive at the truth. If you disagree with your mother's interpretation of the situation, you're quite entitled to your view. Believe me—I've heard many discordant views so far."

He spoke at last, slowly. "The word 'discordant' is hardly up to the job…say rather, disloyal…destructive." He looked at Joe steadily over the table. "What I have to say will destroy for ever my relationship with my mother—whom I love very much—and more than that, it could destroy her. Ruin her life. And what is the evidence of a boy who was seven years old at the time worth? I've gone over and over what I saw. Every day I have lived with it. I can't any longer believe in what I know. In the evidence of my own senses."

Joe was becoming alarmed by the boy's tension, his staring eyes, his hands, clenched and tugging at the table-cloth, and wished he could undo what he'd started. The dog, disturbed, gave a warning growl to the room at large, not quite knowing at whom to direct his unease. But Georges was pressing on, unstoppable now.

"It's been growing in me like a canker all these years. I don't think I can pretend any longer that I don't know. I'll crack up if I don't tell someone and yet I know I risk infecting everyone around me with the filth that will burst out...Sir, will you help me? Will you listen and promise to take no action against anyone I may involve? I could have got this terribly wrong, you see..."

Joe opened his mouth to deliver a formal and clear police warning. "Anything you say, young man, will be taken down..."

But he caught Dorcas's pleading expression and, bewitched—he could only later excuse himself on grounds of bewitchment—heard himself instead giving the asked-for, impossible and thoroughly unprofessional assurances.

"I know that man they're keeping in Reims is not my father," whispered Georges. "He can't be my father because... my father, Clovis Houdart, is dead. But he wasn't killed in battle, sir. I was there when he was murdered. Nearly ten years ago."

Chapter 17

Joe wondered if, over the hundreds of miles of land and sea that separated them, Brigadier Redmayne on his Scottish grouse moor was troubled by the curse he sent winging his way. That mosquito now settling on his left cheek—would Sir Douglas ever attribute the sharp sting to Joe's summoning up of a stab of silent invective?

Dorcas was speechless. Joe guessed that the intimacy of the young pair had not progressed as far as this startling admission and could feel that she too was taken aback.

Joe replied calmly. "Have you never spoken of this to your uncle?"

Georges shook his head. "To no one."

"What a burden to carry by yourself all these years, my poor old chap!" said Joe. "But, you say it yourself, you were only seven years old at the time of this terrible event—if indeed it ever occurred—and I agree, a seven-year-old is quite likely through simple inexperience to put a wrong interpretation on scenes he's witnessed. Why don't we all look at it again with adult eyes and see if we can make sense of it?"

Georges looked at him more hopefully.

"Tell me some more."

Judging by the boy's silence that he had no idea where best to begin, Joe led him into a conversation, pouring out more coffee all round and trying to avoid anything resembling a police interview of the "Where did you last see your father?" type. He remembered a Victorian painting with that very title. Sentimental, colourful and full of narrative power, it had been his favourite. A Royalist family had been arrested in their own home at the time of the Civil War by a company of Roundheads. The Cavalier father was missing, fled. His young son, a boy of about six, stood proudly, stiffly upright, in his blue satin suit on a stool facing up to interrogation by a squad of frozen-faced, dark-clad and totally menacing Parliamentarians. The boy's older sister stood behind him in her white satin dress trimmed with pink rosebuds and she wept into her hands. His sister Lydia wouldn't have wept, Joe always thought. She'd have given them what for. He identified with the boy and sent himself to sleep each night making up stories of increasing complexity with which he might have fooled the chief interrogator. For a change he sometimes played the part of this man who, on closer examination, seemed to have a more kindly face than the other soldiers. He leaned forward over the desk, keen and clever.

Instinctively, Joe had always understood that it was here the danger lay. They would never have succeeded in beating information out of such a boy but one sympathetic word, one well-placed question politely asked and he would be in the net.

Very well. Time to play the kindly chief interrogator.

"How often did your father come home during those war

years?" he asked. "I know leave was hard to come by... men went for years sometimes without seeing their families."

He was on the right track. Georges replied at once. "Hardly ever. That's the problem. I'm very confused about the times when my father came home. Once, he came home in the night and he'd had to go away again before I woke next morning," he said. This had obviously been a sharp cause of distress. "He left a toy horse on my pillow. My mother was always waiting. When she wasn't out in the fields or at the hospital working... She would sit moping by the window or sometimes on the top step with the dog... we had a greyhound in those days. And she would talk all the time about what my father would say and do, how proud he would be of me when he came home. And he did come home. Three times in as many years. I marked them down in my day book. But it was always for a very short time and he'd have to ride off again. I'm not complaining, sir. It was like that for every child at that time. Millions of us were left fatherless. Some lost both parents. I've been lucky."

Joe was glad to hear the boy's refusal to indulge in self-pity.

"Were you not evacuated to a safer place?" Joe asked. "Couldn't help noticing the bullet holes on the façade."

Georges smiled. "Maman refuses to have them filled in. She says they're a part of the history of the house and there they'll stay. And yes, we did go away sometimes to my grandparents in Paris when the war came dangerously close. But mostly we stayed and hoped for the best. We had lots of soldiers through the house, billeted on us. And glad to have them. We always felt safer with men about the place. Maman cheered up when the house was full. She forgot about waiting and moping. And she felt she was doing her bit. She was very good at it. She'd sing and play the piano for them, cook whatever we had. Dress their wounds." He grinned at Joe. "She may look like a butterfly but she's actually as tough as old boots. And she expected everyone to pitch in, even me, though I was only small. I remember working in the fields with frozen hands in winter, keeling over in the heat in summer and never daring to complain. I've never lost the habit." He held out with pride large square hands callused like a coachman's.

"Maman had a poster fixed up at the gates to encourage us all. A call to action to the women and children of France from the Prefect." He smiled and spoke the remembered words with emotion: "'*Debout femmes françaises, jeunes enfants, filles et fils de la Patrie! Remplacez sur le champ du travail ceux qui sont sur le champ de bataille. Debout! A l'action! Au labeur!*' 'On your feet! To action! To work!' Hard work, though! But we did it. We managed—just about—to take in the fields the places of those who were on the battlefields. We were even used as an overflow for the hospital once and I had to help with the laundry." He shuddered and pulled a face to disguise his passing horror. "That was a low point."

"Yes, you did it, old son, you did it!" murmured Joe. "Kept the country going." And, after a pause, "I'm wondering what nationalities you had here? Actually—you might well have had me! I was based very close by."

"We did have a few English. Maman liked them the best. So did I. They were my good friends while they were here. Some of them came back several times. And some wrote to me when they got back home after the war. They missed their own sons, I think, or their little brothers, and I got quite spoilt. We still get Christmas cards from one or two. I have a friend called John who never forgets to send me a birthday card even when he's soldiering abroad. And we had French units of course. Mostly French. There was a day when we almost had Germans!"

He smiled. "They made a terrible mistake. It was at the time when the whole area was swarming with all three armies. No time to get away—we just had to sit it out. We had a squad of English cavalrymen with us at the time when suddenly someone shouted that the Boche were on their way. And a German staff car was spotted coming down the drive. Just driving down as bold as brass! An officer and his driver. They'd taken the wrong turning and thought they were approaching their billet for the night. Sitting ducks for the English marksmen. They fired warning shots over their heads and called to them to surrender. The Germans fired back and those are the holes you see in the front of the house. They were taken alive but wounded and sent off for interrogation."

"Good Lord!" said Joe. "I may even have carried out that questioning myself!" He was reasonably sure that he hadn't but Georges seemed excited at the coincidence and he decided to spin out the story. "I was with Military Intelligence recovering from a shoulder wound. We were brought an officer with a leather bag in his possession. Lots of blood-stained rubbish in there but also a map which quite obviously showed von Kluck's forward planning. We were delighted to have it. Particularly as it showed he was planning a manoeuvre that played straight into allied hands. We didn't get an awful lot else out of the officer but his side-kick, a taxi driver from Berlin, sang like a song thrush."

His confidence won, Georges listened to a few more extracts from the war diaries of Captain Sandilands. "I say, sir, would you like to see my record of the war? My notebook? It's very...well...naïve and badly written but it does give the dates when my father was about the place."

"I shall probably shed a tear or two but if you wouldn't mind—that would be a great help. Good to have something concrete to go on in this shifting affair," said Joe. "No hurry."

"Well, the last date of interest you'll find is in the summer of '17. My father came home for a couple of days. And after that, nothing. No letters. No news. No sightings." The words were coming from him in uncontrolled staccato bursts. "It was said he'd been killed—disappeared anyway—during the battle of the Chemin des Dames. His body was never found. For good reason. He's still here. He never left the château again. He was killed here. Buried here. My mother killed him."

Chapter 18

Joe fought down his instinctive Englishman's out-
burst of incredulity. "I say, old chap, hold on...let's not be
fantastical now..." would have been the wrong response.
But what could possibly be the right one?

While he hesitated, Dorcas asked in an interested voice:
"Can you show us *where* you think all this happened,
Georges? You say it happened here. 'Here' would seem to be
about a hundred acres of house and grounds. If we could go
with you to the scene, it might help."

The practical suggestion seemed to stir him from his
paralysis.

"It's not far," said Georges. "In fact, I've been detailed to
take you there this morning. It's on the tour we give every
guest." His hands began to shake again and he bent to hide
them, pushing them deep into Bruno's fur. "Every day for
nearly ten years I've passed within a foot or two of my father's body and I've never been able to acknowledge him."
His chin went up in defiance. "But today I will."

They followed him from the house and across a cobbled

courtyard. A single-storey wing in the same classical style to their left Joe guessed to be a run of stables ending in a charming dovecote and, on the right, balancing, but of a later age and of a more simple and workaday appearance, was the cellar. Georges, relieved to be active again, had fallen into his accustomed role of guide around the family winery. His talk rolled on smoothly: "Natural caves in the chalk dug out and enlarged, possibly by the Romans... storage for more than a million bottles...steady temperature...ten miles of corridor...if you get lost, just follow the arrows..."

They paused at the oak door at the entrance to the galleries and Georges took a sweater from around his neck and helped Dorcas to pull it on over her head. "It's warm enough out here but down there don't forget it's at a constant 11 degrees Centigrade. The wine enjoys it—you won't." He clicked on the electric lighting system, closed the door behind them and led the way down a twisting staircase.

They started on the tour, Georges full of information and well-rehearsed jokes, and Joe began to wonder if he'd imagined the scene in the kitchen. All was normal if not even slightly boring. The chalk walls hewn out over the centuries were whitewashed. The smell was pleasantly musty and made Joe think of mushrooms, forests and ferns. The storage corridors were lined with wooden triangular racks, double-sided, containing champagne bottles tilted at an angle, dimpled bases outwards. Georges set to, working along the rows, deftly demonstrating with flicks of the wrist the technique used to give the bottles a quarter of a turn each day, a movement which kept the deposit in the bottles on the move down towards the neck of the bottle.

"But why do you want the filthy bit at the top?" Dorcas asked. "In red wine the dregs are always at the bottom and you can easily decant the wine and leave the nasty bits behind."

"Ah—we do it this way to achieve absolute purity," said Georges. "At the very end of the maturing process we have skilled workers who release the temporary cork..." He took a bottle from a rack and, holding it between his knees, carefully pointing it away from his guests, eased out the cork with two strong thumbs. Joe was prepared for the explosion but the effect was so shattering in that narrow space as to make him jump and thrust his hands into his pockets. Out shot a spray of gas, champagne and a smear of detritus. A split second later, Georges had clamped it shut again.

"*Á la volée!* With an explosion! That's how they do it. And what you've just seen is called *dégorgement*. Clearing the neck. All the nastiness gone in a second and we're left with the purest wine."

"But what is that black stuff?" Dorcas wanted to know. "How did it get in there in the first place?"

"It's the remains of the dried yeast. Actually it's been doing a valuable job in the bottle. It plays its part in developing the character of the finished wine. There'd be little aroma or flavour without it. Then after release, we recork, label and sell it!"

"But there's a space in the bottle now," Dorcas said. "Look, the bottle's not full. I don't know much about wine but I know Granny's butler would never accept a bottle with a space between the wine and the cork."

Georges was pleased with his pupil. "Well noticed, Dorcas. We top it up with *liqueur de dosage*—vintage champagne containing sugar—and this allows us to control the degree of sweetness. Uncle Charles has a good deal of fun with this—he's discovered that some countries like it sweet, others, like England, prefer it very dry. He always gets it right. And he has sensitive antennae when it comes to tuning in to changing tastes and trends." Georges grinned. "Sometimes I think it's Uncle Charles who *sets* the trends. A word in the right, influential ear, a well-placed advertisement…"

They strolled on, ready for the next sensation. With some excitement, Georges paused by a section of wall and held up a torch, directing the beam sideways to reveal a slight roughness in texture compared with the wall on either side. On it was tacked a blackboard with chalked words announcing that the bottles stored below were of the best vintage and not to be touched without the express authority of the cellar-master.

"And are they?" asked Joe, kneeling to examine the bottles more closely. "No labels yet, I see."

"As a matter of fact these bottles are!" said Georges. "It was Maman's idea. In the war she had these signs made and put them over our poorest vintages so when the Germans came they would make off with those bottles first. The best bottles were hidden behind the partitions. There—look—do you see where I'm pointing?"

"Only because you show us with the torch beam," said Joe, being a good audience. "I would have missed it. What's behind there?"

"Nothing now, an empty space, but before the war it was an open corridor. The best bottles were moved into it and Maman got the estate workers to build a partition and paint it over with several coats of whitewash until it looked just like the chalk wall. There were about six of those false walls blocking off corridors and alcoves and after the war we managed to remember which ones they were and tore them down to release the stock. Except for this one. Maman had it put back and preserved. I told you she was a great one for history. She keeps it there as a reminder. Did you notice the pictures of the Virgin Mary and one or two other saints as we came along? Those were the markers of the false walls. Maman thought they looked very natural—like shrines. Winemakers are thought to be rather superstitious in that way. Dependent on the weather and other quirks of fate, as we are, it makes sense. And the hidden wine, when the saints delivered it up to us again, at the end of the war, made quite a lot of money for us. Enough to keep afloat at any rate. Anyone who could afford it wanted to drink champagne to celebrate. We began to sell huge quantities to London."

They walked on, mesmerized by the serried ranks of bottles, Dorcas asking the expected questions: "How many grapes does it take to make one bottle of champagne?...If you use red grapes why is the wine pale yellow?...How do the bubbles get into the wine?" and Georges replying patiently and accurately.

"And here we are at the Piccadilly Circus or the Place de la Concorde of the underworld," he announced as they entered an area where the gallery widened and other tunnels radiated from it.

"Ah, there's another saint, on another of those walls," said Dorcas. Darting ahead, she shot across for a closer look, drawn to the brightly painted image, glinting with gold in the beam of the torch. "I don't recognize this man," she said. "He doesn't look very saintly! You're going to have to identify him."

"See if you can work it out," Georges challenged them. "The two of you ought to be up to it."

"Well, he's clearly a saint," said Joe. "He has a halo round his head, look. But he does look much more like a soldier. In fact, he looks like a *Roman* soldier to me. Cavalryman?"

"Mounted on a horse at any rate. Crested helmet," said Dorcas. "He's drawn his sword and he's sliced his red military cloak in two and he's offering half to the naked beggar sitting on the ground at his horse's feet. Haven't a clue."

"Yes, you have," said Georges, choosing to take her literally. "You've come up with all the evidence you need."

"I've got it!" said Joe. "It's St Martin of Tours! But I've still no idea what he's doing here in a wine cellar. Friend of beggars and the poor. Hardly a qualification for presiding over choice bottles of champagne?"

"Where else would he be? Very appropriate! St Martin is the patron saint of wine growers and winemakers. And he's a local boy. Born in 316 AD, in Roman Gaul, he was in the army up in Amiens. His saint's day is 11th November. Remembrance Day. And, yes, he was a cavalry officer."

There was a pride and a sadness in the boy's tone that prompted Dorcas to ask: "Did *you* put him here, Georges?"

He nodded.

"And the flowers?" Joe said quietly. He had noticed, on the ground underneath the icon, a jam jar containing three wilting white roses.

"I put fresh ones in every week," said George with a touch of defiance.

Dorcas had begun to shiver in spite of the thick jersey which reached down to her knees. She turned a desperate pale face to Georges and came slowly back to join them. She took both Georges's hands in hers and asked a silent question.

"Yes, it was here," he said simply. "It happened here. I put up a cavalry officer to mark a fellow officer's grave. I believe my father, whatever remains of him, lies behind that wall."

"Would it distress you, Georges, to tell us what you remember happening down here?" asked Joe with a quick look to left and right.

"It's all right. Don't worry—Maman never comes down here. She hasn't been in the cellars, as far as I know, from that day to this." He pointed to St Martin. "There was just a deep alcove there ten years ago with bits and pieces of cellar equipment in it. It was a summer evening in 1917. I'd been out in the fields with Felix, working. I was angry with my mother for sending me out because my father had come home. He'd been with us for two days and I wanted to be with him every possible moment. Now I can see that I must have been the most awful little nuisance," he said sorrowfully, "shadowing my father everywhere. I finished my work and ran back to the house but my parents had both disappeared. I went to the kitchen and asked the housekeeper where my father was. She said she'd last seen him come clattering downstairs in his uniform and call for his horse to be saddled and then he'd gone off across the courtyard and into the cellars. But that was about an hour earlier.

"I was distraught! This meant he was leaving again. So soon. And apparently without intending to say goodbye to me. I was furious with my mother. I blamed *her*. She'd been quarrelling with him. I'd heard them shouting at each other and she'd been crying on and off for a whole day. I wanted to find him, tell him that whatever was wrong it had nothing to do with me.

"I ran to the cellar. I wasn't allowed to come down here by myself but I knew my way. Could have found my way blindfold, I think. The lighting wasn't so wonderful in those days—oil lamps and home-made candles—but it was adequate. I raced along until I got to that turning there." Georges pointed down the way they had come. "And I stopped. I could hear the most awful noise." He shuddered at the memory. "It was a wailing and then a scrunching, dragging sound, repeated rhythmically every few seconds. I was terrified. I shouldn't be there. I would get a spanking if I were caught. And there was something frightful going on in the corridor ahead, I knew it. I peered round the corner and…and…I saw the hunched shadow on the wall first."

He paused, lost in his nightmare.

"One shadow?" Joe prompted gently.

"Yes. My mother. She had long hair in those days—all the women had—and long skirts. She was sobbing and tugging at something on the ground. I thought at first it was a sack of some kind. But it wasn't. She was dragging my father's body over into the alcove. It was leaving a dark trail on the floor as she pulled it along. I don't know how long I stood there frozen but I couldn't move forward. I couldn't go to my mother. I turned around and began to creep back along the gallery. But I had only gone about twenty yards when I caught a metal pail with my foot. Maman called out at once. 'Who's that? Is that you, Felix?'

"I turned around and called back. 'No, it's me, Maman. I'm frightened. I didn't know where you were.'

" 'Stay where you are!' she shouted. 'Stand still!'

"She came towards me round the corner and I nearly fled. She looked like the Greek women in my books—you know, the Furies or Medea or the Gorgon even. Her hair was hanging over her face, in damp strands, she'd been weeping and her eyes were dilated. She was panting and I could smell her terror. I would have run away but she knelt and seized me by the arms. 'Georges, you are to go and find Felix,' she said. 'Tell him he's to come to me here. At once. And then I want you to go straight to your room. Speak to no one else.'

"I was only too pleased to be sent away and I ran back

and found him and delivered the message. When I got up-stairs I went to the bathroom as I always did to get ready for bed. I saw myself in the mirror. My old white linen shirt was stained with blood where my mother's hands had held me. I was daubed with my father's blood. She'd stabbed him to death."

Dorcas asked quietly: "You were only seven, Georges. Did you understand about death and bodies at that age?"

He looked at her wonderingly for a moment. "I knew about death. I killed things every day. Vermin. Birds. It was my job to keep the vineyards clear. I snared rabbits for the pot. Food was always short. And we were living in the middle of a battlefield. We were always coming across corpses…dead soldiers in the fields. Runaways hiding in ditches. One winter we found two deserters, wounded, starving, who'd crept into the cellars for shelter. They hadn't dared to ask for help in case someone turned them in, I suppose. They were dead when Felix and I came across them. Dead for several days. We buried them in the church-yard in the village and sent their name tags in. I saw sights no child should see. Yes, I know it was a lifeless corpse my mother was hauling across the floor."

Dorcas's next question was inspired by a quick glance up at the icon of St Martin in his cloak and helmet. "The housekeeper told you he'd left in his uniform. Was the body you saw in uniform?"

"Well, you know, it's odd, but it didn't occur to me for years but—he *wasn't* in uniform. She'd stripped the body down to his underwear. I suppose she burned the uniform later or got Felix to do it—just as the stained shirt that I'd hidden under my bed was never seen again. Felix knew how to put up the partitions and all the materials were to hand in the cellar. If he worked all night he could have sealed off the alcove. And then, in the future, long after her own death, if someone were to pull it down they would find a body not so easily identifiable."

"What are the chances of hearing from Felix...?" Joe began.

"He died three years ago," said Georges, subdued. "But he would never have spoken of it. Not to anyone. He was devoted to my mother."

He slumped suddenly, like a string puppet at the end of his act. "This is as far as it goes. I've given you all I have."

Joe put a comforting arm around Georges's shoulder and hugged him, feeling his dejection. He recognized that the boy's desperate courage in sharing his hideous memory deserved an acknowledgement rather deeper than the "Well done, old chap...better out than in—what!" which came instinctively to him. "That took some determination, Georges," he murmured. "I can understand how difficult it must be to speak of such horrors. But equally—how difficult to remain silent! In your present situation, which gets daily more tricky, you will want to do justice to your father or his memory as well as show loyalty to your mother. And perhaps there is a way through...If there is I'll find it," he finished encouragingly. "*We* will find it. And you can count on our discretion." He wondered whether to add a few words about lancing the boil of suspicion with the scalpel of truth and decided he'd said enough.

"But this is all fascinating, Georges! Aren't you fascinated, Joe? I am!" Dorcas's voice rang out suddenly, gushing with excitement, as her eyes flashed a warning. "Do you know—in all the years I've been coming to France this is my first visit to a cellar. But you must be getting cold, Georges? I feel quite guilty, hogging your nice warm jumper. Why don't we all go to the stables next and show Joe the horses? I warn you though—he's quite an expert!"

"Dorcas, really you exaggerate…" Joe spun on his heel, hearing a slight sound behind them. "Ah! Madame Houdart! There you are! You discover us halfway round the tour. We are offered the horses next. Will you join us?"

Chapter 19

Aline Houdart came towards them, smiling her pleasure at tracking them down. She looked fresh and charming in riding trousers and yellow blouse, a tweed jacket thrown over her shoulders. She showed no sign that her appearance down here in the cellar involved anything but her regular stroll around the property. She greeted Joe and Dorcas and, taking her son by the arms, reached up and kissed him on each cheek. "They told me I'd find you down here. What it is to have a son who wakes with the lark! Such energy! It makes me feel old and sluggish! But I'll do my bit now. Better late than never. Georges, darling, you may stand down—I'll show our guests around the stables."

"Dorcas has already seen them, Maman," said Georges, recovering. "We went out this morning. Early. I thought I'd take her to look at the vineyards next."

"Then we shall have the horses to ourselves, Joe," said Aline, slipping her arm through his. "But first I have a rather charming little ceremony to perform. And you can help me."

The two young people had gone ahead and were out of sight by the time Joe emerged with relief into the fresh air and sunshine of the courtyard. He had been trying to reconcile the maenad image of destructive madness Georges had conjured from the haunted depths of the chalk galleries with the cheerful presence and inconsequential chatter of the woman leaning so lightly on his arm, and he could not. What had that looming vision—black, chalk-white and blood-red—to do with this bird-like creature, all chestnut and gold, at his side? With many questions still to put to Georges, he was resentful that Aline was setting the pace and organizing his morning, a feeling he instantly dismissed as churlish. He had made this journey specifically to talk to her and help resolve her problem, hadn't he?—and here she was, gracefully making his task easier.

She paused by the door and pointed to a lidded wicker-work basket on the ground outside. "Would you mind, Joe? We're going to take that to the dovecote. Today you will be witnessing the founding of a new dynasty!" she announced playfully. "A dynasty of doves."

He picked up the heavy basket, catching flashes of white through the holes. "What have we got here?"

"It's a pair of doves a kind neighbour has sent me. Ours died out soon after the war and it's high time we restocked. We have a perfect home for them over there, you see."

She pointed to the round, stunted tower with its grey-tiled pepper-pot roof and started towards it. "A house looks so pretty with doves perched on its roof, don't you think?" She pushed open the door of the *pigeonnier* and Joe stepped inside, an earthy-scented darkness closing in around him, muffling his senses. Aline swung the door shut and as his eyes adjusted to the gloom he found he was just able to see by the soft light filtering in from under the tiles.

"Before we release them we'll close their escape hole at the top of the roof. Look, we use this rope to open and close the louvres. Now, what you have to understand about doves is that you've got to keep them shut up together for at least two weeks, feeding them well, of course, before you can let them out into the open air. They have to be kept together in their place so that they learn it is their home to which they must always return and then they will mate. They are very faithful birds, you know, and mate for life, so it's important to get the pairing right. See how pretty these are!" she said, taking one gently in her hands and spreading its wing. "This one is the female—a pure white. Here, hold her for a moment, Joe."

Joe carefully took hold of the soft round shape which nestled perfectly happily into his cupped hands and began to smooth the silky down with his fingers.

"Men have kept doves for at least seven thousand years, you know," she went on, seeing his interest wakening. "The ancient Egyptians used them as messengers. The Romans probably first brought them to France. And in Persia they were the sacred birds of Astarte, the goddess of love."

Her close presence in the gloom, her murmuring voice and the gentle rustle of straw under his feet were disturbing. He was conscious of the smooth hands that closed over his to take back the dove; he was surprised by a warm waft of her perfume—an innocent country scent he thought he recognized. It was a moment before it came to him: that unique natural blend of flowers and spice was honeysuckle.

"It's very generous accommodation," he said awkwardly, looking around at the large number of nesting holes provided and rather regretting the slight tone of billeting officer he heard. "There must be room for hundreds of birds."

He sensed she was smiling at him. "In earlier centuries, in

winter when all the stock had been killed and eaten, doves often provided the only source of fresh meat. I suppose you would judge that a frightful gastronomic solecism? How typical of the French!"

"Not at all," he said easily. "Cushat pie is not unknown in my country."

"We had a hard time towards the end of the war," she said. "There were many people to feed. Our stock was exhausted. The ones we didn't eat we attempted to use as messengers. The English took away the last of our flock, intending to release them with goodness only knows what significant information taped to their feet, but none ever returned."

"I expect those also ended up in a stew," said Joe. "Cooked up in a dixie over a British camp-fire. So you're intending to keep these two unfortunates prisoner in here until they agree to get on with each other?" he added briskly. "I think I ought to be arresting you for something but I can't imagine what the charge would be." He couldn't shake off the suspicion that she was attempting to manipulate him in some way and yet her voice was cool, her attention entirely on the doves. "And how certain can you be that this pair *will* get on with each other? Who has had the selecting of them? Are they mates?"

"I don't think so. Not yet. These are young birds and I don't think they have chosen a mate yet. They may get on well from the start but sometimes they do not and will peck each other quite savagely. But if you can keep them locked in together for two weeks it will do the trick. They will be lifelong lovers and they will become attached to their new home."

"Does that always happen?"

"Just occasionally it doesn't work and then the male—it is

always the male—flies away when you release them. Sometimes the poor female has to fly in pursuit and herd him back."

He was aware that she was smiling. "Sometimes it happens that the female—and it's usually the female—will tear her unwilling partner to shreds. But don't worry—I don't think you will witness any bloodshed today. What bird would be insensitive enough to reject such a good home? Such a beautiful mate?"

She took the dove from his hands, spoke softly to her and released her. Taking the second dove from the basket she held him up to show the bronze markings on his feathers. "This breed is very rare. Very handsome. They were brought back from eastern lands by Crusaders who went off with Good King Louis—or so I'm told. Off you go and join your mate!"

The dove fluttered upwards, bronze streaks glinting in a shaft of sunlight which bisected the tower far above their heads.

"I shall always think of them as Joe's doves. Why don't you give them a name, Joe?" she invited.

"Well, if it's a pair of timeless lovers we're contemplating—what about Abélard and Héloïse?" he suggested.

As he spoke the two birds began instantly to dispute possession of the same nesting hole with loud squawks and much flapping and pushing.

"Or should that be Punch and Judy?"

"Oh, dear!" He heard her gentle laughter. "Not a good start! Well, let's hope for the best. They have two weeks in which to settle their differences. And when we've got a whole flock of them going we'll collect up the droppings—wonderful manure for the flower beds."

He was happy to hear her common-sense tone and

dropped his guard, to be taken unawares by her next question.

"You know I lured you in here so that we could be alone and not overheard by anyone? Impossible in the house to snatch a moment's intimacy! Come and sit with me over here."

She went to settle on the bottom tread of the circular wooden ladder that revolved around the building providing access to the nesting holes, and Joe seated himself tentatively in the straw at her feet.

"There are two things you must understand about this sorry business, Joe. Firstly, my son declares that the patient is not his father. I think quite honestly that the boy has a damned cheek! And if I didn't love my son so much I'd box his ears. How dare he! He saw his father so few times and with the eyes of a child all those years ago...how can he possibly say that he can identify him more accurately than I? It's my theory that he expects Clovis to be unchanged from the glamorous and heroic figure swishing about in black-plumed helmet that he remembers. He cannot adjust to the idea that his father is now a wreck of a man and will, most probably, remain so for ever.

"Secondly, my cousin by marriage, Charles-Auguste, is a dear man. We quarrel, we sometimes disagree about the running of the business but much more often we agree. He's an inspired winemaker. I couldn't have made the firm so profitable without his assistance. He's also a clever businessman and this is still a world where the word 'man' is important. He feels, I know, that his position here would be threatened were Clovis to be brought back. Nonsense, of course. I have tried to reassure him but I don't think I have succeeded. And once again I must think—how dare he! He was never particularly intimate with his cousin before his disappearance and to deny him so firmly now speaks of priorities other than discovering the truth. Well, there you are. They will each confide in you, no doubt, and you will draw your own conclusions."

"Tell me why you want him back, Aline."

She leaned forward in astonishment at the question, trying to catch his expression. "I love him. He's my husband. Whatever state he's in, he's mine and always will be." She looked at him with curiosity. "Are you married?"

Joe shook his head, dismissing the irrelevant and intrusive enquiry.

"Are you in love?" she persisted. "Have you been in love?" She turned to him, grey eyes black and huge in the gloom, and scanned his face. "Ah! I thought not. It's no good shaking your head and squirming with embarrassment and preparing to tell me this is not police business! As long as you *are* a policeman and your word on the matter is heard by the authorities, it *is* police business and it is mine to make certain that you understand. Hop up here and sit next to me, I can't speak to you when you're wriggling about in front of me like a five-year-old."

Resentfully, Joe toyed with the notion of disobedience. In that moment she was for him nanny, mother, mistress, sister. A beam of sunlight knifing through the slats made a golden helmet of her Titian hair and he added to his list of tormentors—goddess. He sighed and obeyed.

Joe perched uneasily shoulder-to-shoulder with Aline on one half of the tread. He glanced up at the doves over their heads, still, with a hundred holes to choose from, disputing possession of the same hole. Blood and feathers would soon begin to fly. "Know how you feel, old mate!" he thought grimly, identifying with the male bird. But his unkind thoughts vanished in a moment when abruptly Aline began to weep. "I had thought that showing you the doves would explain more clearly than words what I feel," she whispered. "As with them, it was for life. I fell in love...and it didn't take two weeks to know it. Two seconds. It was enough."

So completely had her voice changed he felt he could be listening to a different woman. The self-confidence, the mocking insouciance had gone and he was hearing the hesitations of a girl racked with emotion, a girl struggling and failing to find words that could bear the weight of the intensity of her feelings.

"It's painful, shattering, inconvenient even, but if you have never had the experience of falling completely in love, I pray that you will. Now—is that a prayer or a curse, I wonder? But don't think ill of me for it—I do believe any life is a half-life until you have. A man's eyes on yours, his arms around you and your souls spiralling away into the ether together..."

The words were fanciful, ingenuous even, but the emotion behind them was true and deep. He knew he was hearing a woman talking of a love so overwhelming that she had remained through the years possessed by it. He knew instinctively that for Aline nothing else—home, family, the war—nothing ever was able to—or would—rival it in power.

"So, my reason for bringing the man back here to his home is a simple one. Elemental. It springs from love."

"I understand all that you have to say, madame," said Joe. "And am well able to feel for you in your sorrow. I must ask though, if I'm to do my job adequately, whether there are any indications of a practical rather than emotional identification of the patient. Look, I wonder if you were aware that the doctor in Reims, who, I do believe, has grown fond of our man, calls him Thibaud. Would it offend you to use that name for the time being?"

"Not at all. Thibaud. A good name. I approve of that. And yes, there are aspects of Clovis's body that are distinctive and could well prove that he and Thibaud are one and the same. We could hardly look for mental similarities though I do wonder whether all possibilities have been explored. I have thought, Joe, that we might be able to have him, Thibaud, taken to Austria to a clinic. Or even to London. You must advise me. I understand that wonderful results in cases like his have been achieved through hypnotism. The process is not much practised here in France but I would like to try it and will pay all expenses incurred."

"It is an avenue which, I think, should be explored," said Joe.

"But in the meantime all we have to go on is physical clues. I have provided the obvious information like size and colouring supported by photographs of course. That ought, along with my word, to have been sufficient but I understand that there are now three other claimants vying for him. I shall have to play cards I was holding in reserve."

For a second Joe had a sickening feeling that he'd heard this before and was struck by the similarity, if not in circumstances, then in determination between Aline Houdart and Mireille Desforges. Each, he did believe, motivated by undying affection.

"Clovis has marks on his lower abdomen. His was a difficult birth, a breech birth, and force was used. He has the marks of those...pincers...on either side of his hip. His right hip. But there is more. Come back to the salon with me, will you? I wish to show you further evidence."

Stopping to order coffee to be brought to them in the *petit salon*, she made her way back to the room where they had taken tea the previous day. Judging by the piles of novels and magazines and the cashmere throw draped over a chaise longue, this seemed to be where she spent her leisure time. Joe sat down in an armchair while she went to hunt about in the drawers of an escritoire. She brought over to him three photographs.

In the first, a man very like Thibaud stood looking aloof and aristocratic, slightly embarrassed perhaps to be modelling his cuirassier's uniform for the camera, his presence in the studio insisted upon no doubt by a doting family. He wore a flamboyant helmet which covered most of his head and it was impossible to tell the colour of his hair.

The second, larger, photograph showed a group of young men in evening dress posing informally at the end of a party. A dozen of them were seated around a table strewn with the debris of an elaborate meal. They had reached the brandy stage and all looked very drunk.

"Clovis is the second on the left," said Aline, pointing. "Taken in Paris—a passing out celebration with his contemporaries at the academy of St Cyr. In those days you couldn't go to a dinner party without it being recorded by a photographer. A hard-riding lot! So much hope, such talent, such dash! I danced with all of them in my time. It breaks my heart to look at them and realize that, of this dozen, only two have survived. Clovis and the man on his left, both held prisoner until the war ended or they would have been killed too, no doubt."

She was trembling with emotion at the sight of the twelve bold, laughing young men, her voice husky, and snatched it away to replace it with the third photograph.

This was more natural. Clovis was sitting in everyday clothes, relaxed and smiling and holding on his knee the young Georges clutching a toy train. His hair was fair, his eyes sparkled with intelligence and love and, yes, the man was the spitting image of Thibaud.

He said as much to Aline.

"You haven't noticed it, have you?" She moved behind him and pointed. "It would take an expert in the Bertillon system of identification to spot it and if it becomes necessary, believe me, Commander, I will certainly employ one. Concealed under the straps of a helmet of course but here where he's bare-headed you can see it clearly. Look at the ears!"

Joe looked and saw.

"The lobes. They are joined to the side of the face, not free like these." She tugged at her own dainty ears. "Now, I know—because I've been doing my own research on this—that a small percentage only of the population has this characteristic. One person in four, I understand. That, taken in conjunction with the other signs I have given you, ought to be more than enough proof."

"I hadn't remarked Thibaud's..."

"Attached lobes," she said. "He has them! For the good reason that Thibaud is Clovis and these are his ears!"

Chapter 20

Halfway—and, Joe suspected, a calculated halfway—through coffee, they were joined by Charles-Auguste. Aline withdrew, content to leave the two men to talk to each other, perfectly confident and assured.

Left alone, Joe said as much. "Aline would seem to have a watertight case to make for the man in the Reims sanatorium being her husband?"

Charles-Auguste nodded. "I know! Believe me, Sandilands, I've heard it. Over and over. And it grows in strength. I can't imagine why I bother to demur and throw an occasional, feeble 'Ah, but...' into the mixture." He paused and, invited by Joe's sympathetic silence, went on, pulling a rueful face: "But I do! Who am I to say this isn't my cousin, you may well ask, when his wife of eighteen years, mother of his son, says otherwise? And we were never particularly close. All I can say is that every instinct I have is telling me that there is something very wrong... very disturbing... about this identification. And it stems, not so much from the mental patient himself as from Aline." His voice had lowered and he cast a quick glance at the door. "It's *her* sanity I fear for. She's unnaturally obsessive about this whole business!"

"A bit harsh?" said Joe. "The desire to have one's husband restored can hardly be regarded as abnormal? I have spoken to Aline. She held...and still holds...Clovis in the deepest affection."

Charles took a fortifying sip of coffee and levelled a sharp glance at Joe over his cup. His eyes were shining with cynical amusement. "I see she's got you where she wants you, old man! Oh, don't be concerned—she captures everyone." He stirred uncomfortably. "But, look here, the thing is...and you won't believe me...I say this unwillingly anyway but... quite the reverse. Um. I'd say they positively disliked each other.

"Once he'd got over the initial starry-eyed enchantment, Clovis became over the years, first cool, then irritated and then uncaring. He adored his son, of course. But even so, as soon as war became a possibility he rejoined his regiment. He was a second son. He trained as a soldier at St Cyr. You knew that? And you're aware, I take it, of the French rules of inheritance? Our crazy Napoleonic law! Everything to be divided equally between the male heirs whether there's two or twenty. Ridiculous! It's ruined many a grand—and lowly—estate. And you'd be surprised how many families cease to expand after the birth of the first son. Though, if *he* dies, a second seems, miraculously, to appear in short order. Clovis's older brother died and he inherited everything— threw himself into viticulture and was very effective. Then came the war. Brave man, intensely patriotic. I do think his country meant more to him than anything. In short he was gallant, to use an old-fashioned word. He would always put himself in the thick of things. Surprising that he lasted as long as he did.

"But, as I say, I think he was not unhappy to leave his wife behind. From what I gathered from her complaints he rarely, suspiciously rarely, I'd say, came home on leave. Avoiding her. But he needed to see his son so the man must have been torn in two. He wasn't a cold man, Sandilands, don't think it. Reserved perhaps but…" He reached forward and picked up the photograph of Clovis holding his son on his knee. "That was Clovis. Loving. That's the man I remember and it's the man Georges remembers."

"Well, he seems to have inspired deep emotion. Aline tells me she is motivated by love to pursue her claim on this man," said Joe. "But if *you're* saying—not love on her part or his—then what? She is preparing to go to some lengths, involving experts in the fields of criminology and psychiatry, to make her case."

"And there's where my concern lies. I was delighted when we were told they suspected he was English. A jolly good solution all round, I thought. Best possible outcome. And that's when I contacted Douglas and stirred up the French police. At that stage the forces of law and order were not involved and the whole cat's cradle was being handled by a sanatorium and the Ministry of Pensions. Hardly adequate, I thought, considering the increasing complexity. I knew I could depend on Douglas to send someone to shine a light on all this. And, Sandilands, I'm very glad you're here. We need to know the truth—we can all work with that."

"You don't think Aline would try to circumvent the truth?"

"She wouldn't see it like that. She thinks she's above it. What Aline decides *becomes* the truth—if you see what I mean. It's her unwavering sense of purpose that troubles me. She's up to something we have no idea of. And if she succeeds in her schemes it will bring her into head-on collision with her son. Georges is as convinced as anyone can be that this man is not his father. And I'm not prepared to stand by and see his home and his future put at risk by one of Aline's delusions.

"I've worked—yes, worked—alongside Georges for some years now, taught him all I know that's worth knowing. I'm proud to say in many ways I've stood in for his father. It can never be the same, of course, but, well, I'm not a married man, Sandilands, no children of my own, so you can imagine how I feel." He gave Joe a manly smile. "Don't go in for self-delusion myself. No time for it. I've examined my own motives in denying this man and I have to say that's all I can come up with. The chance that I'd lose my paternal role in regard to Georges. Sounds feeble perhaps but it's something I've required myself to face. I would be distressed to give all this up..." He glanced around and then looked back directly at Joe. "But not so upset it would occur to me to give false statements, to try to effect a wrong outcome. Never!"

"Tell me, Houdart—Georges *has* seen the patient, hasn't he? I say, can we call the patient by his hospital name of Thibaud? Good Lord, I never thought to ask him. I just assumed that..."

"He has seen him. Yes. Once. I took him in one day with his mother."

"I'd be interested to hear your view of the meeting."

"Awkward, embarrassing even. Aline talked to the man... Thibaud, you say?...as though he were fully *compos mentis*. 'Do you remember, darling, the day when you...And I simply can't leave without telling you that...When you come home, of course...' There was a lot of that! Thibaud just stared through her. Then they brought a very unwilling Georges into the room. The lad was taken aback. I was sure at first he knew him. He knelt at the man's feet and took hold of his hands, staring into his face."

"Did Thibaud respond?"

"Not really. He put out a hand and stroked Georges's arm once or twice. The doctor got quite excited but it wasn't much to an onlooker."

"And Georges's impression?"

"He was very shaken but when he could get his thoughts together afterwards, he said: 'It's very like him but it's not my father.' And he repeated it. 'It's not my father.'"

Chapter 21

Joe took off his shoes and jacket, loosened his collar and lounged on his bed, eyes closed. A moment later with a sigh of irritation he gave up his attempt at siesta and went to sit at the bureau to make notes on the morning's events. After lunch Aline had announced that the family generally retired for an hour's rest in the hottest part of the day in the southern tradition and Joe and Dorcas were invited to do the same.

A tap on the door had him padding across the room to answer it. "Dorcas! Something wrong?"

She ducked under his arm and slipped into the room. "Look! I've got Georges's notebook!" she said, holding up a school exercise book. "You're not to let anyone know this exists. Not even his mother knows he's still got it. He thinks she'd have got rid of it long ago." She put it down on the desk and pulled up a second chair for herself. "Good. I see you're working. Tell me—how did the lovebirds get on in the dovecote?" she asked innocently. "I wasn't sure I'd ever see you again when you disappeared in there with Queen

Guinevere. Don't you think she looks like the grieving queen in that picture by William Morris?"

"If you're going to be silly, this conversation ends here," he said sternly.

"Sorry, Joe. Let me try again. Did she manage to convince you that Thibaud is her husband?"

"As a matter of fact, yes, she did present what I would regard as convincing evidence. It is indisputable and therefore I think we have to conclude that Georges is deluded. The victim of a nightmare of some sort? He seems to have led a pretty nightmarish existence in his childhood. It's possible!"

He outlined the evidence Aline Houdart had presented, missing out the allegory of the doves so carefully constructed. He didn't want to see Dorcas's lip curl.

"Well, I'd call that a bit rum!" said Dorcas. "Wouldn't you? You realize we've got three women who all claim an intimate acquaintance with Thibaud's bum?"

"Dorcas! You'd do well to leave such language to the Eton boys!"

"Derrière, then. Mireille was the first one to report a birthmark on her Dominique. 'Conclusive,' you said. Then Madame Tellancourt described in accurate detail her son Thomas's birthmarks fore and aft. 'Decisive,' I remember you saying. And now here's Madame Houdart making exactly the same claim. 'Incontrovertible,' apparently. It must be straining all your powers of detection, Joe, to work out there's something fishy going on! Now, Thibaud *has* got those marks just as described and it's certain that only the one genuine claimant would have been aware of them, so the other two are lying. But where do they get their information? They're rivals. They're hardly likely to pass it on."

"Keep going, Dorcas," said Joe. "You're getting there!"

"It was Mireille who brought it up. She gave the information *before* you asked the doctor to have him checked. Which makes me think... Who else knows about the birthmarks? Dr Varimont... The two orderlies. They know! And perhaps somehow the information got out of the hospital? Perhaps they sold it? They know how the competition is hotting up. The knowledge had a value."

"I think the information got out of the hospital down a telephone wire," said Joe. "Telephone! We need one."

"Georges showed me the office. They have one in there. There's no one about. Madame Houdart is swooning away in her room and Georges and his uncle have gone to organize the gypsy grape-pickers. They turned up just before lunch about a month before they were expected. Come on!"

Joe slipped the notebook between the leaves of a Michelin atlas. "Good staff work, Joliffe," he grinned. "Right! To the communications dug-out! Lead on."

To his relief, the telephone system worked efficiently and he was soon put through to Varimont in Reims. Amused, Joe heard the doctor reacting in just the same way as Dorcas: "*Three* word-perfect identifications? This is ridiculous! This is not to be believed! They're making monkeys of us, Commander! Two, at least, possibly all three, are lying. But the question is—where do they come by this information? Ah. Ah," he said as he silently answered his own question. "An internal malfunction, obviously. Leave this to me, Sandilands. I'll have your answer in ten minutes. What was that? Ear lobes? Good Lord, never noticed. I'll check that myself. Ring me back in, say, half an hour and I should have something for you. Wonderful instrument, the telephone." And the communication was cut.

"Gosh!" said Dorcas, who'd been listening, ear clamped

to the other side of the receiver. "I wouldn't like to be in their shoes! He'll have them on a charge." She turned Joe's wrist and looked at his watch. "Well, while we're waiting…"

Joe took out the notebook and laid it on the desk. It was a school exercise book, the pages secured with a stout paperclip. A quick check of the dates showed that it had been kept sporadically between the summer of 1914 when Georges was five years old and barely able to write and Christmas 1918. His mother had clearly helped with the earlier entries but her contributions ceased when the writing became confident, the comments individual.

Pasted inside the front cover was a copy of the photograph of Georges sitting on Clovis's knee. The entries were for the most part cursory, of the *went away on the train to Granny's* kind. The weather was a preoccupation evidently: *Late frost… heavy snowfall… high wind… another hot day…* as were the comings and goings of various elements of the allied armies billeted on the family.

The situation of the château, in a sheltered position a few miles south of the front, made it a perfect place to station officers recuperating from battle or reservists preparing to go up to the front line. There seemed to have been a constant procession of these from the late summer of 1914 until the Armistice. Their comings and goings had punctuated the boy's life. Georges had noted their nationality (French and English, usually separately, occasionally messing together) and identified their units. If they were infantry their brigade was noted; if cavalry, their squadron; artillery, their *groupe.* The excited seven-year-old had given half a page to the arrival of a twenty-strong detachment of *chasseurs à pied,* mounted on bicycles.

Some officers were mentioned by name:

Yves and I caught three rabbits!

Ten centimetres of snow. Very cold. This was December 1916. Joe shivered at the memory of that winter—the hardest in living memory in Champagne—and read on: *Edward brought in a fir tree from the wood and we made decorations. We painted fir cones with white paint and stuck them on. I made an angel for the top. Maman let us use her old necklaces as trimmings and she let us light candles for half an hour. We sang an English song. Edward shot a partridge and we roasted it with some chestnuts over the vine trimmings.* Carefully printed out on the page opposite the entry, in an adult hand, were the words to "Away in a Manger." The first carol every English child learns to sing.

"Well, good for you, Edward, whoever you are," murmured Joe. "Never let a little thing like a world war interfere with Christmas."

Clovis's appearances were easily identified. The writing took on a weight and a flourish and the entries were marked in the margin with a star. Just as Georges had told them, they were sparse and short; the last recorded arrival was on 20th July 1917. It was followed on 22nd July by a short entry: *Papa gone.*

There was no more until 11th November 1918. *It's finished. I will remember* were Georges's last words.

But there were other reminders of the war collected together in a large envelope tucked into the back. Joe tipped them out on to the desk. A boy's magpie collection of precious mementoes spilled out. Cap badges from English regiments clattered on to the wood and Joe turned them over with keen interest. Dorcas counted out twelve. "These are pretty. What's the galloping white horse?"

"The West Yorkshire Regiment. It's the White Horse of Hanover."

"And this creature? A dragon, I think?"

"Ah, yes. That's the emblem of the Buffs—the East Kent Regiment. And this silver bugle? It's the King's Own Yorkshire Light Infantry."

"Is there a Royal Fusiliers badge among them? Edward's listed as a Royal Fusilier."

"Yes. It's this one."

Dorcas looked puzzled. "What on earth is it? It looks like a chrysanthemum."

"It's meant to be a grenade. An exploding grenade. It's a design common to all Fusilier regiments. The round bit at the bottom is the body of the grenade itself and carries the device that distinguishes it from the rest. This one has a tiny white rose in the centre, do you see? And the rose is set within the Garter and ensigned with a crown. The excrescence spouting out at the top, which you took to be petals, represents the flames issuing from the explosion. This is made of bronze so it must have belonged to an officer."

Dorcas continued to play with them, turning them this way and that and finally counting them carefully back into their envelope. "I can see why he'd want to collect them. They're very attractive."

"And have you seen these drawings?" Joe put them in front of her. One was an accomplished sketch of a trench system with arrows marking out assault and defence manoeuvres, another an affectionate cartoon of Marshal Joffre, easily recognizable by his luxuriant white moustache and his corpulence. And there were cards: birthday cards and Christmas cards from England, some of recent date. There were letters. Some in English, some French, all from officers writing with good humour and happy memories to a child they had grown fond of.

Reading them, Dorcas looked up to comment on this. "They admired him, Joe. You're right—he was the son they all missed or hoped one day to have."

"He must have been a great comfort in those terrible times," said Joe. "And, yes, *hope,* you say. It was hard enough to think of the world as we'd known it ever continuing. Men got very sentimental—I've seen exhausted, hopeless soldiers fall on their knees in the Flanders mud, crying their eyes out at the sight of a clump of snowdrops. The presence of that little boy, clever, hard-working, determined to survive, must have inspired them. He must have represented for them all that they were fighting for."

"Oh, look, Joe! I think this says it all." She passed him a pencil sketch skilfully done, a portrait of Aline sitting holding Georges in her arms, heads together, smiling.

"A modern Madonna and child?" Joe remarked. "It only lacks the haloes."

"Well, of course they're idealized. Anyone can see that. This artist is drawing a mother and child he is fighting for. They aren't *his* wife and child. Look—there's a signature and it doesn't say Clovis Houdart. But at the moment he drew it they were his. You can see that. If he and his comrades were to give way, this little family would be overwhelmed, anni- hilated, and this oasis poisoned. You'd jolly well go out and fight for them, wouldn't you, Joe?"

In her emotion she'd forgotten for a moment that he had.

"I know you're right, Dorcas. It's a very primitive re- sponse. Like the Athenians when they squared up to the Persians on the sea at Salamis. They'd evacuated Athens hours ahead of the Persian advance, fled to the coast and put their wives and children crowded together on a tiny is- land in the bay of Salamis and there, with their families at their backs and the huge Persian navy blocking the channel, the men of Athens turned and fought. It was death or slavery for those women and children if they failed. And more than that—it was the obliteration of their civilization. No men, I believe, have ever had a heavier load resting on their shoulders. Fathers, sons and brothers hauled on the oars of their galleys, rammed, destroyed, shot and slashed their way to an incredible victory.

"It's the most powerful motivation of all," he finished thoughtfully. "Defending your own flesh and blood."

He fell into an awkward silence, remembering too late that Dorcas's father had abandoned her and her brother to the doubtful care of their grandmother when he went off to spend the war years in Switzerland. Should he say anything?

She patted his hand. "It's all right, Joe. I'd have been there, standing on the shore with the rest of the women and children, and I'd have whacked on the head any Persian who tried to swim on to the island."

"Ah! You know the story?"

She nodded. "I'd fight like anything if someone provoked me. Perhaps I get that from my mother. But now, Joe, speaking as my *father's* daughter, I'll tell you—I'm very impressed by this sketch. Orlando's smart friends would sneer and call it sentimental, representational and outdated but I like it."

"Ah, yes. The artist. We have a signature, you say?" Joe fought down an impulse to snatch the drawing from her fingers.

Dorcas peered at the signature in the corner. "Edward Thorndon. July 1917. I wonder if that's the Edward of the Christmas tree?"

* * *

"Time to ring Varimont," said Joe, beginning to pack up the sheets in their remembered order. "Are you ready for this?"

Dorcas settled down, ear to the telephone again as Varimont's voice boomed out.

"Got them! Well, one of them," he announced. "One of the orderlies, a Frédéric Lenoir by name, is actually married to a woman who was a Miss Tellancourt. There you have it! A phone call was made, he admits, to the mayor's secretary in St Céré from where the message went out and, overnight, the family made their plans. Thomas's mother rehearsed her lines and, word perfect, impressed you with her piety. I've crossed the Tellancourts off my list. And dealt with Lenoir."

"And the Houdart family? Any connection with them? Any possibility that Madame Houdart showed gratitude for information rendered?"

"Gracious! You don't let anything by, do you?" He thought for a moment. "No. I honestly don't think so. The man was a family member simply marking the card of the Tellancourts. He says he didn't (and I believe him) tell anyone else. But at least that reduces the claimants to a manageable two. Mademoiselle Desforges and Madame Houdart. Oh, and yes, Sandilands, you were quite right. Thibaud has neat ears but they *are* attached to his face at the side. Look, do you want me to convey all this to Bonnefoye?"

"I'd be most grateful. I'm planning to call on him again when I can extricate myself from this scene and perhaps we can even come to a satisfactory conclusion. Thank you for all this, Varimont."

"Not at all, my man! Not at all. Give my best wishes to Mademoiselle Dorcas."

"I will, indeed. She's right here."

He put down the telephone with a smile of satisfaction. "Well, that's it, Dorcas. The ears have it! Did you catch that? Thibaud's are attached just as Aline said and the photographs show. Now—the question is: why didn't Mireille think of mentioning that if her bloke were indeed Thibaud? She could talk about the chevrons on his sleeves till the cows come home—and you'd expect a seamstress to know all that—but she didn't mention the oddity of the ears."

"Well, you don't notice much!" said Dorcas with deep scorn.

"What do you mean?"

"It didn't occur to Mireille to declare it as an oddity for the good reason that for *her* it is not. Didn't you see? Her *own* ears are attached! She's one of the one in four people who have them, apparently. She was wearing the most lovely pair of silver earrings but I don't suppose you noticed them either?"

Joe continued collecting together the contents of the notebook, unhappy with the ruminative silence that ground on.

"Tell you what, Dorcas," he said cheerily to show he bore no grudge. "This lad, this Georges, is a very good sort. Don't you think? If ever you decided the time was right to whisper in his ear, I'd give you my blessing."

He was pleased with his comment. Unstuffy. Marcus would have approved.

"I'll be sure to bear that in mind, Joe," she said, stuffily.

On the point of clipping the notebook together he was struck by a thought. "Hang on a minute...there *is* something more we can do before we give this back. Sit down again, Dorcas. I'm going to read out names, pack drills and dates. Write them down, will you? Here's a notebook." He produced a Scotland Yard–issue pad and a pencil. "I'm going to work backwards from July '17. Right? We'll start with Edward the Partridge Slayer...surname Thorndon... and he's listed here with a Captain John. They seem to occur as a pair," he said, looking back. "Same regiment—10th battalion of the Royal Fusiliers. London men, most probably...This John is still alive since I see we have a birthday card sent for Georges's sixteenth birthday, and it was posted in India of all places."

"Is that John as a surname or John as a Christian name?"

"Could be either. Just write it down. Then there's a Raoul and an Yves and a Jean-Pierre, no surname given, 1 Corps of the Fifth Army—Lanrezac's outfit. May 1917...In April '17 le Colonel Pontarlier and a contingent of cyclist infantry... Oh, I say! In February 1917 we've got a rather splendid English General! Staying at the same time as a rather splendid French General." He chuckled. "I bet it took all of Aline's grace and charm to get those two to be polite to each other. And I wouldn't have cared to arrange the seating at the dinner table. Now we're back in 1916...November, and here's a contingent of recuperating wounded. Aftermath of the Somme, I expect. Not letting them get too far away from the amphitheatre—a quick recovery and back in the arena, I shouldn't wonder. And we have Edward bobbing up again. Must have been a casualty...He stays for quite a time. Longer than a regular leave at any rate."

A feverish quarter of an hour later and the list was drawn up. Dorcas presented it.

"We've forgotten something," said Joe. "The most important incidence. Let's just add to the list Clovis's appearances, shall we? Mark them with a C alongside in the margin. That'll do."

"Oh, Joe! Do you see what I see?" she asked.

"Certainly do! Stands out a mile! And perhaps we weren't the first ones to see it? Look, Dorcas, I think I must make one more call."

He asked the operator to connect him with a London number. Whitehall 1212. From there he was put through to Ralph Cottingham's office. He had expected a duty sergeant to answer but was delighted to hear Inspector Cottingham himself.

"Sandilands! Sir! How good to hear you! How are things in Champagne?"

"Fizzing along nicely, thank you, Ralph," Joe gave the expected answer. "But listen—two things. I'll make this quick. First: when you've performed in accordance with number two below, you are to go home. That's not a suggestion—it's an order. It's Saturday here in France and I expect it's much the same in London. Number two: I want you to call the War Office. I need urgently to contact a chap in their ex-servicemen's records department. Quicker if you do this from your end. Bates is the name. Ask him to ring me on this number from his office—that's important, I want him with his records to hand—as soon as he can." Joe read out the house telephone number. "Tell Bates he is to announce himself as 'Scotland Yard,' not the War Office, would you, and hold until I answer."

"Got that, sir. Will do. Right now."

"I can see where you're going with this, I think," said Dorcas. "Raking up a witness to a murder? But, Joe, before you go asking about, don't you think you ought to know for certain whether there ever was a murder? It seems to me there's a quick way to find out. You're a policeman, aren't you? Can't you just knock the wall down using all the clout of Interpol?"

"I'd rather use all the clout of one of those trolleys they keep down there," said Joe. "Did you notice? Very substantial. Made of oak with iron-bound corners. Perfect for the job. Perhaps with a pickaxe in reserve? But I think I'll wait until I've heard from Bates."

"Who on earth is Bates? It's the weekend—you said it yourself, Joe. And it's August. There'll be nobody in the War Office. They'll all be licking ice-cream cornets in Brighton or killing things on Exmoor."

"Ah! You don't know Bates! Bachelor. Fanatic. He lives under his desk. But—fingers crossed! Ralph Cottingham will roust out someone who can help us. He's well connected in the military world. And he'll start at the top. Probably find we're answering the telephone to a Field Marshal before the day's out. Anyway, I think we should go back to being good guests now—as far as we can. Keep our heads down. Go to your room, finish your siesta and be discovered awaking refreshed in…" He looked at his watch. "In ten minutes. I'll do the same. Off you go! And, Dorcas— thank you for your help. It's as good as having Ralph by my side."

Joe did not need to feign sleep half an hour later when Georges banged on his door and put his head round.

"Awfully sorry to disturb you, sir, but there's a call for you downstairs in the study. He was most insistent. I'm afraid it's Scotland Yard."

Chapter 22

"Captain!"

Bates's well-remembered voice rang out. He persisted in calling Joe by the rank he held when they'd first met on the Marne, disregarding his fast promotion. Joe accepted it as a mark of affection and a reminder of those desperate days when they'd struggled together, the only two men on their feet at times, to turn around an exhausted army. Water, food and a decent billet had been their priorities. Joe's knowledge of the language with Bates's phenomenal memory and organizing skills had been an effective combination. They had met several times over the years of peace in a professional capacity and Joe could picture the balding head and the sharp eyes as he appreciated the cynical cockney voice.

Each man was aware of a necessity to keep the pleasantries to a minimum.

"Scotland Yard, 'ere!" began Bates. "Shoot!"

"Tracking two British servicemen. Any details welcome. Edward Thorndon, Royal Fusilier. Marne region 1915–17.

Billeted here at…" Joe gave the location of the château. "And a fellow officer known to be a captain in the same regiment, name of John. Surname? Christian name? I don't know. Be grateful for anything you have."

"Easy-peasy. Ten…twenty minutes to be on the safe side. Ring me back on this number, Captain."

Joe wrote it down.

He was joined a few minutes into his vigil at the telephone by Dorcas, who waited with impatience for Joe to pick up the receiver.

Bates answered at once when he got through. "Got 'em, sir. Both of 'em. Thorndon, Edward Alexander. 1st City of London Regiment. Royal Fusiliers, as you say. Educ. Harrow and Cambridge. Entered the war early, rose to Major by 1917. I have a list of wounds and decorations but that'll keep, I expect? Send a copy to your office, shall I? Right-oh. Disappeared at the time you mention, end July '17. Posted 'missing in action, presumed dead' on his way up to rejoin his regiment at Ypres. They were bivouacked in Vélu Wood if my memory serves me right. Overcrowded." Joe could imagine Bates's mouth curling with disapproval. "Weather wet and cold for August. Not much comfort after his château accommodation!

"I have a letter here—well, copy of—condolences to Thorndon's parents (can let you have their details if you want them) written by his fellow officer, John. Then Major John, DSO. That's Sebastian John. Now serving in India. Lieutenant Colonel John is up in Peshawar. Anyway—at the time, he was already stationed two miles north-north-east of Bapaume at Frémicourt. His pal never turned up for the party. With German Uhlans known to be patrolling the environs, he guessed he'd been shot, shelled or taken prisoner.

All too likely. Several of our patrols went missing on the roads up there."

"Mists of war, Bates. Mists of war. Hang on a tick, would you?"

Dorcas was mouthing something at him. Catching it, he nodded and added, "You don't happen to have a service identification photograph of Thorndon, do you?"

"Hang on, there's something in the correspondence. Stack of letters here from the parents. Enquiry after enquiry. Went to the very top. Looks like they refused to accept his death. The usual heartbreak. Yes, thought I'd spotted one. Here's a photo. Not a military one. Civilian. Taken *before* the war I'd say. He looks young … middle twenties tops."

"Describe him, will you?"

"Nothing out of the ordinary. Very English-looking. Hair: light. Rather more than his fair share. I expect his mum took him to the barber's before he marched off. Eyes: pale … grey? Blue? Moustache: neatly trimmed."

"Sort of man ladies might find attractive?" Joe persisted. "Ronald Colman type perhaps?"

Bates gave this suggestion his serious consideration. "More in the way of Douglas Fairbanks, I'd have said. Cheeky expression. He's grinning like he's just cracked a joke. Smartened up and in uniform, he'd have been a sharp lad. 'Follow me, chaps!' Up the rigging or over the top— they'd have followed him all right."

"One last thing, Bates. Look at his ears. Tell me about them."

"Eh? One on each side of his head. Usual thing."

"Look closely and see if the lobes are attached to the sides of his face."

There was a clunking of the receiver and a rustling as Bates tweaked experimentally at his own lobes. "Not easy to say from this print. Reconnaissance rendered difficult, Captain, by presence in target area of thick ground cover. He's got dundrearies."

"What was that, Bates?"

"Sideburns. Down to an inch below the ears."

"Bates, thank you for this. A bit of a mixed bag there. But I'd say you've managed to shine a light on a murky little area down here. Sent up a Very light, you might say! We might not like what we see but at least we've got a look at it."

They signed off with mutual expressions of regard and Joe filled in the details for Dorcas.

"There's only one thing we can do, Joe, isn't there?" said Dorcas. "You can't go to Bonnefoye with this and you can't tell Uncle Charles either. You said you wouldn't. We've got to tell Georges. He ought to know about the scene the doctor witnessed at the hospital when Thibaud spoke in English and mimed killing someone. He ought to know about the identifying marks on his father. Someone ought to suggest to him that there is a possibility that the body— if there is a body—in the cellars may not be his father and his mother may not be a murderer. Nothing will ever be known for certain as long as the truth stays walled up. You've got to speak to him, Joe."

"Correction—*we*'ve got to speak to him."

"He said he'd be in the stables," she said, a little too readily perhaps.

They made their way unobserved over to the stables and slipped inside. Georges was busy polishing up an already gleaming black stallion and Joe wondered if the boy's hands were ever still. Seeing them, Georges closed the stall and dismissed the groom he was talking to. They approached, remaining a respectful distance from the large black, Joe noting its wicked eye and waltzing hooves.

"Ah! This'll be the God of Thunder?" he said admiringly. "Knew a fellow just like him in the war. Early days. Name of Gatecrasher, for obvious reasons. Crasher for short. Hell on the hunting field but he knew what to do, faced with a contingent of German cavalry."

Georges smiled, stowed his brushes and beckoned them over to a pile of hay bales in the corner farthest from the doors. A bucket by the side of the bales contained a scattering of cigarette ends and, seeing Joe's eyes on this, Georges remarked with an easy grin: "Dangerous habit, I know. But smoking, swearing and whistling are three vices you can only indulge in in front of the horses. Banned from the house."

And, as they settled down one on either side of him, "You have news for me?"

"We have, my friend, and it's a bit mixed. Not quite sure what you'll make of this," Joe began ponderously.

"It concerns Edward," Dorcas said impatiently. "Edward Thorndon, the English officer who was billeted on you." She produced the notebook open at the page showing the frequency of his visits and the two heads bent over it. In a few short sentences Dorcas set out the extent of their discoveries and outlined their suspicions and speculations. "Do you see, Georges—they were never here at the same time. Not until that July in 1917 when they clashed. The day they both disappeared. Neither was seen again."

Georges listened without interrupting, finally sighing. "I loved Edward," he said simply. "You're right—he did come...not often...leave was scarce in the British Army as well, and whenever his company took leave they went to

Paris, of course, but he always came here, sometimes with his friend Captain John. I think it must have reminded him of his home because he fitted in at once. He never asked what jobs needed to be done, he rolled up his sleeves and just got on with it. I followed him about everywhere, copying what he did, correcting his French. It was good to have a young and vigorous man about the place. Even when he was wounded and couldn't do much he still... would *radiated* confidence be too strong an expression?

"The first time I met him... I was just returning from the fields... he was out in the yard. A squad of six or so had arrived an hour earlier. He was splitting logs for firewood. He looked up and said, 'You must be Georges. Here, Georges, have an axe and let's get this pile stacked before the stable bell rings five, shall we?' I'd never been allowed to use an axe before."

"Did you do it?" Dorcas asked. Irrelevantly, Joe thought.

"I'll never forget putting the last log on the pile as the first note rang out," said Georges with quiet pride. "I think, looking back, it was a stage-managed moment but," he shrugged, "it was one of many lessons I learned from Edward."

"Did you ever think he might be... regard him as... your father?" Dorcas asked bluntly.

"No. I never confused them. And he never tried to be a father to me. More like an older brother. My mother liked him too. She was always cheerful when he was in the house. I remember she was delighted when he came to us wounded with permission to recuperate. She was a nurse, you know, and she gave him the very best attention."

He went silent and stared at his boots for a very long time. Then he looked up at them angrily under his brows. He swallowed and said stiffly, "Well, you must think me the most awful fool—not realizing what was going on all those years until two foreigners arrive and spell it out for me. I am supposing—nine years too late—that *something* was going on. You must think me incredibly naïve!"

"No, we don't!" said Dorcas. "Young, trusting and betrayed by the adults around him."

"Papa, Edward and Maman," he said. "If something frightful happened that night in 1917, how could I ever assign blame? I loved them all."

"Georges, we don't at present know what, if any, blame there is to be assigned," said Joe. "The answers are blocked up in the cellars under the auspices of St Martin. I think you know what we have to do. A little *dégorgement* has to take place, wouldn't you say, so that whatever poison is gathering behind there is released, identified and dealt with. The pressure's building, the bottle's at the right angle... and the thumb on the cork is yours, old son."

Georges's head went up. He attempted a smile and even acknowledged Joe's extravagant metaphor. "Nine years in the bottle—that's too long. And I'm sure you're thinking I have my own internal dead yeast to get rid of?"

"You said it yourself, don't forget," said Joe softly, "—it's nasty stuff but it plays a necessary part in producing the final aroma and flavour. Release it and the '26 vintage could well turn out to be the best Houdart for decades."

Georges had come to a decision. It was a difficult one to deliver but he had no hesitation and, Joe knew, would never go back on it.

"Two things," he said. "First: my uncle Charles must be made aware of all this. I rather trust you can find the words to tell him, sir? May we leave that to you? Second: we cannot do this in the presence of my mother. That I cannot allow. Tomorrow is Sunday and she goes to morning mass in the village. She will be gone for about two hours. Time enough, I think, for us to perform our investigations. So—will you parade at eight hundred hours? At the *rond point* St Martin? Dorcas, you may be excused...No, I thought as much."

"And if we find nothing, she'll never be aware of the suspicions raised by two interfering English," said Dorcas.

"Exactly."

The understanding between these two was instant, Joe recognized, with a twinge of concern. It had taken only one day for them to be confident of reading each other's thoughts.

"The difficulty will be in acting as normally as possible for the rest of the day." Joe thought he ought to raise this problem.

"I find if you want to deceive, the best way to go about it is to have lots to prattle on about," said Dorcas in a practical way. "If you're boring someone they're not paying much attention to what you're saying. Have you ever ridden bareback, Georges? Then we'll start now. I'll show you how. We'll take two of the more docile horses and make for that wood beyond the vineyard. And we'll have thrills and spills enough, I daresay, to chatter about over dinner. If there's time we could ride over and talk to the gypsies. I know a few words of Romany...We could return bubbling with stories. I say—do you mind, Joe, if we just disappear?"

Joe was irritated enough to say, "Not at all! Run along and play!"

Joe found Charles-Auguste, although it could well have been the Frenchman who did the finding, on his way back to the main house. On hearing the seriousness of Joe's tone when he asked for an interview, he steered him along to the study, leaving instructions with the footman that they were not to be disturbed.

Joe set out his story succinctly and without emotion, managing, he thought, to get his facts in the right order from the scene of nightmare witnessed by Dr Varimont in Reims to Georges's account of his own nightmare in the cellars, on the evening his father disappeared. He mentioned the presence in the château of the billeted Englishmen and talked of Edward Thorndon who vanished from Georges's life and from the records of the British Army at the same time. He spoke of Georges's undisclosed horror at the sight of his mother with the body, the bloodstains on the child's shirt and the covering over of a burial place.

All of Charles-Auguste's concerns were for his nephew. "How can any child have hugged this appalling vision to himself all these years? My poor Georges! Why did he never confide . . . ? Well, of course, I can imagine why he did not . . . It's a child's device—pretend something's not really there and it will disappear. But this never did. I wondered, not very energetically, you see, about the flowers and St Martin. So many shrines down there, I just took it for one of a series, one personal to Georges. But I can't believe Aline would be mixed up in anything of a homicidal nature. She's a bit mad—I've said so—and rather wish I'd kept my mouth shut now! But she's not violent. Oh, no! Nurse, you know, and a damn good one by all accounts. In the business of preserving life not taking it. None of this makes sense, Sandilands."

"And won't begin to until we've taken a look at whatever rests behind that partition," said Joe.

He outlined Georges's suggestion for an inspection on Sunday morning.

"I have to say that's a sensible idea, if very distasteful," said Charles. "And it does amount to out-and-out deceit of Aline." He shuddered. "If she were ever to find out... Still, I agree—if we make the most colossal fools of ourselves, we can just put the cover back over things with little harm done. And the cellar men will have a laugh at least... 'You got it wrong, Monsieur Charles!' they can turn on me and say. 'Whatever made you think there were vintage bottles hidden away behind that wall?' Very well. Eight o'clock? I'll be there."

Chapter 23

Four silent figures gathered in front of the icon of St Martin, looking shifty rather than respectful, Joe thought.

"Eight o'clock," said Charles-Auguste. "I think we can count on two hours, judging by previous form, what do you say, Georges?"

Georges nodded miserably.

"I didn't ask any of the men to attend these proceedings," said Charles. "Thought we could probably manage the work by ourselves. Three strapping fellows. Ought to be enough. But I say, Sandilands, er—Miss Dorcas? Not perhaps a suitable thing for her to witness?"

"You can try sending her away if you're feeling reckless," said Joe. "I've tried. On her own head be it."

"Very well, then. Let's have at it. Picks, Georges? Two. Shovel? Bring that trolley over, will you? That will smash down the partition once we've made a hole in it. What do you say it's made of…? One thickness of brick? And a skimming of plaster over. Shouldn't take long, then. Well, stand back there, I'll take the first swing."

He made the sign of the cross, signalled to Georges to re-move the picture of the saint, raised one of the pickaxes and attacked the wall. Joe took the other pick and, working to-gether, they had soon opened up a gaping hole. No waft of fetid air emerged, as Joe was half expecting, no cold draught, and he remembered that Georges had said this was no more than an alcove behind the partition and not a fur-ther corridor hacked out of the chalk.

Georges held up a torch as the hole enlarged. They could dimly see behind the wall wooden racks, leather straps, a row of jugs still graded by size standing on a shelf. All the paraphernalia of a wine cellar. As the lower bricks crashed to the ground around their feet, a table became visible. Ladles were lined up on it, undisturbed, ready for use.

Joe looked at Charles-Auguste and the same thought flashed between them: "This is all a nonsense. When we've finished here, we'll sheepishly go back up to reality again and crack open a bottle of the best to celebrate having got this spectacularly wrong."

Joe took the next swing, a mighty clout that signalled his impatience to get it over and done with. He held up a hand to Charles-Auguste and peered into the hole. "Dorcas," he said in a voice suddenly tense, "if you've changed your mind, this would be a good moment to leave us."

She shook her head and, clutching Georges's hand, came nearer.

Silently Charles grabbed the shovel and cleared piles of bricks and plaster dust into one of the trolleys. Joe chipped away at the bottom row and Charles cleared some more. They pressed round staring, trying to make sense of what they were seeing, and then Charles-Auguste made the sign of the cross again. Automatically, Joe made the same gesture.

A huddled shape lay underneath the table, wrapped in the remains of a carpet or rug.

"That rug—it's the one Felix used to stand on when he was working the bottling machine," said Georges. "He suffered from rheumatism. Maman had it brought down from the house for him to stand on, to insulate his feet from the cold ground."

Joe took one end of the bundle and Charles the other and together they slid it out from under the table and into the light.

Reverently, Joe pulled back the end of the rug where he judged the head to lie. He went on tugging, and revealed, inch by inch, to a subdued moan from Dorcas, a pitiful, shrunken corpse. Almost mummified, by some trick of the ambient conditions in the dry, cold cellar, it lay, stiff and brown as any ancient Egyptian taken from the sands after thousands of years. But this body was not bound in linen wrappings: the rags clinging to the emaciated shape were rags which had once been army-issue white cotton underwear. Spreading outwards over the vest with its centre at the heart, a brown stain of blood, much blood, trailed down towards the ground and lost itself in the swirling pattern of the Indian rug. His feet were bare. His head, which Joe could scarcely bring himself to look at, bared improbably white teeth at them from shrunken brown lips. It was crowned by a shock of still-bright fair hair.

"Sir," whispered Georges. "Tell us! Who do you think this is?"

"Well, it's perfectly obvious who this is! Silly boy!"

Aline's voice rang out, shocking in its sharpness and lack of emotion. They whirled around to see her, standing watching them from the corner, silhouetted in black dress and black veiled hat against the chalk walls. She still clutched her service book in black-gloved hands. Joe could not begin to guess how long she had been standing there observing them, a silent, malignant presence.

She came on, moving slowly towards them, with never a glance at the body.

"A deserter, of course. Probably French or German—they usually were. The English made for the coast, I think. How clever of you to find him! Poor Georges discovered a couple in…1918, was it, Georges?" Her voice was controlled. An interested adult was joining a group of children up to something slightly reprehensible. "And now another one. Felix must have failed to notice him huddled up in the alcove. The lighting was particularly erratic in those years and Felix didn't have the keenest sight by then. Poor chap! I expect the curé will give permission to have him interred in the local cemetery. He's very accommodating about these things. Better have him checked for identification, of course. Charles, arrange for the men to take over, will you? I really don't think this is a proper use of your time on a Sunday morning. And what on earth you think you're doing letting little Dorcas witness such a scene, Commander, I have no idea. Shame on you!

"Now," she finished, ticking-off over apparently, "why don't we all withdraw to the house and open a bottle of the…'13 vintage, Charles? And drink a farewell toast to an unknown warrior?"

In a few short sentences, Aline had offered a solution to the case, rapped a few knuckles and shown them the acceptable way out. Georges and Charles were looking shocked and sheepish, Dorcas had unconsciously crept over to stand behind Joe.

Recovering from the shock of finding her amongst them, Joe rallied. She had gone too far in questioning his judgement. Spurred by a jab of icy anger, he decided to break through her thin crust of pretence. He had noticed that she still had cast not one curious glance at the corpse. Well, he would make her confront the victim.

"Identification," he repeated, nodding acknowledgement of her suggestion. "Yes, it all comes down to that, doesn't it? I wonder if this poor fellow has a name tag around his neck?" He bent over the corpse, careful to avoid contact with any part of it. "Ah, sadly—no. But then, some soldiers, particularly the French, were known to carry theirs wrapped around their wrists. No again, I'm afraid." He straightened and made a dismissive gesture. "Here was a gentleman who did not wish to be known to posterity, apparently. Oh... hang on a tick... what's that?" He leaned closer, every inch of him on the alert. "Ah! Do you see that, Charles? Over the other side... There, gleaming in his left hand... there's something, I'd swear!"

All eyes were drawn to him, even Aline's, wide and staring under her veil.

"Do you want to do the honours, Charles? No? Very well, I'll retrieve it. Your light over here, please, Georges!"

With some distaste, he bent across the corpse and detached something small which glowed golden in the wavering torchlight.

Joe gave a low whistle of astonishment. "Well, well! The very last thing I'd have expected to find clutched in the hand of a dead man in a champagne cellar!" he said. "Just look at this! I think this speaks volumes, don't you, Aline? You may even wish to remove your veil to take a close look at it?"

He held up in front of her face between finger and thumb

a small gilt object, no more than two inches high. Tormentingly, he moved it from side to side with the air of a satisfied conjuror.

Ashen-faced, Aline stared, her head moving as though hypnotized by the object in Joe's hand. Too shocked to respond, she opened her lips but made no sound. And still she would not crack. Joe decided to play his last card.

Chapter 24

"It's a cap badge," he announced, showing it to the company. "The flare at the top identifies it, do you see? It's an exploding grenade. The cap badge of the Royal Fusiliers, I believe. London regiment. Damn good soldiers. Could fire fifteen rounds a minute! Poor bloke. But now at least we can identify him. Shouldn't be too difficult to come by the names of any Fusiliers who went missing on the Marne in—when did you say this alcove was blocked up? In 1917? Summer? I'll get on to it."

With a scream of fury mixed with despair, Aline turned and fled away down the gallery.

Georges turned on Joe. "Did you have to be such a swine?" he shouted. He hurled his torch down at Joe's feet and ran after his mother.

"Oh, my God!" said Charles. "What a mess! What the hell was she doing here? How did she know? Look, don't be upset, Sandilands. The boy was bound to react like that—I'd think the less of him if he didn't. You did what you had to do. *We* did what we had to do." He patted Joe on the shoulder and his back stiffened in resolve. "And we haven't finished by a long chalk. Leave Aline for later. She's not going to run away. We're going to have to clear this lot up. I suppose there's a good deal here," he indicated the body, "a policeman will need to check over. Stroke of luck him dying clasping his cap badge though, wasn't it? Could save us hours of research, I'm thinking."

Was there a slight question in his voice?

There was more than a question in Dorcas's voice when she spoke. It was heavy with sarcasm. "Joe doesn't trust to luck just happening like that. Sometimes he engineers it. Like that little scene of discovery just now. I bet if I were to count out Georges's collection of badges there'd be one missing and it would be an exploding grenade!"

"Dorcas! How can you be such a cynic? Georges's collection is complete. I didn't make off with one."

"But then…what…?"

He held up the badge again. "Sleight of hand, misdirection…Aline knows who this man is and she saw what she expected to see: a Royal Fusilier's badge. But it isn't! This one belongs to me—it's the emblem of the Royal *Scots* Fusiliers. Very similar, to a civilian's eyes. A grenade going off with flames curling out of the top—but mine has the lion and the unicorn on the base, not the white rose, you see. And mine is gilt, not bronze."

Dorcas peered at the badge and nodded. "Do you always walk about with your old cap badge in your pocket?" she asked, her voice slow with suspicion.

"In my pocket? Well, of course not! You were so interested in Georges's collection, I dug mine out of my kit and brought it down to give to you. I thought you might like to start your own collection—have it made into a sweetheart pin if you like—many girls do! I've given away dozens of these in my time. You find them all over London. But give it to Georges if you don't want it. And if you're going to be so sniffy..."

"Children! Children!" said Charles with weary good humour. "Pressure's mounting, I know, but do you think we could get on with the job in hand?"

Contrite, Joe was instantly on his knees, going carefully and impressively through his post-mortem routine. With no possibility of taking notes on the spot, no photographer or fingerprinting facility available to him, let alone the supportive presence of a Scotland Yard–appointed pathologist, he did what he could.

He gave a running commentary on his findings for his own benefit as well as to allay the curiosity of Charles and Dorcas: "I am assuming from an inferred identification on the part of a witness that this is the body of Edward Thorndon, Royal Fusilier, record of disappearance available from the War Office in London. Physical details of corpse concur with known characteristics of said Thorndon. Dental records, if such exist, and fingerprints ditto will doubtless give further information, probably confirmation. In the absence of any medical assistance I will carry out a preliminary and non-invasive examination of the fatal wound on the spot."

"I say, should we look the other way?" said Charles, moving to shield Dorcas from the sight.

"I'm not digging very deep," said Joe. "Haven't got the equipment. And you're a valued witness."

He took a penknife from his pocket and carefully cut a cross in the fabric over the centre of the bloodstain. With delicate movements of the blade, he peeled back the four corners from the wound. Murmuring, he lengthened his cuts and revealed a larger extent of the chest. "Wounds!" he said. "Plural. There's enough of the skin and flesh preserved to allow me to make out five at least. They appear to be one and a half inches in width, consistent with a cut from a sabre blade. Not a slash—a plunging cut. A great deal of blood was spilled and…" Joe shuffled on his knees all around the corpse, observing closely, "and, oddly, the victim would appear—from the path of the blood flow—to have been recumbent at the time the blows were delivered. Do you see? If I'd stuck a blade in you, standing face-to-face…" He got to his feet and offered up his penknife blade to Charles's chest. "The initial outflow of blood would cascade down your front, staining your breeches and your feet. Here we've got a ponding of blood around the wound and a general overflow around what I think must have been a supine form. No stains, you see, on his lower limbs. But why would a chap be lying on his back in a cellar waiting for someone to come along and stab him? He clearly didn't wander in here to die after a wounding that occurred somewhere else. You wouldn't survive an attack like this for longer than a few seconds. Death must have been just about instantaneous."

He bent to examine the right arm, again cutting away remaining shreds of fabric. "No sign of an old wound to the upper arm visible."

Puzzled, he looked at the man's face. "Either of you got a working torch? Thank you, Charles. Shine it closely on the face, would you, there on your right, his left. There! Are there signs of a blow to the head? Too faint to make out. The features are decayed, extremities show depredations by rodents. Broken cheekbone, though, I think. Pre-mortem?

Someone kicked him unconscious and, as he lay there, stabbed him to death?"

He looked at Dorcas, the doctor's appalling mime of Thibaud's nightmare performance vivid in their minds.

"Check, Joe, can you see if his hands were tied? He wouldn't have just knelt down to wait for the blow, would he?"

Joe lifted each hand in turn. "Hard to tell, honestly, without a microscope but there's something there. On both wrists. A slight mark. A ligature he struggled against? It's possible. And, significantly—it's been removed. The man has been overpowered, we must assume, here on this spot, kicked unconscious and repeatedly stabbed."

"But who on earth could perform such a despicable act?" said Charles. "Hard to believe that anyone we know and who—we must presume—was acquainted with his victim, could kill in this cruel and brutal way."

"Oh, I don't know..." said Joe bitterly. "I've known much worse meted out by men who hadn't even been introduced to their victim."

He got to his feet, clicked shut his knife and dusted off his knees. "That's all for the moment. I think—and it doesn't please me to say this—that we now find ourselves in a position where we have little choice but to go along with some of Aline's suggestions. Or were they orders? We must turn this sad relic over to the men to have it conveyed upstairs. And—opening a bottle? I could do with a whisky, if I may make a suggestion of my own."

"Right. Right," said Charles, shuffling his feet in the dust. "Look, Sandilands, why don't you go on ahead? Speak to Aline? She'll be expecting it. She'll be in the salon. Planning her next move and rehearsing her lines, shouldn't wonder. You've been warned! Leave me to make all the necessary

arrangements for our friend here. I'll have the local under-
taker sent for."

Joe smiled and mimed stiffening his shoulders to take a
command.

"Bon courage, mon ami!" said Charles as Joe stalked away
down the corridor.

Chapter 25

Joe went first to the stables, aware that he was dragging his feet, reluctant to encounter Aline once again. He took off his jacket, and stripped off his shirt, and began to wash his hands and arms and face thoroughly, making use of the cake of carbolic soap available in the grooms' earthenware sink. He dried off on a towel hanging on a hook and finally, feeling clean but smelling disgusting, he put on his things again. He straightened his tie, squinting into a cracked looking-glass and grimacing at his strained face. "Can't put it off any longer, Sandilands," he confided to his image. "Shift yer arse!"

Crossing the courtyard he encountered a stern-faced Georges. "My mother's in the salon," he said curtly. "She's not obliged to—don't think it—but she'd like to have a few words." And, challenging and suspicious: "What have you done with Dorcas?"

Joe was suddenly angry. "What the hell do you *suppose* I've done with her? Knocked her on the head and sealed her up in an alcove? Not the kind of behaviour we go in for in my family! She's with your uncle, desperately trying to clear up *your* family's mess!"

Georges's head went back as though he'd been slapped and to Joe's dismay tears began to trickle. He sniffled noisily and put a large hand in embarrassment across his face.

Instantly, Joe threw out both arms and seized the boy in a tight hug. "Forgive me, Georges, old man. Awful thing to say! Insensitive! Unforgivable! Be kind and put it down to strain—the strain of having to go in there and speak to your mother—will you?"

Georges nodded his understanding.

"And, I say—before you rush off to find Dorcas—any chance you could rustle up a drink?"

Georges gulped, raised a dim smile and found his voice. "A twenty-year-old Glenfiddich?" he offered. "Would that fit the bill?"

Joe tapped on the salon door and entered on hearing the quiet instruction to come in. He was carrying a tray loaded with whisky bottle, glasses and a jug of iced water.

"Well, I wasn't quite sure what would appear round the door," she said. "The local gendarmerie flourishing hand-cuffs perhaps? I didn't hope for a Scotland Yard commander bearing a tray of refreshments. I'll have a large one, please. Neat, no ice."

He poured out her drink, taking the same measure for himself, and they sat and sipped the whisky silently.

Her hat and hymn book had been abandoned on the floor at her feet and she was sitting perched anxiously on the end of her chaise longue, puffing rather inexpertly on a small cigar. Her tawny hair was dishevelled, her face tear-stained. She looked small and frightened and Joe could no longer imagine what about her had so disconcerted him in the cellars. But, whatever that quality, it was not so much to be feared as this new show of vulnerability, he decided, taking out a little insurance.

A few more sips and puffs and she had recovered sufficiently to look up and sketch a wan smile. "I'm sorry I frightened you all," she said. "Making an appearance like that and spoiling your moment. I didn't go to church. Guilty conscience, I suppose, made me fear to leave what you'd probably describe as 'the crime scene' for too long. Not with a sharp and determined bloodhound like you within a few yards of a concealed body."

He was relieved to hear her light tone.

"So you know about Edward?" she said.

"I couldn't say that with any confidence," he replied. "I know that the body we have just found is that of Edward Thorndon and that he died here while sheltering under your roof in late July 1917. I know that your husband, Clovis, disappeared at the same time. I know that you, Aline, were observed dragging the body into its hiding place and giving instructions for it to be immured."

"Yes, yes," she cut him short. "Georges has just told me what he saw. My poor boy! All those years…out of loyalty…I had no idea…I am much to blame for never realizing."

Her head went up and she held out her glass for more whisky. Joe was glad to oblige and poured a second generous measure. He had never suspected that this might be the way to melt Aline's ice crust. She delicately invited him with a gesture to refill his own glass.

"But I did it for *him*, you know. For Georges. I couldn't bear to lose him."

"I think you're going to have to explain that," he said.

"But first—I want you to tell me what you have deduced from that terrible scene down there. No!" she added, seeing his cynical surprise. "No! I did not see the murder, I certainly did not play a part in it. I came across the body of Edward. There was no one about. Clovis had been stamping and raging all day and I feared his temper might lead to some sort of scene...but I never expected this madness. A servant told me they'd gone down to the cellars. Together. And they were both in uniform. Both about to go back to the front. You can imagine what I thought—some sort of awful duel! Clovis was capable of anything. Do you think they fought a duel, Commander?"

Joe outlined as simply as he could the evidence he had drawn from the murder scene and linked it with the doctor's report. "...so, I'm assuming Clovis, having lured Edward down there—issuing a challenge or an invitation of some sort, 'Sabres at seven,' 'Why don't we find a quiet place to discuss this?'—ambushed him, overpowered him and tied his hands. Perhaps some exchange of views took place and as a result of what was said, Clovis kicked him in the head as he knelt begging for his life."

Joe hesitated, wondering how much of his knowledge he should share with her. "Oddly enough," he said, "like a terrifying echo from the past...a recorded scream you might say if you were being fanciful, we know exactly what was said by the victim with his last breath. His words scored themselves on to the mind of his killer to be replayed like a phonograph recording years later in the course of a nightmare. Dr Varimont observed and noted. And that last desperate plea being wrung from him in his native language—in English—was the reason for my involvement. For good or ill."

He repeated Edward's dying words and her head drooped, heavy with grief.

"Having stabbed him to death, I'm supposing Clovis himself cut the ties from Edward's hands, though I can't imagine why…"

"A cavalryman like Clovis would never want to be accused of killing a restrained man, Commander. It's a matter of honour. Like shooting a sitting duck. He would want it to be thought—if discovered—that he had killed a worthy opponent in fair combat. But this is worse, much worse, than I had ever envisaged. My poor Edward…"

She dragged herself free from the cold grasp of her imaginings, steadied her voice and started on the explanation Joe was waiting for. "It was a difficult visit. I had quarrelled with Clovis. He made it clear that he had no regard for me— suggested I return to my parents in Paris when the war ended. He was sure that it would be over by the end of the year. And he proposed to go on living here with Georges.

"If he survived! But I think he wasn't seriously expecting to survive the next battle. He was clearing up things here. He knew I loved Edward. It must have been obvious even to him. And I cannot be certain that Edward did not tell him. He was a very uncomplicated character. Open and good-hearted. He was not, by nature, an intriguer and what was going on here was, on one level, a torment to him, I knew that. I warned him to be discreet but, knowing him, he would have seized an opportunity of telling Clovis all."

"Do you mind telling me exactly what *was* going on, madame?"

"Well, a love affair," she smiled. "You remember the doves? I was speaking of Edward, of course. We had met in 1915. In September. I'd cycled back from my shift at the hospital in the village to find the house full of troops. I assumed they were *our* troops—that Clovis had come back on leave—and I hurried off to the stables where they told me he'd gone. Clovis would never waste a minute waiting about. It was dark in the corridor but there he was coming in through the back door. He was wearing Clovis's old clothes—his own uniform was in the tub. His fair hair was gleaming in the sunshine, he was being trailed by Georges and the dog. I was sure it was Clovis and I ran to him and threw my arms around him. Silly thing to do—he was carrying two bottles of champagne in from the cellar. The last thing he could have expected was a bloodstained nurse hurling herself at him and kissing him! He picked me up and swung me away from the broken glass and I realized."

Her cigar had long gone out though she still clutched it, and Joe gently took it from her and put it in an ashtray.

She breathed unsteadily and her eyes filled with tears. Hardly able to speak she battled on, accepting that nothing she could say would convey the depth of her feeling but impelled to try. "Two seconds! I told you! Nothing we could do about it! Nothing! To say we fell in love is a bit weak—we recognized each other. We belonged to each other from that moment."

Joe was becoming uncomfortable with the high swell of her emotional revelations. "And Clovis ran into a confession from Edward, you think?"

"More than a confession. He was determined to tell him that, if he survived the war, he would come back for me and we'd make a life together in England with Georges. He refused to leave Georges behind."

And Joe understood. "A dynastically minded man like Clovis with his honour challenged would never accept that. And he loved his son. He thought he was not likely to return from his next encounter...where did you say he was bound? The Chemin des Dames? Ah, yes. He would have known his chances of surviving that were low. He would not want to ride off leaving behind his wife and his son to be acquired by a despised Englishman who'd usurped his position, stolen his life. Aline, this was always going to end disastrously! It was madness to think otherwise."

"Madness? What are you talking about? We were surrounded by madness! We lived in a daily hell of madness. Every day could have been our last. Our love was an escape from that—it was the only sane thing in our world."

"Not quite the only thing that meant a good deal to you, I think," said Joe. "This conversation started with Georges..."

"I couldn't let it ever be discovered that my son's father was a murderer. He was a clever boy, Commander. I was certain he would work it out. I had to hide the body. It was for his sake I hid it. Concealing it in the cellar was the easy part! I had to get rid of their horses in the night so it would appear they'd gone off to rejoin their troops. I rode one and led the other. I let them loose within a whinny of a French army camp where I was sure they'd be welcomed with open arms. They were good horses, it broke my heart to let them go. And I walked back through the lanes and helped Felix finish the wall."

Joe was smitten by the reserves of strength, emotional as well as purely physical, that unforgettable night must have called for from this woman.

And he still had not guessed at the extent of her resilience. She gave him a calculating look. "There's not a great deal you can do about this, I think, Commander? You have a corpse to which it will be difficult to assign an identity—I was not deceived for long by your confidence and your sleight of hand. And what authority is going to be interested enough or have sufficient time on their hands to get to the bottom of it? There are thousands of bodies coming back to the surface every year. The land itself disgorges them: French, German, British, Belgian, men from the colonies, they still appear. And you know as well as I do—better perhaps—how the authorities work. The French will hand the file over to the British who will hand it back again with a few superior and dismissive phrases. And it will spend more months...years...gathering dust on a shelf somewhere. Eventually all those who might have an interest or a memory will be gone themselves."

"We are speaking of a man who did not die in battle, madame. He was murdered."

"A soldier's body pierced by sabre cuts? In the middle of the corpse-strewn Marne? Who will care? My dear Commander, if you pursue this, you will be a laughingstock."

She had drawn up the battle lines. Over-confident.

Joe strolled to the table to put down his whisky glass and turned, replying with chill formality: "*I* will care, Madame Houdart. And, for me, the derision of a deskbound official or two in London or Paris is as nothing compared with the silent cry for justice of a fellow soldier."

He took his cap badge from his pocket and studied it. "Edward of the Fir Tree: I feel I know him. He was a soldier just like me. A Fusilier, miles from home, trying to cling to some semblance of civilization and tradition...snatching at love and warmth where he could find them. I'm a pretty traditional sort of man myself, madame, and in an old-fashioned way I'm going to give you my pledge that I will bring this matter to a conclusion that would have satisfied *him*. And here's my gage on that!"

With a scornful gesture he tossed the badge across the room to land at her feet.

She stood up, glowing with fury, indicating that the interview had ended. As he bowed and made to leave her she called after him: "I had a black hound once...an English breed...a nonpareil when it came to following the quarry. But he was too keen, Commander. Sadly one day, in his eagerness, he outstripped the rest of the dogs and fell into a boar-trap. Broke his back. A terrible thing but someone had to give the command to administer the *coup de grâce*. I gave it."

Chapter 26

Joe closed the door quietly and stood outside, grinning and shaking his head to dispel his disgust at the melodramatic performance. "Pompous English idiot!" was his judgement. "Against lying French schemer! Wonder who'll prevail?"

He was disturbed enough by his conversation to wish to share his concerns with Charles-Auguste, recognizing now the man's prescience in calling in a little help from a discreet quarter, and set off back towards the cellars. Charles was at the door, leaving directions with one of the men. Dusty and tired, he made his way over to Joe.

"Kitchen, I think. I'll put on a pot of coffee."

Settled around the table and by themselves, they set about producing a second breakfast.

"Here, have some bread," offered Charles. "It'll soak up the whisky. You smell like a distillery, man! Trying to keep pace with her, were you?"

"What? You're not saying that...?"

"Oh, no! Aline's by no means dependent on the stuff.

She's a winemaker, after all. Knows exactly where to stop. Usually doesn't start but when she does...! She was probably trying to drink you under the table. Seen her do it with buyers. But she should have known better than to try that on with a Scotsman, I'd guess?"

"The capacity comes in useful sometimes. Even so, I'm ashamed to say I'd reached the loosening-of-inhibitions stage and made a gesture or two I regret. But, Charles, I want you to listen to Aline's account and tell me what you're thinking. I hardly know the woman. You do. I don't want to come to a wrong conclusion about her and base my further actions on something false."

Charles listened and asked an occasional question as the conversation and Joe's interpretation of it were laid out for him. He grimaced and drew in a whistling breath as Joe recounted her Parthian shot. "No, actually she wasn't making up that story about the dog...I remember the brute. Black as night, keen as mustard and he died as described. Ouch! You're for it, old man! But tell me—what are you going to do now?"

"Head straight for the boar-trap, I'm afraid. Nowhere else to go. I won't stand by and see Edward Thorndon shovelled into the earth as a nameless deserter, in a pine box in a French graveyard, with no one to mourn him but the woman who indirectly brought about his death. He has loving parents in England. They continue their search for information. They will want their son's remains returned and, believe me, Charles, this is one missing soldier who's going home if I have to carry him on my back!"

He paused to fill his coffee cup.

"And that's the easy bit," said Charles. He gave Joe a level look. "We're both skirting round mentioning the obvious, aren't we?"

"Yes. And it goes right back to the beginning of all this. It was *you* who raised the matter with Sir Douglas, Charles. It's *your* concerns I'm here to investigate. And I can tell you I *have* been picking up the hints. Now stop me if you think I've got this quite wrong but—it all hinges on a single simple question: Why in hell does Aline want her husband back again?"

"There we have it," said Charles with relief. "I've always suspected she hated my cousin—though I had no idea what good grounds she had for that hatred! And now we're looking at a woman who's prepared to move heaven and earth to have this husk of a man brought back here into her life so that she may care for him. She knows how difficult that will be for her and for Georges. It would have been easy to have ignored the appeal in the paper—'Great heavens! What a surprise—doesn't this man look incredibly like poor dear Clovis who was killed up near Craonne in '17? I do hope they manage to locate his family. I can imagine how they suffer.' And that, if any comment were called for—which it wasn't—would have sufficed. But she went straight after him—like that bloody old Diabolo she told you about—hounding the doctor, spending time and money on research and bribery I shouldn't wonder, determined to get hold of him."

"I'm bound to say there is a perfectly reasonable motive. She must know (as you say, she's done some research on this) that the condition of shell-shock, *Kriegsneurose* or *la confusion mentale de la guerre,* whatever you want to call it, is not invariably irreversible. She must have considered the possibility of his recovering his memory with a click and a bang one of these days. There are many well-documented incidences. And what happens then? Clovis comes racing, hands down, back to his home to confront his faithless wife and reclaim his long-lost son? She'd lose everything. Would Aline be prepared to take even the slightest risk of this happening?"

"Certainly not. She would not want that. She would prefer to have him under her control. Here. Not in Reims or anywhere else speaking his mind—should it ever come back to him. But—and I think you've seen it, Joe—there's something else. Something darker."

"Yes. I think I have. The patient in Reims is not just a pathetic leftover from the war, he's Clovis Houdart, the man she hated, the man who would have taken her son from her, the man who stabbed her lover to the heart and killed off her hopes. I'd guess that she's pinned the blame for all that has gone wrong in her life, the disasters and the sorrow, on him. Oh, yes, she wants him back all right. But not to care for him. No. Not that." Joe shivered and rolled to a halt.

"To torture and torment him," Charles finished for him. "She's a vindictive woman who's not happy unless she has someone in her power and if she can't charm them into submission, she'll resort to other means. I really believe—and, Joe, I would be only too relieved to hear that you think my suspicions absurd—that she means to have her revenge in her own twisted way. If she were to acquire him, be granted custody, I think I would be sent away back to Provence in short order and, after an almighty row, Georges would flee. With me? Perhaps. Into the army? More likely. He's still maintaining, by the way, that Thibaud is not his father. And she would be left head-to-head with that poor, dribbling wreck. I can't think any further." He stumbled to a halt, shaken by his own dark thoughts. "You'll think the worse of me for even entertaining such dreadful suspicions."

"No, Charles. My mind has plumbed much the same depths. Look here—you have said to me, lightly and on one or two occasions, that you thought Aline might be 'a bit mad,'" said Joe tentatively.

"Just a manner of speaking," mumbled Charles. "And if you're talking medically, I'm no authority. Indeed, I have no personal experience of the condition and my views are not worth an airing. But—oh, why be so mealy-mouthed!—her behaviour is occasionally worrying. Her reactions, excessive. I've always put it down to her sufferings in the war—they were enough to have brought down a strong man, you know—and with this further evidence of mental torment uncovered, well, one understands and sympathizes."

"I think your fears may not be unfounded," said Joe. "I agree we could risk terrible consequences if the man—Thibaud—were to be turned over to her."

"But, I'd guess the ultimate decision rests with the French authorities, am I right? And they will act without the benefit of witnessing the little scene down in the cellar just now. You begin to see why I would so have liked you to arrive and declare him English! Our problem would have been carted off over the Channel to live out his days in some comfortable south coast clinic for officers instead of festering in a lunatic asylum or cooped up here being—"

"Cooped up?" Joe's memory was stirred. "'Sometimes the female has to fetch him back...and sometimes he's ripped to shreds by his mate...'" he muttered, remembering with horror. With all the assurance of Athena she had told him the truth and had never attempted to conceal her intentions. She had no fear of interference by a foreign policeman, however deep he dug. His enquiries could only lead to the inevitable truth: the patient was her husband, her claim indisputable and she would have him returned to her.

"Charles! I must return to Reims! At once."

Chapter 27

"No, it's not a rout! Let's think of it as a strategic withdrawal, shall we? Like the retreat from Mons. We're going to regroup with Varimont and Bonnefoye, turn again and start on the march to the sea."

"If you say so. It feels like a defeat to me. And let's hope the hotel can offer us a billet when we turn up a day earlier than expected. What are we waiting for?"

They were sitting, luggage stowed away, engine running and bonnet towards the open gate.

"We're waiting for Charles-Auguste. He's bringing me something from the house. And here he comes."

Charles hurried over and placed a large brown envelope on the back seat. "No problems. She's brooding upstairs in her room. Tell Bonnefoye to return it to me here when he's done with it, will you? And it's farewell, Miss Dorcas—for the time being. I'll just say I've been delighted—*we've* been delighted that you were here. And I know we'll see you again. And, Joe? What can I say? You know you have my thanks and my apologies and, look here—it's not over by a long chalk yet...don't leave me worrying and wondering, will you? I'm always about early in the morning."

He turned away and slapped the car on its rump as Joe put it in gear and started off down the drive.

"Not saying goodbye to Georges, then?" Joe asked.

"We said our goodbyes in private," Dorcas said. "I hate all that fussing about round car doors."

"How is he bearing up?"

"Not well. But what would you expect? His main concern is for his mother. She's suffered a shattering blow today."

"I'm not sure I'd waste my sympathy on Aline Houdart," Joe commented.

"What? She comes across the murdered corpse of a man who is either her husband or her lover being uncovered by a foreign policeman who proceeds to hypnotize her into a confession of goodness knows what—of course she deserves sympathy. You're jolly lucky it was Georges who threw a torch at you—I'd have aimed a little higher."

"Dorcas, if you'll just stop fizzing with indignation for a moment, I'll explain about Aline Houdart. I'll tell you everything I know."

It took longer than he had expected and three villages had rolled past the windows before he'd finished but at least she didn't interrupt his account.

"But she's so charming and pretty and brave," she said finally. "And Georges thinks the world of her. The sort of woman anyone would want for their mother. Hard to believe. Have you thought you might have misinterpreted something she said in the dovecote, Joe? Head-to-head in that charged atmosphere...you know how easily you get carried away."

He refused to rise to this bait and let her mull it over in silence. At last she said: "And I wonder if it's occurred to you that the two women whose claims are still being considered have something in common? They both claimed to have fallen in love at first sight. Oh, dear! I've got a useful piece of advice for anyone who declares they've fallen in love at first sight: take a second look. I said that to Elsie when she decided to go off with the knife-grinder. She didn't listen. Disaster! People use it, you know, to excuse any amount of bad behaviour. 'Can't help losing my virginity . . . betraying my wife . . . bashing my old man on the head . . . we just fell in love, you see, at first sight.' Huh!"

"Heavens, girl! You'd give Romeo and Juliet a wigging, then?"

"Certainly would! I've no time for romantics like them. Think of the mayhem they caused."

Joe interpreted this nonsense as a warning not to enquire into her friendship with Georges and heeded it.

"Aren't you bursting with curiosity to see what's in Charles's envelope?" he said. "Take a look, if you like."

Dorcas scrambled over the seat to retrieve it. "Addressed to Bonnefoye. Photographs," she said. "Three. Of Clovis. Surely he must have seen these already?"

"Yes. But we've had further information. Don't forget the ears. A magnifying glass on these should come up with evidence one way or another."

"And Thibaud will be handed over to Aline? Is that what you want, Joe?"

"I'm here to find out the truth, Dorcas, and see that justice prevails. I'm not a fairy godmother, granting wishes to my favourites."

She looked sadly at the photograph of the small Georges on his father's knee. "You know that Georges is adamant that he should not return?"

"Yes. Charles said as much. And there are doubtless

complicated reasons for that. But I'm no psychiatrist, Dorcas. Nor are you. Leave it alone."

"And this framed one is a party of some sort?" she said, trying to make sense of the third photograph.

"Passing out of his year at St Cyr, according to Aline."

"Ah, yes. I can spot Clovis. He's here on the left, with his arms around two of his friends. It's funny, Joe, we've always seen him as a total solitary…no one to talk to even if he could talk. But here he's…well, a bit drunk, obviously… but matey, popular, supported. What wonderful young men! And now I suppose…"

"I'm afraid so. French cavalrymen didn't hang back," said Joe. "One only survived of that merry band, Aline says. Apart from Clovis, of course. And for the same sinister reason—held prisoner in some German hell-hole."

"Well, perhaps there's another contact there? Ah, yes. Of course. Now Bonnefoye can set to work to find him."

After a moment's thought she spoke again, tentatively. "Joe, you know what people do with these photographic records? So that they won't ever forget old so-and-so when they've grown decrepit and ga-ga? I've got a souvenir photo of my last class at the village school and I did it. They write the names on the back. Shall I have a look? It's only a cardboard frame stuck down at the edges."

She was already sliding a thumbnail along the join and Joe pulled into the side of the road, intrigued by the operation. Neatly she withdrew the original photograph and scanned the back.

"Yes! There's a name in pencil over the head of every one of these men! Now Clovis is on the bottom left…" She turned it over again and got her bearings. "So this would be him, the centre of the entwined group of three. The Musketeers! And look, Joe, it says 'Self.' Well, that's it! Your final proof, I'd have thought. No need to go hunting after the missing survivor."

Joe took the photograph from her and studied it. His hand began to shake.

"No. You're quite right, Dorcas. But there's one man on here we must chase after, to the grave if necessary. What the hell! Sorry. But this is really rather unsettling. You see the man on the extreme left—that's on Clovis's right? Musketeer number one? Dark-haired, dishevelled and devilish handsome? Now turn over and look at his name!"

Chapter 28

Bonnefoye was looking mischievous, Joe noticed with apprehension when he entered his office early on Monday morning.

"Sandilands! My poor fellow—what an unpleasant weekend you must have had! Unearthing bodies much better left lying, I hear. How tiring! Sit down, sit down! Alone today?" He enquired with warmth after Dorcas. "I won't send for coffee...Tell you what—I haven't had breakfast yet so why don't we go out into the square and have a *café complet* when we're done here? That suit you?"

"It certainly would," said Joe. "I dashed out breakfast-less too." Then, picking up on the word that had disturbed him in the Inspector's bland and friendly speech. "You *hear,* you say? From whom do you hear?"

"Madame Houdart herself telephoned to fill in the details about half an hour ago. She had some pretty disparaging things to say about the methods employed by the arm of the British Law. Bounder? Perfidious Anglo-Saxon? Tool of the Interpol Inquisition? Recognize yourself? She was calling for your head on a plate, I'm afraid, but don't worry! I squashed her complaints with ringing references to the Minister of the Interior, the Foreign Office...everything that occurred to me. I think I quietened her."

"She jolly well ought to keep quiet! Concealing a murder is, I presume, something of a crime here in France?"

"A murder? Would you say so? I understand the body to be that of a runaway, a wounded escaper from the battlefield. Dead of sabre wounds, I'm told."

"That's *her* story. Now listen to mine. And prepare yourself for some surprises."

Bonnefoye sighed and paid attention.

"I understand. And I accept your account of events, Sandilands," he said simply when Joe had finished. "But you know as well as I that there is no action I can reasonably take. Even if we allow that a murder was committed—and by Clovis Houdart—we'd have insurmountable difficulty in putting a case. We'd be laughed out of court—would that be the phrase?"

"I think Madame Houdart would approve it. You might even have heard her use something very similar," said Joe bitterly.

"We wouldn't actually get this as far as court. And the alleged murderer who committed this *crime passionnel*—which may even have been a case of self-defence—has officially been dead these nine years. If he is still alive, he's insane. And we aren't in the business of sending to the guillotine men of unproven identity who are not in possession of their senses. Forget it, Sandilands! Antibes calls."

"I agree. I'm not trying to persuade you to follow up this crime, Bonnefoye. I'm asking you to do whatever you can to prevent a *further* one."

He laid out his fears for Thibaud should he end up in the

dubious care of Aline Houdart. "Though how we would ever account to anyone for assigning the patient elsewhere—or nowhere at all, which I suppose is always an option—I have no idea. Since he *is* her husband, we'd have our work cut out," said Joe.

"Ah," said Bonnefoye, his initial spark of mischief rekindled, "this is the moment for a revelation of my own. I acted on the suggestion you left with me before you set off into the country. The fingerprinting? I had it done and the results sent off to our laboratory in Lyon by police messenger. They came back last night."

He pulled a file across his desk. "You may take this away and study it. You will be impressed," he promised. "You will admire the technical skills and the speed. You will tell of it in Scotland Yard when you return."

"Come on, man!" Joe smiled. "Put me out of my misery. The last page? What does it say?"

"Thibaud's fingerprints we already had on record. When a comparison was made it was discovered that there were thirteen distinct points of agreement... ample to declare an absolute identification. Page 16. Got it? And what all those bifurcations, arches, whorls and loops are spelling out is this: our Thibaud and Mademoiselle Mireille Desforges's soldier-lover are one and the same! The man who'd reached Chapter 52 of *War and Peace,* who sat drinking her brandy, who put his feet up at her hearth and stoked her fire is the patient in Dr Varimont's care."

"Good Lord!" said Joe faintly. "It was an outside chance, Bonnefoye. I wasn't certain that after all these years the prints would still be usable."

"We took the pipe and the book you mentioned but it was the dirty brandy glass that gave the best evidence. Sentimentally, she'd left them untouched just as she told you she had and on a surface like that a print is virtually permanent. So, if you think I'm treating your run-in with la Houdart a little lightly—well, you see, I can afford to. Her claim has suddenly begun to look very shaky. We're now down to one tick—Desforges—one question mark—Houdart—and two crosses."

He was pleased to see Joe's raised eyebrows. "We've been busy, Sandilands, while you've been off sampling *la vie de château*. I despatched two sergeants in opposite directions to the country. Smart lads! One extracted a confession from the Tellancourts and they have grudgingly retracted their claim. Though the old girl stuck to her story throughout. With those ingenuous saucer-like blue eyes of hers and her mourning clothes and lace-edged hankies, she very nearly put one over on my chap. She only caved in when he called her bluff and threatened to take a second look at the evidence buried in the churchyard. My other bloke, following instructions, grilled the grocer's wife, Langlois, closely followed by the local schoolmaster, Barbier. My instincts proved sound," he said with satisfaction.

"Blackmail?"

"Some naughtiness of that kind. Coercion perhaps? Madame Langlois has the goods—would you say?—on the schoolmaster. A nasty snakes' nest of low-level corruption came hissing into the daylight. And yes, I will be following it up. The man Barbier has been betraying his pedagogical trust for years. His time is up. And, Madame Langlois decided that her time had come to put certain information that she had to use: 'Support me in my claim or I'll tell the school authorities the stories the children have been circulating for decades.'"

Could it be so simple, in the end? Joe wondered. Did Thibaud's pipe and slippers beckon? Dorcas, at least, would be pleased. To say nothing of Mireille, so longing for her

Dominique to come home from his last campaign. No, of course it could not be so simple. Joe cleared his throat.

"Sorry, Bonnefoye, but we're not quite done yet. I'm about to throw another spanner into the works. I want you to take a look at these photographs we brought away from Septfontaines. In particular, I want you to study the man who's sitting on Clovis's right."

He waited while Bonnefoye turned the photograph this way and that, around and about, hissing with disbelief. "This is crazy!" he said eventually. "But—'Self' it says here on the back. This is surely Clovis Houdart? Attached ears and all. And he's the man Dr Varimont is holding at the sanatorium. Are we agreed on this much? Yes? But the man Mireille Desforges has identified as her lover, one Dominique de Villancourt, is actually sitting here in the photograph, next to Clovis—entwined with Clovis you might say—and, Sandilands, he's dark-haired and at this moment, very dead. Quite clearly he is not our mental patient."

"Yes. There are three of them, you see, three friends. The closest of friends. My niece jokingly called them the Musketeers."

"I see where you're going, Sandilands. 'One for all and all for one,' are you thinking? I am." He pursed his lips and looked tenderly at the photograph. "Didn't we all read Dumas at an impressionable age? So young! So gallant! Tell me, Sandilands, you were a soldier and must have been young once—would you have allowed your closest friend to make use of your identity to conceal his own in an affair of the heart? An affair played out rather too close to home for comfort?"

Joe smiled. "Oh, certainly. The least one could do for a friend. These men would have cheerfully given their lives for each other. Some probably did, I'd guess. What's the loan of a name in comparison?"

"And may I remind you of the motto of the cavalry—was it the dragoons or the cuirassiers? *Je secours mes chefs et mes frères d'armes.*"

"I come to the aid of my commanders and my brothers-in-arms. Hmm…"

"You remember I told you of an officer who survived a German cavalry ambush and spent the rest of the war in prison? The one who reported the dying actions of Dominique de Villancourt?" He tapped at a face on the photograph. "Here he is. This chap here. I remember his name. We have his address. I can contact him and ask for information on his other friend Clovis."

Joe sighed wearily. "Well, yes, you could. But it might be more informative if you were to contact someone quite else. I don't know about you, Bonnefoye, but I can tell you—I'm getting a bit fed up stirring around in all this sticky speculation, personal opinion, bad memory, good memory, downright lies. It's like snatching at moonbeams. You think you've got it and then the light shifts and your hand's empty. Let's get some verifiable, recorded-in-black-and-white factual information, shall we? The fingerprints were a start. Now I think I see how to conclude this."

"Who've you got in mind?"

"Someone rather prosaic—Houdart's bank manager. In Paris. Any favours you can call in to wring a little information out of him?"

After a sweaty half-hour on the telephone, threading his way through departments, alternately charming and threatening, Bonnefoye finally hung up the receiver with a smile of mild triumph. "He's agreed to give us what we want! He'll ring back in an hour. Sending someone up to the attic probably to dust off a file. At least he still does have the file. Had Houdart banked in Reims, it would have been destroyed. Now, we can't sit here waiting—let's nip out and have that well-earned breakfast, shall we?"

They got to their feet, grinned at each other and both began to speak at the same time: "Bonnefoye, had you thought…"

"Sandilands, shall I say it, or will you?"

"I have an old aunt who has a very annoying saying: 'There's an elephant in this room, is there not?' We're skirting around, pretending to ignore the huge truth that's staring us in the face."

Bonnefoye took his képi from a stand, put it on and adjusted it to his favoured rakish angle. "I think I saw the elephant first," he said confidently. "But have you realized how very much *worse* this makes everything? What we've got on our hands is a genuine tug of war, a life-or-death tug of war. And we have to decide which end of the rope we are heaving on, Sandilands."

Chapter 29

They ordered breakfast sitting on a café terrace in the sunshine while it was still cool enough to be comfortable. Crunching his way through his first croissant from the pile of still-warm rolls served in a napkin inside a silver basket, Bonnefoye stopped chewing, wiped his mouth and spoke to Joe in a low voice.

"I wonder if you've noticed...will be surprised to hear... that your niece is also taking breakfast at the Café de la Paix? And she's not alone. She is accompanied by a gentleman. Odd choice of escort, I'd have said. They're sitting four tables away, north-north-west."

Joe was alarmed and puzzled. He'd slipped a note under Dorcas's door which clearly said he'd left instructions for breakfast to be brought up to her in her room and she was to stay there until he returned. He risked a quick look over his shoulder in the direction indicated. Dorcas caught his eye and waved to him. He identified her escort at once and turned back to Bonnefoye with a relaxed smile.

"All's well. I know the gentleman. Nice chap. He's staying

at our hotel. He's a mayor from a small town in the Ardennes, I think he said. Poor fellow—I'd say he's on his last legs. He had a heart attack or something very like it just after dinner the other day. I suspect there's not much one can do for him. Don't worry, he's quite safe with Dorcas. The child has had a rather sparse and unsatisfactory family for the early years of her life and it's my theory that she goes about collecting relations. She picked up an older brother in Georges Houdart and now she's acquiring a grandfather figure, I'd say. They were both alone in the hotel—much better to have someone congenial to chat to over the *café au lait* in the sunshine. All the same, I don't think we'll ask them to join us."

"A mayor? What did you say his name was?" said Bonnefoye.

"I didn't. But he's called Didier Marmont and he's an old soldier."

The telephone call came, as promised, exactly an hour later and Joe was able to infer from Bonnefoye's responses that there had been results and the results were confirming their suspicions. After effusive thanks, Bonnefoye put down the receiver.

"There we have it!" he exclaimed. "A large amount of money was withdrawn from the account of Clovis Houdart in late August 1914. It was in the form of a cheque made out to one Dominique de Villancourt. Now we can't get at *his* banking details but what's the betting that this same sum of money made its way through agents and lawyers carrying the signature of de Villancourt and ended up paying for the purchase of a flat overlooking the Bois de Boulogne—it's about the right price for such a property in

1914. The legal papers which, er—" Bonnefoye flashed a disarming smile "—you may possibly not be aware that I had seen…"

"Mademoiselle Desforges, at least, would appear to be the epitome of honesty and forthrightness," said Joe. "She told me you had them."

"Indeed. These papers, as she avowed, bear his signature and this I have been able to authenticate. The same signature also appears on the subsequent transfer of the deeds to the grateful lady. A good friend! A man happy to lend his name to a bosom pal anxious to hide his amatory activities from family and acquaintances—activities carried on within a few miles of the home he was determined to protect? Time to say hello to your elephant?"

"I'm afraid so," said Joe. "Our Thibaud was a busy boy. Leading a life of danger on the battlefield and off it… But I'm thinking, Bonnefoye, that from what I've perceived of the French way of going on over the years—and I know you'll shoot me down if I'm wrong—keeping a mistress, in whatever state of luxury, is not held to be a cardinal sin or even anything out of the ordinary. Not a reason for all these expensive manoeuvrings, surely? And he had, from the start of the affair, told Mireille that he was a married man."

Bonnefoye nodded his agreement and waited to hear more.

"So why the rather desperate attempts at concealment? I think we're looking at this from the wrong perspective. I don't think Clovis was hiding his wife from his mistress. I think it was the other way around. Don't you think that perhaps Clovis was all too aware of the strength of his wife's emotional surges—her unpredictability? And was at pains to shield his lover from her," he added thoughtfully. "Having seen the lady at close quarters, I must say, I'd rather face a charge of Uhlans than an Aline Houdart who'd just discovered that her husband was madly in love with another woman, intending to leave her for a nobody—a little seamstress from Reims. Or even worse—intending to send her back to her parents in Paris and retain his son and his life at Septfontaines. I'm just surprised that he managed to get away with his throat uncut. On that occasion."

"But you tell me that Aline was herself conducting an affair…"

"The fact that she was betraying *him* would not weigh heavily with Aline. Charles-Auguste said it—'What Aline believes to be the truth becomes the truth.' He thinks his cousin may be a little… there may be a slight cerebral… not sure what the correct medical term would be…" Joe finished delicately.

"Crazy?" said Bonnefoye. "I had wondered! And if you were married to her, wouldn't you want a Mireille in your life? I've got to know Mademoiselle Desforges slightly in the course of this case and I have to say, Sandilands, that were she not so earthy, so worldly, so full of life and mischief, we'd have to say she was an angel."

He sighed a very Gallic sigh.

"But she's about to be a disappointed angel, I'm afraid," said Joe. "Clovis and Dominique are one and the same and there's no separating them. I suppose we could take a leaf out of King Solomon's book in the matter of assigning possession but I've always thought that a very chancy procedure. In law the man must be returned to his rightful home and the bosom of his family. You're going to have to make the decision, Bonnefoye. Sign the forms. Yours is the finger on the pen."

"Correction," said Bonnefoye. "*We'll* have to make the decision. I'm not bearing the weight of this alone. We will summon the good doctor to a conference and he as the medical authority in the case, you representing Interpol and I as the case officer, will come to a unanimous decision. This afternoon. This has gone on for quite long enough. We'll do this at the hospital. Can you attend, let's say after lunch at two o'clock?"

"I'll do that." Joe nodded. "So—we have an identity. The unknown soldier is unknown no longer. I wonder if the general public will remain enthralled by the story?"

"Perhaps—if we were to tell them the whole tale. But I shall give out a severely edited version. I don't know about you, Sandilands, but I got quite fond of the old bugger— Clovis, I suppose we should get used to saying. I'd like the rest of his semi-life to be as uncomplicated as possible. And I'll deliver a strongly worded warning about patient-care to la Houdart before she takes delivery, don't worry!"

"Poor old Thibaud," said Joe sadly. "I shall always think of him as Thibaud, I'm afraid."

Chapter 30

"I have the strongest misgivings about this. You may only come if you swear to stay in the background and not protest about the decisions taken. You know what you're like. This is official business. A man's life and future are at stake, to say nothing of three men's reputations—I won't have you sticking your oar in." He flicked open his napkin in a decisive manner.

"Very well, Joe. Of course, Joe. If you're going to be such a fusspot, I'd really rather not go at all. I'll stay behind and do a little souvenir shopping. And your appointment's for two o'clock?" Dorcas looked at her watch and frowned. "If we have a quick lunch we'll have time to pack up the car and get straight off afterwards and then we could be in Lyon by this evening."

He was pleased to be distracted by a practical arrangement.

"Never sure you're to be trusted. Going off on your own like that this morning! Marcus warned me to treat you like Carver Doone…"

"Who?"

"His pet ferret. Rabbiter. Half trained he was. Never lived to be *fully* trained. Nine times out of ten he'd do what was expected of him but on the tenth, he'd run away and go wherever the fancy took him. Gone for hours. One day, poor old Marcus was discovered shouting vainly down various rabbit holes one after another, ordering the villain to come out at once or else. Suddenly, there was the most awful scream and Marcus raised his head from the hole with Carver Doone attached by his fearsome little teeth to his nose. It led to a painful separation. Now, something light, I think you suggested... And while we're choosing, why don't you tell me what you were talking about so earnestly with old Didier?"

"He's a wonderful man. A soldier. Something of a Bolshevik, I'd have guessed. He was telling me about his daughter Paulette and her American husband. He's devoted to his family. He's got a baby grandson called John. Only six months old. He knows he's dying, Joe, and can talk about it as though he's just going on holiday. So matter of fact. I expect it was the truly awful time he had fighting on the Chemin des Dames that ruined his health." She thought for a moment and then went on: "Have you noticed, Joe, that throughout this case that name has kept coming up like a chorus in a song? Everywhere we turn it seems someone's whispering about...what would you say in English? The Road? Path? Of the Ladies? Which ladies? And which road?"

"The Ladies' Way," said Joe. "A pretty name for a blood-soaked piece of country. North-west of Reims. The ladies were the two aunts of Louis XVI—the one who was guillotined after the Revolution—and the way was their favourite coach-ride along a high bluff overlooking low-lying plains to north and south. A fearsome strategical position since the Stone Age. Any army wanting to defend Paris has to hold that height.

"And—chorus, you say!" Joe shivered. "Have you ever heard it, Dorcas, the song that came out of that battle? The song of Craonne? The song of the mutineers? It has the most haunting of choruses."

"I don't know it." She looked around her. "We're out of earshot and we're English eccentrics anyway—why don't you sing it? You can always stop if the waiter comes."

"I warn you—I rarely manage to get to the end of it, it's so sad," he said, and, self-consciously, but confident of his baritone voice, Joe leaned over the table and began to sing.

> Adieu la vie, adieu l'amour,
> Adieu toutes les femmes,
> C'est bien fini, c'est pour toujours,
> De cette guerre infâme.
> C'est à Craonne, sur le plateau,
> Qu'on doit laisser sa peau.
> Car nous sommes tous condamnés,
> Nous sommes les sacrifiés.

Unusually, Joe managed to get through the lilting song dry-eyed but hurriedly passed his handkerchief to Dorcas.

"Sing it again slowly and I'll translate as you go, if I can keep up.

"'Goodbye to life, goodbye to love and goodbye to all women...It's all over—for ever, this terrible war...It's up there in Craonne, on the plateau, where we must all leave our skins?...Die, does it mean?...For we are all condemned. We're all to be sacrificed.' They don't sound like—what did you say?—mutineers, Joe. They're saying goodbye, they know they're going to lose their lives. It's far too sad, too hopeless to be a song of revolt."

"It was a very strange revolt. And yet the army authorities were so afraid of the power of the song to move a whole army, a whole people perhaps, that they banned it and offered a huge reward to whichever soldier would turn in the man responsible for writing it. And, do you know, Dorcas, the money went unclaimed. No one betrayed the songwriter. And they all went on singing it."

"I've never heard of this. But then I don't know much about the war."

"No one knows very much about this part of it. Even the English army fighting on the flank were not aware that the French had downed tools and declared they'd soldier no more. And yet that's not exactly right—they never surrendered. They were not traitors. They held the line but declared that they would not advance another inch until peace had been declared. They were holding out for a settlement."

"You say the English didn't know about it? Did the Germans find out?"

"Those of us in British Intelligence who knew conspired with the French to keep the lid firmly on. And—goodness knows how—it worked. The German trenches were only a few yards away from the French front line in places and no rumour reached them." He shuddered. "One man caught in no man's land and made to talk, one man deciding to go over to the enemy, and it would have all been over for us. They would have called up forces from the east and poured everything they had on to the weakened French lines and broken through."

"Poor Didier. And poor Clovis. He was up there too, wasn't he?"

"I believe he was. He killed Edward and then rode off into the night and back into battle as far as we know, expecting to leave his hide up there on the plateau with all the other sacrificial victims."

"I wonder what happened to the rebels? Do you know, Joe?"

"I know. It's very unpleasant and I'd really rather not talk about it, Dorcas. Not for your sake—for mine. Now—omelette do you? Or would you prefer steak-frites?"

Varimont, Bonnefoye and Sandilands sat down together around the table in the doctor's office as the hospital bell sounded two o'clock. Bonnefoye produced the papers to be signed and succinctly set out the case for assigning custody of Thibaud to Aline Houdart.

Joe intervened at this point to voice his concerns about the welfare of the patient if such action were followed, and this was seriously considered by Varimont, who questioned and evaluated his information. "This is indeed a cause for concern as Sandilands says, Bonnefoye," said the doctor. "Look here—there is a third way of doing this which perhaps in the light of Sandilands's insights we ought to consider. Don't assign him to anyone. I'm perfectly willing to hang on to him here if, truly, no better situation is available to him but—well, you've seen it. It's not ideal. I am, however, very interested in Thibaud and his condition—and neurasthenia of war as it affects other unfortunates—and I'm making something of a study of these cases. It would be interesting to see how he reacts if transplanted into neutral surroundings.

"Look—I would be quite prepared to tell the press and anyone else who's interested that his identity remains unproven and he is being lodged with a third party, nominally under the control of the hospital, so that our experiments may continue and observations be made. Should this type of care prove successful the government will be only too pleased. Too many such cases clogging up the public health system."

"It's a thought," said Joe. "Find and register a caring townsperson willing to liaise with the hospital."

"He's Aline's husband," objected Bonnefoye. "He's Clovis Houdart. We can't get around that. We have the widow's identification, which I would now declare to be incontrovertible."

"But an identification which is stoutly questioned, let's not forget, by his son and his cousin," the doctor objected. Then, startled, he looked at his watch and exclaimed: "Oh, great heavens! I have to tell you—I have a further appointment this afternoon. No, don't be concerned—we won't be interrupted. I'm intending to run it alongside this one. I had a most insistent call from a witness the other day. A man who claims to know Thibaud. An old army colleague. He's only just recently come across the photograph apparently but is one hundred per cent certain—aren't they all?—that he knows our man. As he was able to give me a name and rank—Clovis Houdart, Lieutenant Colonel—I thought it might be worth giving him a crack at it, bit of extra weight in the scales, one way or another. I wouldn't see him right away—Thibaud has been disturbed by all the comings and goings and I thought I'd give him a weekend off. But now—he's due in ten minutes' time—we could all go with him to Thibaud's room and chalk up one more positive identification. Or not. You never know!"

* * *

Joe could not be certain that Didier Marmont was pleased to see him. The one short flash of uncertainty was so soon followed by a warm and gracious recognition that he thought he might be wrong. He had clearly not been expecting a reception by two policemen as well as the doctor but took the introductions in his stride.

Approaching Thibaud's cell he showed signs of nervousness but made a joke and entered following Varimont.

Eyes turned immediately on Thibaud. He was sitting, exactly as before, forlorn, on the edge of his bed, staring into the wall. His hair had been freshly washed and trimmed and he was looking smart, slender and almost waif-like in white pullover and black cord trousers. Joe's eyes, however, were fixed on Didier. He wanted to catch his first reaction. What was he hoping for at this late stage? A derisory "What's this? No—that's never Clovis Houdart!" Yes, he could not deny that was his hope.

But Didier knew the man at once. His eyes widened, he caught his breath. He strolled over to Thibaud and looked carefully into his face. Putting out a finger, he gently traced the line of Thibaud's broken jaw and nodded.

He turned to the assembled company. "This is Clovis Houdart. Lieutenant Colonel Houdart of the Fifth Army, last encountered serving under General Pétain. Summer of 1917. Soissons-Auberive sector."

"You served in the same company?" Joe asked.

"I was just a corporal, called up as a reservist. My age, you know. By that stage they were using even old wrecks like me. There were three generations shoulder-to-shoulder in the trenches."

"But it wasn't the first time you'd soldiered?"

"No, I fought at Sedan. Experience was a help, in fact. I tried my best to calm the troops. Father-figure, you know.

'Think this is bad, lads? You should have seen . . .' You know the sort of thing."

"Soissons, you say?" Joe asked quietly. "You were caught up in the Mutiny?"

Bonnefoye and Varimont exchanged looks.

"I know—I'm not supposed to know anything about that," said Joe. "But I do. I was in Military Intelligence."

"Then you'll know how low morale had sunk by April of '17?" Marmont was pleased not to be called on for an explanation. "I was given a squad of boys, fresh meat, straight off the farm. One day in the front line was enough to send them mad. They couldn't understand why we'd suffered such an assault, accepted such a stalemate for three years. They were fighting from the trenches their dead predecessors had dug and occupied three years before. Not an inch had been gained and the trench walls were revetted with the bones of French and German alike. General Nivelle had built up our hopes. One last push, he'd said. One more concentrated attack and we'll carry the day. We went into it with spirit but months on we were bogged down, thousands dying every day. Food disgusting when we had any. No leave. Weeks sometimes in the front line with no reprieve. My lads were given suicidal orders to go over the top. Few ever came back.

"But one lad kept coming back. Grégoire, his name was. Seemed to bear a charmed life. You see that every so often. Must have come in for all the luck allocated to his family— his brothers had all copped it. His parents were dead. No family left. I took him under my wing. Tried to advise him when he went over to the rebels. He lived long enough to get a short leave in Paris. The men were bombarded at the stations by pacifists. Bolsheviks? Patriots? I still don't know. But Grégoire and others like him returned and spread the word. Rebellion was raging through the troops. Unpopular officers were stoned...disappeared quietly in the night... Trains were commandeered and driven to Paris... Desertions increased...Forty thousand men grounded their muskets. The lads said they'd man the trenches, hold the line, but they wouldn't attempt to go forward another inch until they got what they wanted: peace. Someone was going to have to sign a treaty. I'll never know why we weren't instantly overrun by the Germans. But they never seemed to catch on to what was happening in front of their noses."

Joe's voice broke into his monologue, an interested fellow soldier going over a battle plan. "Might have something to do with the discreet though disastrous attempt by the British top brass to distract them from the French lines. They knew the dangers of the Soissons-Craonne sector. We made a feint—a push to draw the German forces away from the French and on to ourselves. And our effort to help out resulted in the appalling losses of the third battle of Ypres. You may know it as Passchendaele. We were suffering along-side you, Didier."

Had he heard? The content of Joe's short speech would normally have been provocative enough to stoke a whole evening's conversation and argument. But Joe's tone seemed to calm him. Marmont turned, his attention caught, and spoke directly to him, needing to explain himself, a link es-tablished with this friendly stranger who seemed to under-stand him. An elderly doctor and a young policeman were a less acceptable audience, it seemed, than a man who had survived Ypres. "Don't blame them. They weren't traitors! Poor buggers just wanted the noise to stop, to be able to go home. They wanted the war over by the fastest means. They had honour. They loved their country. They still had within them an unquenched spark of independence and the spark flared into something uncontrollable up on that ridge near Craonne.

"And this is where our hero comes into the story." He indicated Thibaud who had heard not a word. "I expect you wonder why on earth I'm rambling on, wearying you with my memories. Where I'm going with this."

"Nowhere good," thought Joe, but he assumed an attitude of entranced listener. Not difficult as he was fascinated to hear more of Clovis from someone who had known him on the battlefield. Instinctively, he moved forward a few paces, steady and unthreatening, positioning himself in front of Varimont and Bonnefoye, focusing all Marmont's attention on himself.

"Top brass kept the lid on but it couldn't last. Nivelle was sacked and Pétain was brought in to clear up the mess. Better food, more leave and promises got the men back at it again. But there was a stick as well as a carrot in this equation. We were going to be made to pay…"

Joe felt an icy trickle of foreboding along his spine.

"An example had to be made. Thousands of mutineers were arrested and court-martialled. Over twenty thousand were found guilty. Whole companies, every man jack of 'em. Four hundred were condemned to death. Fifty were actually executed. They say fifty…" He shrugged his shoulders. "And the rest! Nobody ever declared the retributions carried out in fields and ditches. And the red-tabs who organized all this—not worth our spit! *Becs de puces! Peaux de fesses!*" The *poilu*'s crude curses burst from him. "They made us kill our own men using firing squads made up of their fellows. '*Pour encourager les autres!*' they said. '*Pour l'exemple!*'

"They drew lots to decide who would be punished! Can you imagine that? Can you? Lining up and shuffling forward to take your life or your death from a tin cup! Funny though—I don't know if many noticed, but the lads who were picked out for execution had something in common. They didn't count for much with anybody. Lads with no family to make a fuss about their execution afterwards. Lads like my Grégoire."

Joe didn't want to hear any more but they all listened on in awful fascination.

"I was put in charge of the squad detailed to execute him. He took it bravely . . . wouldn't have expected anything else. I sat with him all night holding his hand and praying before that dawn. I'd done everything. Pleaded with the commanding officer. Offered a substitute . . . Deaf ears. 'Orders . . . orders . . . nothing we can do . . .' You've heard it.

"We fired. Of course, we all shot wide. I damn nearly swung round and put my bullet through the commanding officer who was officiating. Wish I had. Grégoire didn't drop. He was wounded in the shoulder but not dead. And then the CO stepped forward, cursing us, and drew his pistol. It was routine. It was expected. But it still churns my guts. The swine put it to Grégoire's head and shot him.

"It was a pistol just like this."

Marmont pulled a Lebel service revolver from his pocket, took a step towards Thibaud and held the gun to his temple.

"And this was the officer."

They waited, helplessly, for the shot, the *coup de grâce* so long anticipated.

Joe didn't think Marmont was savouring the moment—there was no triumph or gleam of vengeance in the man's face, nothing but disgust, loathing and pain. "I lost my rag. I rushed him and clobbered him with my rifle butt. Glad to see he bears the scars. Hope it hurt like hell. I spent the rest of the war in a punishment squad. Shouldn't have survived.

And I thought this bugger must be dead. Lieutenant Colonel Houdart. And then I saw his photograph in a newspaper a week ago.

"There are two bullets in here. The first's for him and the second's for me. Gentlemen that you are, I count on you to do the decent thing and just give me time to turn the gun on myself, will you?"

They stared, unbelieving, at Clovis Houdart's expressionless face, chlorine pale, a fragile thing against the black gun barrel. A vein throbbed in the temple and Joe wondered for how many more beats it would pulse with life. Each man knew that there was a soldier's steady hand on the pistol, a determined finger on the trigger. The skull would shatter before a move could be made towards him.

Into the silence Joe's voice spoke, light and conversational. "If that's really what you want, then I'm sure we can do as you wish. And you will go, knowing you have our sympathy and our understanding because, Didier, we've heard your story. And these tears running embarrassingly down my face in an unmanly way are for Grégoire and all the other poor sods who suffered."

For a second Marmont's eyes flicked sideways to Joe. Joe pressed on: "But isn't there another name we should be hearing? John—your grandson, John! How old is he? Six months? John." He repeated the name with deliberation. "He too plays a part in all this."

Marmont directed another look at him in dawning surprise. "Grégoire," Joe said again respectfully, acknowledging with a nod of the head the presence of the dead soldier in the room as an honoured guest, "Grégoire is remembered. He stands with us. For as long as you are with us to tell us his story. But Grégoire is the past. And John is the future. John will never hear your words of suffering—of explanation.

What will he grow up knowing of his grandfather? That he was a brave soldier who gave his all for his native land, who survived against overwhelming odds to hold him in his arms and tell him stories, or—that he is a man never spoken of in the family? A man surrounded by silence and mystery until one day someone tells him his grandfather murdered a defenceless lunatic and then turned the gun on himself. Will he understand, do you think?

"Look at your target. Take a good look at him. There's nothing there, Didier. You might just as well fire your bullet into that pillow. Don't sacrifice your honour, your years of suffering, your grandson's memory of you, for this empty shell. Give me the gun. And that's an order, mate! And, Didier, let's make it the last order you ever take from an officer. From an officer who's listened, understood and suffered alongside."

Marmont made no move to lower the gun but his eyes were looking from Clovis to Joe and back again.

The first sign of indecision.

Encouraged, Joe spoke again, taking his time. "Look—in the circumstances, I'm supposing you haven't made any plans for the rest of the day? Well, I have, but I've decided to put off my departure today to take you out to dinner. My niece, on whom you seem to have made quite an impression, would insist. This calls for a bottle of the best. Not champagne perhaps but a Château Latour. And here's a joke—we'll put it on the expense account of the British War Office! Mean buggers! I'll tell them it was drunk to celebrate two lives saved. Yes, a Latour. I'm sure they'll have something good to eat with it?"

Confidently, almost casually, Joe started to cross the room.

He reeled back as the gun crashed out once and then again, deafening in that small space. Bonnefoye threw himself to the ground, drawing his pistol as he dropped. Varimont cursed loudly. Joe, shocked, found himself unable to move forward. He began to cough and sneeze and then burst into nervous laughter as he flapped at the snowstorm of feathers descending on all their heads.

The old man stayed for a moment, frozen, staring at the unseeing Thibaud. The officer's face was only inches from the blackened pillow which had taken the blast but he registered no emotion. Marmont shook his head and looked at his gun, uncomprehending. But Joe understood. Understood that the gap between the height of emotion to which the old soldier had hauled himself and the depths of bathos to which he knew he must plunge could only be bridged by an explosive reaction. The two bullets were always going to tear their lethal way down the barrel and Joe thanked God that Didier had, in the end, had the strength to divert them by a few inches.

He handed his smoking revolver to Joe and slumped in exhaustion as the doctor hurried forward, clucking with concern and reaching for his pulse.

"We must try not to bore her with too many old soldiers' stories, then," Didier grated out at last, and added, with a wheezing grimace, "as we enjoy our . . . ah . . . what would you say to *civet de lièvre à la bordelaise*? Or they had a *bisque de palombes aux marrons* on the menu for today, I noticed." He shook for a moment with silent laughter. "Can't say I studied today's menu at length. Wasn't expecting to eat again."

"The jugged hare would be perfect," said Joe. "I don't think I could be tempted by wood pigeon, even accompanied by chestnuts."

* * *

The conference broke up at four o'clock. Two hours which seemed like a lifetime to Joe. And the course of two lives had been decided in that time. Didier was still alive and a free man, Bonnefoye having gallantly offered to look the other way. "What's the charge?" he'd shrugged. "Killing a pillow? I'd be a laughingstock!" And Thibaud's identity was established beyond any possible doubt.

His wife had known it all along. He was Clovis Houdart.

And Mireille Desforges had known her man. But he was a phantom. A perhaps loving, but certainly deceitful, phantom.

"So, let me check this," said Bonnefoye. "One last time—you are content with this, Varimont? We're taking a considerable chance, I acknowledge that, and if there are repercussions, I'm afraid you will be the first in the firing line of public opinion. I am a French police inspector—I can extricate myself from anything. No, don't ask! Sandilands will have taken French leave—*English* leave as we would say—and be well distanced from any enemy action and you, the professional in all this, and I have to say the instigator, the prodder of wasps' nests, will bear the brunt of it. And quite right too! It's a bit unconventional what we propose and it could all go very wrong."

"I'm only too conscious of that," said Varimont. "Which is why I am insisting on the inclusion in the report of so many recommendations, so many clauses. I hope I make it perfectly clear that, in these circumstances, for which I see no precedent, it is essential that no doors be closed. I have promised further reports and reviews at yearly intervals. Everyone likes that. No French official will agree to anything that is likely to blow up in his face. This way he can always find someone else to blame. Most important: a close monitoring of the patient and the nurse will be a condition written into the contract."

He paused long enough to receive a nod of assent and a sigh of relief from each of his companions and took out his fountain pen. "Well, if we're all agreed, then," said Bonnefoye, "we can sign this recommendation and get it off to the Minister. The wheels of government moving as they do, and some of the conditions being a little out of the ordinary, it will be a few weeks before any action is taken as a result but I think we can say this is one soldier who'll most likely be home for Christmas."

Joe prayed they had come to the right decision.

Chapter 31

October 1926

"Firing party, present arms!
"Slope arms!
"Volleys!"
From the graveside three fusillades were fired skywards in perfect unison to the vociferous astonishment of the neighbouring rookery. As the noise rolled away, a bugler of the Royal Fusiliers began to sound the Last Post. Joe, standing to attention, flanked on one side by Brigadier Sir Douglas Redmayne and on the other by Colonel Thorndon, listened to the piercing strains and felt his soul snatched up by the music and transported, solitary, to a distant place. The three men, handsome in dress uniform, saluted as one as the oak coffin began its gentle descent into the grave. Edward's father stepped forward and scattered a spadeful of rich Sussex earth on to the coffin, then stood back.

Edward's mother, frail, but straight and determined, approached and threw in a prayer book and, with a swift apologetic glance at her husband, added a small brown toy dog. The firing party marched off and the ranks of mourners broke up and began to mingle, offering each other comforting remarks. Mrs Thorndon made straight for Joe and placed a gloved hand on his sleeve.

"Commander! I'm so pleased you could get here in time. We wanted to thank you for bringing the boy home. Douglas has told us of your heroic efforts, tracking him down to the Marne and digging about in the battlefield to find him and restore him to us. And to think we had imagined that the War Office had given up on our case! We should have had more faith in the Military!"

She directed a sweet, smiling apology at the Brigadier.

Sir Douglas bowed in silent acknowledgement and fixed his eyes thoughtfully on a flock of migrating swifts gathering overhead.

Mrs Thorndon looked around the quiet village graveyard, the only sounds the melancholy autumn fluting of the birds and the occasional damp plop of a falling leaf. The Sussex beeches surrounding the graveyard were aflame in a haze of red-gold, the grass still a lively green.

"We would have been happy enough to leave him with his fellows in a French cemetery—it would certainly have been less complicated and less time-consuming, and they care for our boys so beautifully but…oh, Douglas, do you blame us? I know we've demanded so much of your attention… Do you think we are unbearably fussy to want him back here with us?"

"Not at all, Emily. May all the brave lost souls have the luck to find their way home! I think every soldier deserves to be laid to rest in his native churchyard," was the hearty reply. Followed immediately by: "Where it's possible, of course."

As she drifted away Joe addressed a comment sideways to Sir Douglas. "I'll be presenting my bill for services rendered, then, sir?"

"Bill? What bill?"

Joe was pleased to have startled him. "It's a new thing. French entrepreneurial spirit. You have to admire them! They charge by the kilometre for retrieving a body from the battlefield and returning it. At the going rate you owe me... er...with conversion from kilometres and francs...fifty pounds."

Redmayne grinned. "Take that in champagne, will you, Sandilands? Eliminates the paperwork."

"Maman, I've brought you some camomile tea," said Georges Houdart brightly. "Very calming! Just what you need!"

He carried the tray over to Aline, who was sitting in a state of excited agitation by the window of the morning room from where she had a clear view down the drive. The beech trees were still glowing pale gold in the early October sunshine and scarcely a leaf had fallen to mar the neatness of the gravel.

"Thank you, darling. Oh, and I see you've brought the last of the roses," she said, gently stroking the rusting petal of one of the few remaining blooms to be found in the garden. "How clever of you to remember! These are his favourites! Stay and have some tea with me, will you, while I watch. Oh, and Georges—call on one of the men to open the gate. They've left it closed and I don't want the unwelcoming sight of a closed gate to be the first thing to greet him when he arrives."

"Yes, of course, Maman."

Wearily Georges rang the bell.

"Tell me—did Charles-Auguste remember to bring up a couple of bottles of the '13 vintage?"

"He did, Maman."

Her eyes had been drawn back to the gate and the road to Reims beyond. "And what are we to have for supper tonight, do you know? ... Calves' liver? Are you sure of that? No! No! That will not do! He simply detests liver! You must go and speak to Cook and ask what on earth she thinks she's about."

"Are you quite certain he doesn't like liver, Maman? I thought he did?"

"He hates it. But he adores game. It's the hunting season. Surely a fine shot like you, Georges, can keep the kitchen supplied? You must hurry off and see what you can find. A rabbit will do if you can get nothing else."

"Maman," said Georges tentatively, "you can't go on sitting here, waiting and watching. You're making yourself ill. You're making *us* ill! Uncle Charles is worried witless."

"Of course I shall wait! What else can I do? He's on his way! He's coming!"

"I'm not quite certain, Maman..." Georges spoke hesitantly, anxious to avoid bringing down one of her increasingly frequent screaming tirades on his head, "who exactly you are expecting to come up the drive?"

He hastily moved the hot teapot out of her reach and drew back. She did not scream and stamp at the mild challenge and hurl a cup at him as he'd come to expect over the weeks but turned to him, eyes wide with astonishment at the question, and smiled one of her old, loving smiles.

"But—Edward, of course! Georges, darling, you haven't forgotten Edward?"

Whiskers twitching with anger, the cat shot out of the kitchen the moment the door opened to release him, making clear his displeasure at being shut up in there for a

whole morning. A morning when things had been happening in the house. Things he ought to have been a party
to. Comings and goings, strange smells and sounds and
currents of air. A disruption of his routine.

Holding his tail stiffly to indicate an extreme degree of
pique, he stalked down the corridor and went into the parlour, heading for his chair.

He caught sight and smell of the interloper from the
doorway and went to stand, fur on end, directly in front of
the man lolling at ease in the armchair which had been
empty for nine years.

He waited for a very long moment, assessing the situation,
and then decided on his action. He leapt up on to the man's
knee, eyes narrowed, demanding and holding his gaze, hissing with rage, and one paw lashed out, claws exposed, to tear
at the man's flesh. The sudden pain and the trickle of blood
down the back of his hand drew a startled cry. The cat
paused briefly, then, judging the reaction he'd provoked adequate, he turned around several times, kneading the man's
thighs with unsheathed claws, and finally settled down on
his lap. He began a rasping and unpractised purring.

"There! That'll teach you to stay away for years on end!
What you've just undergone is the traditional feline punish-
ment for going absent without leave. And well deserved too!
I do believe Louis has missed you more than I have...
Oh...!"

The light voice from the doorway, determinedly cheerful,
even matronly, was cut short, stopped by emotion. A tray of
tea things slid to the floor.

His hand had gone out to ruffle the cat's fur in a familiar
gesture. The other reached out to the table at his side to pick
up his pipe. Thibaud looked up, focused on the anxious face
in the doorway and smiled a smile worth waiting for.

Author's note

If, having finished this book, which is—let me make it plain—a work of fiction, any reader would like to find out more about the Great War as it was fought in the hills of Champagne, there are many excellent books available. The following short list contains those I have found most inspirational as I trailed after Joe Sandilands from London to Reims.

Liaison 1914, Edward Spears. Eyre and Spottiswoode, 1930. Reprinted Cassell and Co., London, 2000.
Major-General Sir Edward Spears was a young Lieutenant of Hussars when he was sent to the front at the very start of the war. He became a liaison officer working with the BEF and the French Fifth Army. His meticulous eyewitness accounts are dramatic, humorous and moving.

Tommy, Richard Holmes. Harper Perennial, London, 2004. A brilliant account blending narrative and personal testimony. Contains all you never knew you didn't know about the Great War. The introduction is an education in itself.

The Fifth in the Great War, Brigadier H. R. Sandilands. St George's Press, Dover, 1938.
Understated, crisp account of the war fought by the Northumberland Fusiliers. Excellent maps.

The Living Unknown Soldier, Jean-Yves Le Naour. Arrow, London, 2006.
The fascinating—and true—story of a genuine unknown soldier, an amnesiac, late-release prisoner of war. A compelling and thought-provoking story which reads like a thriller.

About the Author

Barbara Cleverly is the author of nine novels of historical suspense, including *The Damascened Blade*, winner of the CWA Ellis Peters Historical Dagger Award, *The Last Kashmiri Rose*, *Ragtime in Simla*, *The Palace Tiger*, *The Bee's Kiss*, *Tug of War*, *An Old Magic*, and *The Tomb of Zeus*. She lives in Cambridge, England, where she is at work on the newest Joe Sandilands novel, *Folly du Jour*.

If you enjoyed Barbara Cleverly's TUG OF WAR, you won't want to miss any of the electrifying novels in the award-winning Joe Sandilands series or Cleverly's newest series featuring Laetitia Talbot. Look for them at your favorite bookseller.

And read on for an exciting early look at the newest Laetitia Talbot mystery, BRIGHT HAIR ABOUT THE BONE, coming from Delta in 2008.

Bright Hair About the Bone

by Barbara Cleverly

On sale October 28, 2008

Bright Hair About the Bone

on sale October 2008

Prologue

Burgundy, France

The priest smoothed down his white robe and prepared to make his entrance into the Village Hall. Fastidi-
ously, he twitched into place his carefully chosen girdle—a
narrow length of cloth sewn for him by the ladies of this
village. They would recognise it and welcome the discreet
compliment to them. The door swung open and he caught
the buzz of many voices, a whiff of wood smoke and the
scent of home cooking. Bracing himself for the heat and
hysteria generated by an overcrowded room full of emotional people, he turned, a few steps short of the door, and
looked back over the countryside.

He'd known better days for a funeral.

The summer day was still flooding this side of the valley
with mellow light, quite out of keeping with the solemn
occasion which demanded his presence inside that dark
beehive behind him. He stole a few moments, opening his
senses to Nature, saying his own silent farewell to the lady
he had loved, admired, and—on occasion—feared. It was un-
fitting that such a woman should be consigned to her grave,

mourned by humankind, on a day when all of Nature was smiling and fertile.

The priest was a country boy by birth; though schooling and theological college had taken him away from these hills for many years, he had never ceased to read the land with an experienced eye. And the scene he was now contemplating enchanted him. Had he ever seen orchards so heavy with fruit, meadows and pens so full of healthy young animals? The late afternoon sun was slanting over the cornfields, gilding them with an illusion of ripeness. He examined the ear of corn he'd plucked absentmindedly on his way through the village and was surprised to find he was still holding. Green and hard. Another week or so, he calculated, before they would hear the cry of "Harvest home!" along the valley.

And yet, he would expect this farming community to be growing daily more active, more involved with the preparations for the heavy work and its reward—the week of feasting and celebrations, the highlight of the year. This ill-timed death must surely have broken the rhythm. The funeral and the following wake would take up three days, and then everyone would be back at work in the fields according to schedule, though no doubt with headaches all round if he correctly remembered the strength of the local beer. But once the carousing was over, it was the loss of confidence that this lady's passing would impose on the local people that concerned him. Simple, superstitious, and trusting, they found themselves without warning prematurely bereft and he feared for them.

"Oh, My Lady," he muttered, "how long did I know you? Twenty years? And how often have I known you to mistime a single word or action? Never. How am I to make sense of this death—early and unseasonal?" He smiled sadly. How much more appropriate if she had died in November, at the beginning of their year. *Earth to earth ... From decay comes renewal...The seed is Goodness...the conception: Silence...* In winter, the sermon would have come readily to his lips and the congregation would have understood and been reassured. The rhythm of the seasons would have been unbroken.

But here he stood, as unready as the wheat in his hand, casting about for a message. He was certain that there would be purpose even in her dying, and if he could open his mind he would see it.

And then he smiled. This forthcoming abundance was her gift and would be her memorial. Yes, that's how he would present it in his oration...something on the lines of how *fitting* it was that her mortal remains should return to the womb of earth at the very moment when that which she had cared for was full of the promise of fecundity. And then he would send up a silent prayer that summer storms should not come along and ruin the harvest...making him look a fool.

No one can be saved until she is born again... Yes, it would be wise to finish on a triumphant note: *She is not dead but lives...* But in whom? It would be up to him to discover. He would be watchful. Pose a few well-aimed questions. It was likely that she had handed down her gifts already.

He turned and approached the door of the Hall, where a gaggle of children had been set to watch for his arrival. Ducking his head under the lintel, he entered and pulled himself back up to his impressive six feet four inches, standing, ceremonial staff in hand, scanning the crowded room with a searching eye. He noted, without surprise or offence, the subtle movement of the now silent crowd away from him. Who, of these countrymen and women, would be comfortable to be caught standing close to a priest of his rank? The ones prepared to meet his gaze held it for a proud moment before looking deferentially away. A good sign. If all was to go well they would have to talk to him. He needed their information. Most of them, men and women, were clutching tankards of ale; a few more hours of steady drinking would loosen tongues.

But his immediate need was to break through the barrier created by his awe-inspiring presence. He looked around for a child and chose, from among the reception committee by the door, the smallest one, inquisitive enough to be caught staring. He beckoned him forward. Bravely but slowly the child approached. "Take my staff, would you, young man," the priest asked pleasantly. The child took it as though it might turn into a snake between his hands. He held its long length awkwardly and failed to make an allowance for the weight of the carved head, overbalancing and scurrying to gain control. For a few agonised seconds he struggled with the implement, dragging it along the floor like a hobby-horse, and, finally, was helped by an older girl who descended on him with all the clucking concern of a brown hen, to prop it up against the wall.

The priest's shout of indulgent laughter at the performance had its calculated effect: it was echoed instantly by the crowd. "You have learned a valuable lesson in life, young man," said the priest to his red-faced helper. "In a tight spot, always enlist the aid of a big, capable girl."

The ice broken, a woman of the village approached, bringing him a drink. Not the mug of ale he yearned for, but a silver goblet filled with red wine. He thanked her warmly and, as she stood awaiting his response, he swirled the wine gently, admiring its rich colour and bouquet before tasting it. He sipped again, drawing out the moment, then sighed. "I believe this may be the best wine I have ever drunk! Italian? I would guess from Etruria, perhaps?"

She giggled with pleasure, nodded, and hurried away.

The Mayor moved forward to greet him. "My Lord

Aeduan, may I say how honoured we are that…er…your lordship should…"

The priest turned toward him benignly and cut through his hesitations. "She was an incomparable lady and if I may mark her passing by my presence, then the honour is mine. I see you've got all the bigwigs of the diocese under your roof, and I passed hundreds of folk gathering in the square. The arrangements are all made, I trust?"

"Certainly. The bier is prepared and will start on a signal. As you requested, our own village priest is here, ready to assist with the practicalities and accompany you on the journey to the grave. Bran!" The Mayor beckoned to a slender young man in linen robes, whose belt was heavily hung with ceremonial gear.

Aeduan tried not to stare at his assistant, though the bleached hair, fashionably spiked upwards over his head, was clearly intended to mark him out for attention. Having all the charm of an albino hedgehog, Aeduan decided, amused, but he looked clever.

"The equipment you called for is to hand, my lord," Bran murmured in a quietly efficient tone. "Though there'll be little enough for me to do, you'll find, sir. She requested no animals at the burial. The last convention she'll overturn? Of course…if you should wish to counter that order, sir…? I'm sure we could provide even at this late stage…No? Ah, well…the hearse will be drawn by six lads of the village…Oh, there is an exception…She asked particularly that her dog be allowed to accompany her. He's over there." He pointed towards a group of three young girls sitting together by the hearth. The two older ones, arms locked together for comfort, were whispering to each other, subdued; though heavy-eyed with grief, their blonde beauty drew everyone's gaze. The youngest girl, barely ten, was small and dark and absorbed by her own thoughts. As he watched, she put out a hand to stroke the grey-coated hound lying across her feet. A handsome dog. What else? Aurinia had known her horses and her dogs. This one, alert and fierce-looking, was of a breed he'd admired across the sea in Britain. They could run down a deer and snap a bone with ease in their grinning jaws or, as now, play guardian to a child.

"These are her daughters?"

"As you say. The two fair girls, Beth and Saillie, are twins."

Silver Birch and White Willow. The names echoed their fair colouring and the slender grace of their limbs. Aeduan smiled his approval.

"Orphans now, of course," Bran confided. "Their father died in battle. That little spat with the Germans twelve years ago."

"I remember him. He was one of the bravest and best. But the third child? I have no recollection of her."

The assistant priest smiled dismissively. "The Lady's sole mistake. After the death of her husband she took up with…showed favour to…a stranger, a foreigner. Charming fellow. He would turn up here every couple of years, selling things. Luxury end of the market." He pointed to the wine cup Aeduan still held. "That was one of his. The red silk dress she's chosen to be buried in…the amber necklace gracing the bosom of the Mayor's wife…my own belt…he left many markers of his passage through the village!"

"Including the third daughter?"

"Yes, sir. I'm not surprised you were unaware of her. She was not much paraded."

"What is her name?"

"Sirona, sir."

"Sirona? The Star? How exotic! And what happened to the father to whom I take it she owes her intriguing dark looks?"

"He was a traveller." Bran shrugged a shoulder. "He travelled. He didn't speak much of himself but we all guessed that he was from the south, beyond Marseille. Africa? Egypt, most likely, but we can only speculate."

"I should like to express my condolences to the girls."

"Of course, sir. If you'll follow me?"

Aeduan spoke soft, sad words to the fair daughters, causing a further flow of tears, and touched each one comfortingly on her bowed head. It didn't escape his sharp eye that both girls cast swift glances under damp lashes at the gathering, seeking assurance that no one had failed to witness the honour being done them by the priest. At close quarters the pair were even more lovely than he had guessed. They had chosen to wear short dancing skirts and heavy belts from which dangled a single silver disc. Aeduan was impressed and reassured. With their looks, their parentage, and what he guessed to be their wealth, they would have no difficulty in marrying well. They must be very near the age of choosing and there were many young men present from all corners of the province, he noted, young men whose heads turned all too readily, drawn to the swing of a silver disc.

As he approached the youngest, the dog at her feet growled a warning, abruptly cut off at a sharp command from the child. To all appearances unaware of the priest's presence, this daughter remained, head bowed, staring into the hearth. The shapeless grey dress that reached down to her ankles was clearly chosen to deflect attention. Her sole ornament was a sprig of yew fastened to her shoulder with a simple pin. Yew. The tree that grew at the gateway to death. The symbol of rebirth and immortality. Now, who was this? The Ashypet, the Rhodopis, the Clinker-Raker of the folk stories? The fairy-tale tableau the three girls were presenting at the hearth was too obviously staged to have come about by chance. And he rather thought he might be looking at the unlikely dramatist.

"Sirona!"

At the sound of her name, she looked up at him, unafraid, preoccupied. Through his surprise at what he saw when she did so, Aeduan struggled to maintain his expression of kindly concern. Under the thicket of springing black hair he had expected to find matching black eyes with perhaps an eastern cast, but these eyes were light grey: her mother's eyes. The child even had the same disconcerting trick of regarding him in a slightly unfocused way, as though she were looking not at or past, but in some strange way, *into* him.

With a certainty he could only wonder at, he reached on impulse for the wheat stalk he'd stuck back in his belt and held it out to the child. She struggled to her feet and he saw with a pang of tenderness that she was indeed quite small. She could with ease have ridden on the tall shoulders of the hound which had risen with her and now stood flexed and ready for attack, held back only by the power of a slender right hand on the upstanding scruff of his neck. Aeduan thought the time had come to establish precedence: he murmured to the dog until it sank back with a muffled whimper onto its haunches.

But the girl's whole attention was on the stalk of wheat. She looked from it back to the priest, then put out a hand and took it from him, her face suddenly alight with a smile that he would have sworn was complimenting him on his perception.

The service, held out-of-doors in the village square, was a triumph. How could it fail to overwhelm the congregation? The Lady had earned their deep love; the priest himself was visibly moved, his oratory unsurpassed. At the close, a cortège formed up, ready to make its way up the hill towards the burial place. Aeduan's rich baritone voice rang out over the valley, echoed by the mourners' traditional responses, lusty and tuneful. The six young men chosen to pull along the bier with its gold-inlaid wheels and lavish decorations took up the strain and heaved. On it had been placed a couch spread with rich fabrics and on this lay, open to view, the body of the Lady. Her feet in gold-embroidered slippers were just visible under the drape of her red silk gown. Her arms were heavy with gold bracelets and around her neck she wore a ceremonial gold necklace. They had placed a pillow under her head so that the sight of her pale beauty could bless them for the last time.

Many people lined the way to the burial place, calling out farewells and throwing flowers onto the bier. Aeduan, acknowledging their sorrow with graceful flourishes, reckoned that many in the crowd had travelled a considerable distance to say their farewell. The Lady's influence had spread far wider than this valley. Well, he would ensure that the pilgrims had tales to tell when they returned to their own hearths. A bit of theatre was always welcome on these occasions; the antics of the threshing-floor were always remembered and reported. As they passed the last cornfield he held up his hand and murmured a command over his shoulder to his assistant.

Puzzled—for this was not part of the ritual—Bran obeyed at once, and, selecting a knife from his belt, the young man grasped a handful of wheat by the stalks and sawed at them until the bunch came away in his hand. If he'd had warning of this he could have brought a sickle along, he thought resentfully. The priest took it from him and, with a conjurer's gestures, slipped the girdle from around his waist and wound it tightly around the wheat stalks. The assistant was uneasy. What on earth was going on? Had old Aeduan been seduced by some esoteric eastern cult? Been spending too much time in Greece?

He watched, entranced like everyone else, as the priest addressed the crowd.

"You see me gather from the field, not the customary *last* bundle of wheat but the *first*." He brandished it over his head for all to see. "It is unripe. The ears are slender and there is no sustenance in them. But, my friends, they are well formed and they are whole. With the waxing of the moon they will be ready. They will feed you and your children for the coming year. This is the parting gift of Our Lady."

In the holy grove, Aeduan filled a beaker with water from the spring that jetted from the red rock-face and they started on the steep final ascent. He timed the last notes of his hymn exactly to the arrival at the cave in the hillside. The village women had done well. The entrance had been decorated with branches of greenery and white flowers to brighten the darkness. Above the mound a wraithlike crescent of a moon was starting its climb into the still-bright sky. Aeduan noted its position and the absence of clouds with satisfaction.

The shadows had already gathered at the burial place and he was relieved to see that the Mayor had arranged for a chain of lads to hold up flares deep inside the cavern. The entrance faced the east. She would be laid to rest facing the rising sun.

With rehearsed ease, the hauling team took the couch reverently on their shoulders and carried it into the cave's wood-lined interior. In moments, the wheeled bier was dismantled and all its parts carried into the chamber. There it joined the arrangement of rich gifts already in place. Aeduan, his assistant, the twin daughters, Sirona leading the dog, along with representatives of the village, entered to perform or witness the last rites. While Aeduan sprinkled the corpse with water from the holy spring and sang a final hymn before the silver-gleaming image of the Goddess, Bran moved objects about here and there, finally nodding that he was satisfied.

Aeduan lingered, kneeling by the body for a few last moments. He contemplated the strong features, framed and softened by the cascade of pale hair and now, in the light of the last flare, gleaming with an illusion of youth restored. He mastered his startled reaction when, with a clink of gold bangles, her right hand fell from her bosom and swung limply in front of his face. No one heard his murmur. "Aurinia, Lady, forgive me my slow wits! One last time you show me the way."

A further sign. His certainty was growing.

He tugged a bloodstone ring from her finger and returned the hand to its place across her breast.

Bran approached clutching a deep silver bowl. "Excuse me, sir…one more thing before we close down…The hound, sir. Shall I?"

"Ah, yes. Carry on, would you?"

At a nod, Sirona led the hound forward and commanded it to lie down at the feet of its dead mistress. Swiftly the assistant priest placed the bowl on the ground in front of it. Assuming that it was being offered water, the animal stretched its neck forward. Then, from behind, the young priest seized the dog's muzzle tightly in one hand, jerking it upwards. With the blade in his other hand, he cut the throat in one practised stroke. The blood spouted cleanly into the bowl.

Duty done, the party moved back onto the hillside path and the priest cast a measuring glance at the heavens, checking the height of the moon, now an emphatic horned presence poised over the mound. All was perfectly positioned.

In the view of the crowd below, Aeduan caught the small girl by the sleeve. She was already moving towards him and made no demur as he drew her forward a few paces, along the path to the summit. He knew that at the moment he offered her to her people she was colluding with him in the presentation and perfectly aware that those below were seeing her silhouetted against the darkening sky and crowned with a silver crescent. With slow ceremony, he took her hand and slipped the bloodstone ring onto her finger, then, bowing, held out the bunch of unripe wheat. She took it from him, steady and gracious, and held it before her with the pride and solemnity of a girl taking possession of her bridal flowers.